Floss and the Iguana Book 1:

ZOOM

PENNY SPIRLING

Contents

Chapter 1

A Rude Awakening

Floss dragged herself out of bed and over to the window for her daily check on the blackbird nesting between the drainpipe and the wall of her house. She didn't see the blackbird. What she saw instead sent shivers down her spine. It was gruesome. An earthquake had hit May Tree Close! Her road was a disaster area. She squinted and rubbed her eyes, taking another look at the catastrophic nightmare beyond her comfortable bedroom. Bricks were strewn everywhere and the houses, all but her own, had disappeared. The previous evening life had been so simple and normal for Floss Roberts. Her parents, Lin and Pete had invited Bill and Yumiko Gibson to their house for a Chinese takeaway. The Gibsons' were Lily's parents, Lily being one of Floss's best friends and a sporting ace who'd missed the get-together to train with the Carshalton

Athletics Club. The evening had been fun if at times just a little argumentative. Yumiko Gibson worked for a Tokyo art company and entertained the dinner party with anecdotes about mystical creatures depicted in the oriental trinkets her company sold. Some people believed these dumb, inanimate curios actually possessed magical powers! It was ludicrous but Floss's imagination ran wild and now, looking at the devastation outside she wondered if perhaps she was sleep walking, dreaming of Yumi's weird and wonderful reincarnations.

Floss's heart raced. Staring at the confusion outside she blinked uncontrollably, unable to take it all in. It looked like sheer carnage although she couldn't see any blood and gore, just bricks and mortar. She called out to her mum. No answer. She belted along the landing to her parents' room. It was late, 9 am, and they were still sound asleep, unconscious even. Floss had a dental appointment at 10 am so she wasn't expected at school until later but her dad started work at 7 am so he certainly should have been up by now. She checked the view from her parents' window finding it just the same as from her own. Every house except 83 May Tree Close, Floss's home, was a heap of rubble. Could an earthquake strike during the night and yet boycott the Roberts' abode? Of course not! Floss was a light sleeper so surely she'd have felt even an itsy bit of a tremor and besides, nature didn't work like that.

Florence Roberts, the deep thinker of Form 10B cast her mind back to the previous evening. Nothing untoward sprang to mind except that the Chinese dishes Yumi chose had given her a dry throat and her mum had argued it was down to the monosodium glutamate. Yumi had vigorously defended the food insisting that monosodium glutamate had been banned years before. It was at this point that Floss coughed and wheezed!

"Oh no! Floss has a cold!" Her mum apologised in view of their guests proximity to the disease now circulating the room at high velocity in the form of watery droplets.

"There's a flu virus doing the rounds at work," said Pete, trying to be helpful. Pete Roberts and Bill Gibson both worked for the local council supervising rubbish collections.

"No, Pete," Bill corrected, "Elsie's flu turned out to be hay fever. The doc said it was an allergy to tree pollen." Whatever it was, it was the last straw for Lin Roberts. Floss was made to take a spoonful of cough syrup without making a fuss. Thinking about that now Floss wondered whether that cough mixture might have contained an ingredient that put her into such a deep sleep that she'd missed the earthquake altogether? It kind of made sense.

Chapter 2

Help!

Floss's brain was in a spin. What should she do next - wake her parents? It seemed the most logical thing to do. Floss had passed her St. John Ambulance First Aid test so she knew the signs to look out for. She noted the rise and fall of their chests suggesting they were at least breathing normally. She shook her dad.

"Dad, wake up, wake up!" He didn't stir. She dashed around to her mother's side of the bed and tried rousing her in the same manner. It was like trying to wake the dead, an unfortunate analogy, and she chided herself rechecking that they were still inhaling and exhaling. They were. Mr and Mrs Roberts were thankfully alive!

An emergency situation prevailed and Floss, overcome with shock, was momentarily clueless about what to do next. It was deathly quiet outside. Information! She needed information. Remembering her dad's smart TV she took the stairs two at a time leaping the final three and racing into the lounge like a cat who'd spotted a mouse. She switched on the telly, a sixty-four inch model held up miraculously across the chimney breast by a clever metal frame and lots of bolts. The telly was set on a quiz show channel but what Floss needed was news and current affairs. Her mind was playing tricks on her and she couldn't remember any of those channels. Frustrated, she flipped through station after station without luck. Floss didn't watch much telly. It was usually homework followed by *You Tube* and then chatting to friends on social media that commanded her after school attention. She needed to concentrate.

Floss remembered her dad liked watching the BBC's twenty-four-hour news channel. She thought it had a two in the number. She dashed through possible combinations, 220, 203, 213? No luck! Her brain was going crazy with anxiety until she saw the TV guide magazine listing all the stations lying beside her on the floor. It was Channel 231. She punched in the number and Hey Bingo! Squeezing the life out of the remote she plumped herself down on her dad's foot stool in front of the screen and listened carefully to the day's announcements. The Breaking News live feed reported a State of Emergency in the Middle East, something to do with an explosion in Egypt. During the night there hadn't been any earthquakes, tornados, or any other humanitarian disasters anywhere in the world, not even the tiniest rumble and especially not in Carshalton.

Floss's little outpost of south London had been reduced to piles of bricks. Six houses wiped out and no one, but no one was making a fuss about it and to top it ALL, her parents were unconscious at a time when they should have been up and about and at work. Floss's mum also worked for the local council. She answered the phones as a waste and recycling customer services adviser. Surely she'd be missed. Floss felt drained and she'd only been out of bed a short while. She went to the kitchen and ran the tap, filling a tumbler with refreshing cold water. She took a swig of the invigorating liquid and refilling her glass took it upstairs to the spare bedroom to see the view from the back of the house. She looked down on her next door neighbour's property. Mr and Mrs Green lived there and what she saw made her stomach churn. What had been 81 May Tree Close was now just a stack of bricks making an impromptu barrier between the Greens' back and front gardens. The house in the middle had vanished!

Floss accidentally spilled a drop of water onto her bare feet drawing attention to the fact she was still wearing her jeans and t-shirt from the night before. She'd been so tired when she'd gone to bed that she'd just flopped down on it and had fallen asleep without undressing.

"Oh Blubber!" She shrieked. Her school friends had a list of words like, *blubber* they used to avoid using expletives.

"Floss, it's all about hormones," Lily, the font of all knowledge about diet and wellbeing had said once. She'd mentioned feel-good endomorphins or was it endorphins? Apparently they were brain neurotransmitters that could reduce depression. Oh boy! Florence Roberts desperately needed those neurotransmitters right now. She threw on a clean blue and white stripy t-shirt and a fresh pair of socks. She combed her long, brown, straggly hair and attempted plaiting it but she was all fingers and thumbs so she just tied it back with an elastic band to keep it tidy. The elastic band broke. Would nothing go right today? The exasperation of having to do it all over again was too much. She left it hanging loose.

Floss pondered her situation. The Emergency Services should be dealing with it not a fourteen-year old schoolgirl! An earthquake, if that's what had caused this mayhem would be right up their street. Her mum always said, *vital seconds count.* If the Fire Brigade could rescue cats from trees they must be able to find people buried underneath rubble, right? Floss dialled 999. Unobtainable! She tried again and again, still nothing. She texted Lily, but her fingers kept getting in the way and she made silly and annoying spelling mistakes, having to delete and re-type her message several times.

"Emergency! *I'm in tyouble! Imninent risk to life. I nerd uour jelp now. Get to ny houde ASAP! May Tree Close is a mazzive disasyer zone.*" She hit the *send* button and went to re-check on her parents. Lin and Pete were still fast asleep - as snug as a couple of bugs in a rug, completely out of it.

With Lily, hopefully, hot footing it to May Tree Close Floss waited eagerly at her front door for her to arrive. Being as impatient as always she decided to text another best friend, Emmeline Taylor. Emmie lived with her dad, Eric, just a few roads away and was his pride and joy. Eric sung Emmie's praises to anyone who would listen and was particularly proud of her wonderful puzzle solving gift. Her fantastic ability had won her the *Inter-Schools Under Fifteen Code-Breaking Competition* when she was just thirteen years old. Mr Taylor loved telling everyone that if his clever daughter had been around in World War Two she'd have been recruited to Bletchley Park, the top secret code-breaking centre, for sure.

Floss corrected her texting mistakes and sent it on to Emmie. Her thoughts now turned to Edward Kimber, a friend of hers from History Club. She greatly admired Ed. He read lots of books whereas everyone else just read their mobile phones! He seemed to Floss to be clear-headed and unlikely to panic in an emergency; characteristics that would be useful in this current crisis. He also appeared strong, which would be so handy when shifting bricks and just the sort of bloke she needed around right now. The truth of the matter was that Floss had once had a crush on him but he seemed more interested in his studies so she kept her feelings to herself. Never-the-less, remembering this she took more care when composing her message to him.

"*Ed, an earthquake has destroyed all the houses in my road except mine. Please come and help me! Lily and Emmie are on their way*," she added this last bit as an after-thought, hoping it was true. She read the text back laughing nervously to herself. An earthquake in May Tree Close? Ed would think she was insane. If he came at all he'd likely bring a strait jacket and a stretcher to carry her away on!

Floss stared at her phone. It was 9.40 am. With the Emergency Services not responding and her friends hopefully on their way she tucked her mobile into the rear pocket of her jeans and stealthily walked outside to the end of her driveway. No repercussions so far! The sky hadn't fallen in on her head or the ground moved under her feet. She gingerly took a few more steps. Her mathematical prowess told her that if she continued taking steps the same size she'd be outside The Greens' house in a nano-second. Floss regarded the Greens' front drive, twice voted Carshalton's Best Kept Front Garden. Their hedges were usually immaculate with a pretty flower border running alongside the path to a trellis where in June, beautiful yellow roses meandered across the top of their front door.

Floss felt so sorry for her neighbours. The total obliteration of their property meant they had no hope of hanging on to their prestigious trophy, that's if of course, they were actually still alive!

A brick fell from a pile of rubble jolting Floss from her thoughts. May Tree Close was uncannily quiet. The main road was just over the tops of the houses but weirdly, she couldn't hear any traffic noise. Even though she was feeling nervous she forced herself to walk across to a small grassy island where normally there would have been a bench beneath a cherry tree. This morning there was no bench or tree! Both had been upended by the earthquake or whatever it was that had done the damage. Floss thought she heard her phone ping. A reply from her friends? She checked her messages. Nothing. She so wished she could ask her mum what to do. Even though she was a teenager she found her mum's presence comforting even though she was always reminding her to make a good impression on other people and constantly nagging her to mind her *Ps and Qs*, an old saying meaning to be polite. Generally speaking, thought, they got on like a house on fire. Another bad analogy at this juncture in time.

A plane flew overhead and Floss's mind wandered. Her dream was to become an airline pilot. She'd chanced upon an article about aviatrixes - female pilots, and that was it. Flying through the sky became her raison d'etre. The school's careers adviser, Mrs Godfrey acted quickly on Floss's change of direction and urged her to join a school trip bound for Paris. She had inside knowledge that the captain on this Rise Airlines Gatwick flight would be a woman. As luck would have it industrial action at the Paris end meant passengers had to spend an extra thirty-five minutes on the tarmac. During this frustrating time Captain Jackie Ambrose handed round drinks giving Floss the chance to speak to her and confirm that this was what she wanted to do. Passing the time, waiting for Lily, Emmie, and Edward she allowed herself to daydream. Captain Floss Roberts! It sounded wonderful.

Floss's nice memory of her meeting with Captain Ambrose soon faded away being replaced with frustration and anxiety. She walked to 79 May Tree Close where Christy Makepeace lived with her happy little poodle dog, Harriet. Floss liked Harriet but didn't much care for her owner who was rather stuck-up and the most difficult neighbour in the Close. Everyone suspected it was Miss Makepeace who'd complained about kids playing football on the green resulting in the town hall putting up a sign saying, *No Ball Games*, upsetting all the local children. Miss Makepeace's blue car, like all the others in the Close was severely damaged by fallen masonry and peeping out from under a back wheel was a large rag doll, the kind dog owners buy for their pets. She dearly hoped Harriet wasn't lying underneath the wrecked car too.

Floss felt lonely. Where were her friends? There must be people trapped under the rubble! A telephone rang and her hand flew to her mobile but it wasn't her phone.

"What an idiot...," she said out loud. "I should know my own ring tone by now!" A phone was definitely ringing in the distance and following the sound she found herself standing outside the Jaggers' house at 77 May Tree Close. On the front drive sat an old fashioned red plastic telephone persistently calling for attention. Floss surveyed the scene. The Jaggers' were always refurbishing their home. Hardly any of the original interior was left. The kitchen had been refitted twice within Floss's own memory. The driveway hadn't escaped their desire for makeovers. Their piece de résistance was a central fountain around which their cars could just about circumnavigate. Her dad had laughed when he'd first seen it.

"They must have more money than sense, if you ask me," he'd remarked. Both the ruined house and fountain would now need to be rebuilt and their brand new car, covered in brick dust and severely dented, would need some serious panel beating.

The red phone was still ringing, breaking the eerie silence and Floss courageously, but cautiously, lifted the handset, her heart beating madly.

"Hello!"

"Floss, it's Lily. What's going on? I was just going into a session on *Safer Internet Surfing* when I saw your message.

I'm cycling over right now. Stay calm!" Lily obviously didn't understand the seriousness of her friend's situation. Floss could feel palpitations in her chest and they were growing stronger by the minute.

"Great. Just get here as fast as you can," Floss shrieked, adding … "Lily, is the school building still intact?" So far that morning Floss hadn't left her Close so had no idea how widely the earthquake thingy had spread. Lily was dumbfounded. Floss must be going daft!

Lily and Floss had been friends since being fruit monitors at infants school, distributing apples and pears at break times. Lily's shiny, black bobbed hair courtesy of her mother's Japanese heritage and her own slim proportions gave the accurate impression that she was not the type to allow the grass to grow under her feet. She was like a coiled spring with long gangly legs - from her dad's side of the family, the latter coming in useful when she played netball for the high school league. She never missed popping that ball through the hoop. Sanders High won every match when Lily was playing. Floss admired Lily's athletic ability and admitted that in this they were poles apart. Floss's granny told her that opposites often attract. In their case it did seem to be that way.

Chapter 3

The Cavalry Arrives

Floss replaced the red telephone's handset and it immediately vanished into thin air. When she thought about it she couldn't recall seeing any wires connecting the telephone to the cables overhead. She was no telecommunications expert but understood the basics. And, how on earth could Lily know the number of THAT handset? Her thoughts were interrupted by the sound of tyres skidding to a halt as Lily arrived by Floss's side.

Lily was dressed in her beloved trendy black and white striped jeggings, longline white blouse and her favourite black patent clod hopping boots – an outfit that just about adhered to her school's relaxed uniform guidelines. Relief swept over Floss knowing that at last she was no longer alone and could share her burden. Lily nearly fell off her bike when she saw the devastation in the Close. She stood the bike up against the remaining stump of a brick wall and went to Floss, giving her the biggest of hugs. Floss, in return, was reluctant to let her friend go.

"I get the feeling you're pleased to see me," Lily smiled.

"You bet! What do you think might have caused this?" Floss asked, pointing at the disaster area. Lily surveyed the area more closely.

"I've no idea! It does have the look and feel of a very local earthquake," Lily agreed, her words summing up the sheer desperation they were both now feeling.

Floss still needed an answer to her earlier question.

"Has the whole of Carshalton been reduced to a heap of rubble or is it just May Tree Close that looks like a lot of matchwood?" She asked.

"Apart from this neck of the woods Carshalton appears unscathed. There's something very odd going on just around the corner on the main road, though." Lily enlightened her. "They're digging up Wallington Park Road near the zebra crossing. It looks a bit strange if you ask me, not your usual kind of roadworks. The workmen for starters are like zombies wearing shiny silver spacesuits; quite the oddest looking workwear and over the top of the shiny stuff they're wearing those yellow vests like the guys who collect the rubbish… and I saw bumps on their foreheads as if they'd once had antennae attached. I thought they looked like ginormous ants!" Floss's mouth was hanging open. "I know. Ridiculous, right!" Lily continued. "I think, maybe, they might have been wearing ear defenders at some point and they've left impressions on their brows? Health and Safety Regulations!" Lily reasoned.

Peculiar forces were at work for sure. Floss wanted as many details as she could get.

"What are the spacemen-like workmen actually doing?"

"They've dug a whacking great hole – repairing leaks in the water supply pipe? They're turning cars back as they approach a temporary barrier. That's all I can tell you."

"So, how did you get through with your cycle?" Floss asked.

"It was the strangest thing. I approached, just like the cars but the cars were turned back and I was allowed to go through. The workmen appeared to recognise me, opened the barrier and beckoned me through." Lily suddenly realised the full horror of their predicament. "What the hell's going on here?" She wailed, running her fingers through her black locks.

"I wish I knew. I'm as mystified as you are," Floss murmured, shrugging her shoulders. "When I woke up this morning it was just as you see it now. My house was the only one still standing!" Floss looked despairingly towards her own house. "I'm scared for my parents too. They're unconscious! Just lying comatose in their bed. It might as well still be the middle of the night. I've tried shaking them awake but nothing works. Thankfully, they're breathing normally so I have to suppose they're OK," Floss said bleakly.

"Oh, I do hope so. I really like your mum and dad." Lily consoled her friend feeling grateful that her own parents were known to be safe and well. Floss managed a wan smile, short lived due to the re-appearance of the red telephone. It had moved from the Jaggers' driveway to the house next door at no. 75 where it rang noisily beside the front porch of Mrs Barbara Stanley who lived there with her son, Jack.

Jack Stanley was Edward Kimber's best mate. His parents came from Trinidad although Jack was born just up the road at the local hospital where his mum worked as a specialist nurse. Ephraim, Jack's dad, had died tragically in a freak motorway accident on the M6 whilst delivering metal girders to an engineering firm in Birmingham. The loss had hit the Stanley's hard, making money tight. To help out Jack did an early morning paper round and several other jobs to earn pocket money and keep his mum and himself afloat. He was a pleasant young man who always took the trouble to say, good morning. Floss's granny insisted that this was a good trait in a teenager and bode well for his future. Jack and his mum shared their home with Rosie, a black and white angora rabbit.

The red telephone was still singing outside the Stanley's house. The girls were paralysed with fear, their brains not functioning. Slowly they regained their senses and Lily, swishing her fringe back away from her eyes waltzed up to the phone without further ado.

"Hi, who is this?" She asked assertively expecting a ghost to answer.

"Hello Lily," Emmie replied, recognising her friend's voice. "Theoretically, I'm only five minutes away but there's a long queue of traffic. Road works. Cars and pedestrians are being turned back. I'll hopefully be with you and Floss shortly." If anyone could find a way through the maze of road repairs and barriers it would be the puzzle-solving Emmeline Taylor but Lily had an idea.

"Emmie, keep walking towards the barrier and see what happens." If her own experience was anything to go on Emmie should be allowed through.

Emmie followed Lily's advice without trepidation. As she approached the barrier the silent spacemen simply ushered her through just as Lily had predicted. It was only Emmie who was accorded this privilege. A mother pushing a pram, seemingly hypnotised spun around and walked away in the opposite direction. It all seemed so bizarre. Five minutes later Emmie arrived panting and shocked by what she saw in May Tree Close.

"Thank goodness you're here," sighed Floss.

"I might tell you you're very lucky to have me," Emmie tried to lighten the mood. "I was just at the boys' high school for a two-day code-breaking symposium run by MI6, hence why I'm dressed as I am and not strictly kosher as far as school uniform guidelines go." Emmie felt the need to explain. Floss and Lily regarded Emmie's attire. Uniform guidelines were relaxed at Sanders High School but they certainly didn't include seriously short mini-skirts.

"MI6! You're a spy?" Lily teased. Emmie's intellectual brilliance irritated Lily at times whilst Emmie, by an odd turn of events, wanted to be more athletic.

The red phone rang again outside the Stanley's house where their yellow front door was still attached to its frame but only just - hanging loose and about to drop off. Driven by some unknown force Emmie walked directly up the driveway towards the phone believing that if she entered the murky world of espionage, taking the bull by the horns was the modus operandi she would have to adopt. Floss was feeling more edgy by the minute and thinking supernatural powers must be at work she watched Emmie, horrified by her action.

"Stop! Don't go there!" She hollowed after her friend. Emmie nearly jumped out of her skin. "Emmie, I'm sorry for making you jump. I just think we should wait until help arrives. Until then, I'd be grateful if you didn't put us in more danger than we're already in." Floss felt a surge of pride deep within herself for taking charge of the situation. "I wouldn't like you to be gobbled up by a monster from outer space," she joked, taking the sting out of her brusque request and lightening the mood, completely unaware of how true her last sentence would turn out to be. Emmie returned to the fold and the red phone disappeared.

Blown to smithereens, the ruins that were houses just the day before reminded them of images of the London Blitz during World War Two.

"Shouldn't we be doing SOMETHING?" An anxious Emmie pleaded. Her friends seemed rooted to the spot. "There'll be people under this debris. We should be looking for them!"

"Yes, but how?" Floss sounded desolate, praying that Edward would arrive soon.

"Emmie's right," Lily said. "At the very least we should begin looking for the basic signs of life?" Being the school's Equalities Representative she was really into humanitarian causes. "Well, perhaps we could dig where it's easiest for starters?" Lily offered without thinking it through, realising afterwards that neither Emmie nor herself were attired for such strenuous activity.

Emmie's red and green tartan mini-skirt, pink silky blouse, and brown tights with her fave pink fluorescent satchel flung across her shoulder were not exactly digging clobber. A pair of orange trainers graced her feet and Floss and Lily both knew that their friend wouldn't want to get them dirty. Lily looked down at her own black patent boots and sighed. Her boots were her own particular pride and joy.

"I know this sounds ridiculous," Floss began, "but I'm sure help must be on its way! If we rush in now we could get hurt by falling masonry and then we'll be in more trouble than we are now." It sounded reasonable. Lily and Emmie held back, the latter clipping her short blonde hair out of the way with pink hair slides from her even pinker satchel.

Floss re-dialled 999 getting the unobtainable tone again.

"The Red Cross uses heat sensing equipment to locate bodies," Lily informed them.

"That sounds a great idea," Emmie said, sarcastically. "I'll just run home and get my heat sensing equipment, shall I?" Friends falling out in the middle of a crisis was not good. Floss sighed. They needed to pull together.

"I think my dad has a few pairs of heavy duty gardening gloves in his garage. Shall I go get them? Picking up bricks with our bare hands will take the skin off." Floss was being practical. Her friends were all for protecting their hands since they spent shed loads of their pocket money on getting their nails done. As it turned out there was no time to get the gardening gloves because the red telephone reappeared on the front drive of 73 May Tree Close, the home of Mr and Mrs Beck and was making a noise like a garden strimmer. The girls shuffled towards it but as they closed in it stopped ringing. The Becks, Floss knew, were away visiting their son in Australia and would not be back for another month.

"That's one house we don't have to worry about," Emmie announced. "No bodies under the rubble there!"

The phone rang again only this time it sounded like a hive full of bees buzzing furiously.

"Hell No! Bees!" Lily screamed, panicking, and getting ready to run a mile. A bee sting some years before had made her wary of the insects.

"Calm down! It's only that dumb phone," Emmie reassured her. Minutes later and with no sign of Edward, Floss decided that perhaps her friends were right and they should devise a rescue operation. Floss stepped cautiously up to the phone and picked up the receiver just as Edward Kimber accompanied by Jack Stanley came bounding into the Close.

"Hi! We're so pleased to see the two of you!" Floss shrieked, still holding the receiver. Jack was a pleasant surprise and many hands make light work, a saying her granny used.

"What the devil's going on here then? We were just coming to the end of 'Prefects Late Duty' when I read your text and with Jack living at 75 May…." Edward's voice tailed off. Jack and Floss were nodding acquaintances.

"Welcome Jack!" Floss smiled at her neighbour. "It's so good to see you." Jack removed his sunglasses for a closer look at the disaster area.

Edward would be the first to admit that Jack was usually the more adventurous and sociable of the two and the more likely to be voted in as head boy in due course – everyone loved him but they were about to see a less cool Jack.

"How did you get through the roadblock?" Lily asked the boys.

"Ah yes! Slightly odd! The workmen took one look at us and beckoned us through. Most peculiar," Edward explained.

"Yeah," Jack said, not giving them his full attention focusing instead on the havoc surrounding them and then suddenly remembering his mother. "Bloody Hell! My mum's inside our house…It's her day off from the hospital." Jack was yelling manically. "We've got to get her out, now!" Jack moved towards his front drive.

"Don't touch a thing," Floss shouted back, barring his way. "We're trying to decide the best way forward. We seem to be in a time warp. It's all so unreal," she said, trying to keep the sense of panic out of her voice.

With Jack living at no. 75, which was now a heap of rubble it was difficult to understand how he could be with them right now, completely unscathed.

"Jack, what time did you leave home this morning?" Lily asked.

"I didn't. I was playing computer games last night with my mate, Harrison and his mum invited me to stay over." Jack felt guilty now for not being there for his mum. He visualised her body lying cold and lifeless beneath the fallen bricks.

"Floss's right, Jack. Best not touch anything until we've a definite plan or expert help," Ed advised, patting his friend on the back and trying to sound calm and collected. He felt his friend's unease. "We could make things ten times worse - if people are still alive under those bricks we could crush them to death." Edward made sense. Jack nodded dolefully.

Floss was still holding the red phone and she now put the receiver to her ear. The cable joining it to the body of the phone twitched. It changed colour from bright red to green with black stripes. It developed eyes, a mouth, a nose, and a flappy fringe of skin going from the top of its neck and running down along its evolving body and elongated tail. It was alive and wriggling. Floss dropped the plump, scaly, moving mass that had just seconds before been an old fashioned telephone. Shock enveloped them all and Lily screamed as she watched the phone mutate.

"What is it?" She shouted, terrified.

"It looks like a chameleon," Edward mumbled anxiously. The creature had reached a metre in length.

"It looks like a komodo dragon to me," Jack theorised, having got a grip on his emotions. His friend Harrison had a copy of the Komodo Wars virtual game. "Komodo dragons can grow to up to three metres long," Jack shared.

"Oh, please be wrong!" Lily cried as she watched the reptile expand.

"Do Komodo dragons run fast?" Emmie asked, hoping for a negative reply.

Edward took control of the situation, audaciously marching up to the creature and was about to grab it by the tail when it jumped out of the way and spoke to him.

"And what do you think you're doing young man?" The indignant reptile spoke English with a thick Spanish accent. Edward fell back in shock. Luckily, Floss was right behind and broke his fall.

"What are you?" Floss asked the creature from a safe distance.

"I'm a ctenosaur or spiny backed iguana," the chubby reptile replied.

"Where do you come from? I have never seen anything like you around here," Jack asked, knowing very well the animal was not indigenous to Carshalton.

"My long-term home has been Costa Rica in Central America and for your information, ctenosaur is pronounced, tino-sore. It's Spanish and naturally I speak Spanish too."

The iguana's arrogance was obvious to all. He looked enquiringly at them.

"Is it Wodan or Thor's day today?" Talking to an iguana was a new experience and with his thick accent none of them understood much of what he said. "Have I stifled your simple minds?" He asked. "I suppose I'll have to clarify. Wodan and Thor's days are ancient Scandinavian words for Wednesday and Thursday, respectively. I've just been dining with Thor, the God of Thunder. Too much fish for my liking..."

"Today is Wednesday," Floss found her tongue. "Do you have a name?" She asked wondering whether talking iguanas had names.

"Of course I have a name," the iguana paused for a non-existent drumroll, "I'm known as Juan of Malachite!" He gave them a little bow.

Everyone was mesmerised by this odd creature and the way he'd turned up out of the blue.

"Are there any more of you? I mean, do you have any ferocious friends we should know about?" Edward, normally the courageous type suddenly felt apprehensive, wondering if there might be ravenous lions or worse lurking in the piles of rubble.

"Yes of course I have friends. Don't you?" Juan sounded terse. "My best friend's called Rodrigo and then there are the termite commanders... Now let me see, there's Felipe, Alvaro, Joaquin, Gonzalez, and Admiral Mathias..."

"I think we get the picture," Edward interrupted.

"They're all boys names. Don't you have any girlfriends?" Emmie asked innocently, not realising what a can of worms she was opening.

Juan's face took on a sad expression, his stubby iguana snout drooping down to the damaged crazy paving of 75 May Tree Close.

"I had a girlfriend once. In part, she's the reason why I'm here. I would like to tell you my heart-breaking story?" The teenagers nodded, being keen to hear it. "It might take some time," the iguana warned. With people potentially being crushed to death by rubble the teenagers felt jittery about listening to the long winded yarn of a mysterious ctenosaur.

"Mr Malachite, we're a bit short of time." Floss could see that Jack was becoming agitated again and quite rightly so. It was then that the penny dropped and she made the connection between the appearance of this cantankerous reptile and the horrendous events befalling May Tree Close.

"Eh, ...Juan, did you cause this disaster to happen?" Floss asked, pointedly.

"I'm afraid to say it was all me," the reptile admitted, scratching an itch on his chest with a long finger and beginning his woeful tale totally unfazed by the destruction he'd wrought.

When everyone was as calm and collected as they were ever likely to be in the circumstances, the creature started his tale.

"My story begins on the planet Malachite, more light years away than you've had hot dinners!" The reptile chuckled at his apt use of such a well-known English saying. "Please, don't be angry. I just needed to get your attention."

"You certainly did that," the May Tree teenagers chorused.

"Never mind Malachite," Jack shouted, "What about my mum!" Jack was fretting.

"Don't worry about a thing, young Jack," the iguana reassured him. Jack was surprised that the creature knew his name. "Everything's under control. No one in May Tree Close will be hurt, I promise you. You have my word upon it!" The iguana sounded convincing.

Floss thought some background information might be a good place to start.

"Tell us about yourself. Where do you come from," she asked, feeling more confident with every minute that went by.

"Let me start with my planet, Malachite. If you've never heard of it it's because it hasn't been discovered yet. Your astronomers will discover Malachite in 2029. I saw it myself on the Solar System calendar about fifty years ago. In 2029 Malachite will be in the heavenly line of sight for the big telescopes you have on Ben Nevis. Why a man called Ben has telescopes attached to himself completely escapes me!" The iguana looked confused and his new young friends were unable to suppress their giggles at his misunderstanding. "As I was saying, astro-physicists will announce the discovery of Malachite in 2029. I can even tell you the exact day and time but you might think I'm just showing off," he guffawed.

"I thought malachite was a rock not a planet!" Emmie cast doubt on the iguana's words.

"Indeed Yes! Malachite is a rock and my superior planet is built on a gigantic lump of it. It's hot and humid with lots of lush vegetation like your Amazonian rain forest. The main difference being that Malachite is full of clever Malachitians like myself," he said smugly, whilst inspecting his nails.

Edward, the intellectual of the group, felt he should put this extra-terrestrial creature that had come amongst them to the test.

"What's bigger, a universe or a galaxy?"

"Galaxies fit inside a universe. Malachite is just one planet inside a galaxy made up of lots of planets and stars," Juan explained.

"So there could be lots of universes with countless galaxies within them?" Edward asked.

"Exactement! I would have to admit, however, that space is so vast that even I can't be sure how big it is." Edward appeared satisfied with the answers given.

"So where does the Milky Way fit into all this?" Floss asked, innocently.

"The Milky Way is the galaxy that contains your Solar System. It sends out light from so many stars that they can't be recognised individually by the naked eye.

My friend, Galileo, discovered it in 1610," the reptile was pleased to announce.

"How fast do planets travel?" Edward could not let the topic go.

"To give you a few examples, the Earth travels around the sun at 66,615 miles per hour, Mars at 53,853 mph, Jupiter at 29,236 mph and Neptune, which is the slowest at 12,146 mph. Mercury is the planet nearest to the sun and is the fastest, travelling at a whopping 107,082 mph!" It was clear to Edward that Juan knew a lot about celestial bodies.

Floss delved deeper into the iguana's place of origin.

"What about your own planet, this Malachite? Please tell us more," Floss encouraged, believing the iguana when he'd told them no one under the rubble would be hurt.

"My homeland is a green and beautiful place abounding in flowers and tropical birds constantly twittering in our treetops." The creature sounded homesick.

"We get the green thing," Edward commented harshly. He wasn't the romantic type, "If your Malachite is so full of superior intellectuals why were you living in Costa Rica? And, why are you an iguana and not an oak tree?" He'd read that oak trees were known for their symbiotic relationship with insects and birds.

"Trees can't walk and I suffer badly from itchy feet!" The reptile returned, irritated.

Why did these kids keep asking him questions? The iguana was truly exasperated.

Emmie, being the linguist and insisting everyone pronounce their words correctly was quick to criticise the iguana, adding insult to injury.

"Juan, I can't understand a word you're saying." Emmie, Like Lily, never minced her words. The iguana's head bobbed wildly. It's something they do when they feel threatened.

"Frankly, you do need to lose the Spanish accent," Edward agreed.

"OK, OK. I'll do my best," the iguana acquiesced sounding now more like a south Londoner. "People-lets, come closer and sit by me," he invited, indicating that they should sit on the dusty driveway right in front of him. They declined.

"We're not people-lets. We're young adults," Jack told him stridently. Juan felt his hackles rising. Working with these youngsters was going to be a pain.

"On Malachite people-lets are juveniles until they're thirty years of age and since you're all around fourteen you're still toddlers. However, for the benefit of this conversation and any potential future relationship we may have to endure I'll endeavour to refer to you as young adults from now onwards."

Floss normally sat at the back of the class, keeping her head down to avoid being picked to answer questions. The current situation demanded more and she rose to the challenge.

"Please let Juan get on with his story or we'll be here all day and I'm feeling so hungry having had no breakfast. Soon I'll be too weak to lift a single brick!" She told them. The iguana picked up on Floss's words.

"Let's eat first! Rome wasn't built on an empty stomach was it!" He effused.

"Your mixing metaphors," Edward corrected. "It should be, Rome wasn't built in a day or, an army marches on its stomach," he explained. Juan shook his head in dismay. Idioms weren't his strong point.

"I'm sorry. The central Malachitian library doesn't always have the most up to date information. I'll speak to our information scientist when I get home. What I was trying to say was this - if you're hungry I'll create a feast for you. Your wish is my command!"

The iguana was standing up on his hindlegs using his tail to balance, wobbling uncontrollably. He waved his scaly arms around and in seconds had magically created a feast fit for a king of iguanas and set it out on a kitchen table. Before them were plates of breaded locusts, deep fried glass wing butterflies, roasted raccoon babies and bowls of green turtle soup.

"You're having a laugh, aren't you?" Jack remarked. "Who eats this awful stuff!"

"Well, actually I do," the iguana retorted, spinning round, and swishing his tail violently, making everyone jump out of his way.

"My mum makes the most scrumptious Trinidadian curried duck with rice. I want some of that instead of this muck," Jack demanded. Emmie pulled a face at curried duck for breakfast causing Floss to step in with a better suggestion; one with wider appeal.

"Let's have pizzas and Coca Cola to drink," she suggested.

"I'll have still water. Drinking more water is part of my new health regime," Lily told them. Juan swung into action. The fried locusts etcetera, vanished, and set out on a pretty daffodil patterned tablecloth were four pizzas, a dish of curried duck and glasses of Coca Cola and water. The aroma from the hot, delicious food was too much and they descended on it like the plague of locusts they hadn't wanted to eat earlier. Even Lily succumbed.

"Hey, Floss! What would our teachers say if they could see us here in the middle of a bombsite conversing with an iguana and eating pizza?" Floss had her mouth full and remembering her P's and Q's didn't answer.

Chapter 4

Believing the Unbelievable

Breakfast over and hoping there would be no more interruptions the iguana began his grave tale, which was one that held momentous consequences for universal peace. The teenagers gathered around him as requested but were reluctant to sit down on the dusty ground. Juan was resting his sausage-like body on a length of fallen tree trunk and stroking his chin with his long finger, deciding the best way to relate his epic tale of treachery, intergalactic battles and larger than life creatures from planets thousands of light years away. He was so deep in thought that he hadn't noticed that the leggy youngsters were still standing.

"What's the matter now?" He asked. "Can't you get comfortable?"

"Comfortable!" Lily remonstrated. "How can we get comfortable sitting on these cold, dirty, stone slabs? No disrespect intended to your mum's crazy paving," she said to Jack.

"My thoughts exactly," chipped in Emmie, her legs exposed by her mini, mini-skirt and aware that sitting on the hard surface would not be a nice experience. Floss began to wonder if they would ever get to hear Juan's story. The iguana, equally despondent, clenched his fists not in angst but as part of a conjuring trick.

"Cushions Galore!" He shouted at some unknown source of ethereal power. Straight away rumbling noises erupted from the clouds followed by a mass of cushions falling thick and fast, approaching the ground at lightning speed making everyone duck and dive to avoid being knocked out by them.

The cushions were all shapes and sizes. Heart shaped, round, square and rectangular. Giant beanbags in bold colours turned up too. Last to make an entrance were five bed pillows each illustrated with a photograph of one of the five friends.

"Wow," exclaimed Lily, "did you really just do that?" She grabbed an emerald green sparkly pillow with her picture on it and squatted down.

"Enjoy!" Juan invited. "The cushions are filled with the finest soft fleeces of the Malachitian jacacan," he informed them, knowingly. Edward had read Darwin's *Origin of Species* and there was no mention of a jacacan in that profound work. Indeed, Darwin had not mentioned the astro-biology of outer space either.

Edward's scepticism had made the others question the iguana's authenticity too. They listened to his and the creature's exchange of words.

"A jacacan?" Edward asked. Juan prepared to elaborate.

"A jacacan is a cross between a llama and a camel. The big difference setting the jacacan apart from llamas and camels is that they can fly and converse in the Malachitian language. It's a wild beast that lives in herds, willingly presenting itself at our jacacan shearing stations to donate its fluffy wool, which we use to line the Malachitian pod nests," he explained. Pod nests? They had never heard of pod nests. "By shearing the jacacan's wool we're actually doing them a favour. Our all year-round hot climate becomes even more unbearable during our tropical season for a creature with so much woolly insulation."

"I don't believe it," Edward cried out.

"So you've been to Malachite have you?" Juan asked curtly.

"No, but…" Edward was not allowed to finish.

"The jacacan is a reality to those who live within the Malachitian galaxy. I read once that you Earthlings believe the creature is a myth. Untrue! The jacacan is as real as the Abdominal Snowman," Juan told them.

"You mean, the Abominable Snowman," Jack corrected.

"Quite so. Both the Abdominal and the Abominable Snowmen are as real as I am.

Juan noticed Lily's outstretched legs. Her black and white stripy jeggings struck a chord with him as he looked along his own stripy torso.

"Tell me Lily, were any of your ancestors related to the lizard family?" He was in earnest. Lily threw him a look that could have killed. Juan transferred his gaze to Floss and was similarly engrossed by her knee ripped jeans. Poor girl, he thought, the child's parents can't afford to buy her a decent pair of trousers. "Floss, do you have links to the venerable race of reptilia, Squamato Iguana?" He asked, pointing to her blue and white stripy top and ignoring the slashed jeans for now. Floss tittered.

"No! Neither of us are related to the iguana genus in any way, shape or form!" Floss laughed. "Juan, stripes are fashionable right now so I guess that makes you trendy too!" Juan scratched his lizard-like head feeling mightily confused by these strange homo sapiens.

A chilly wind arose and blowing through May Tree Close made the girls shiver.

"It's just like winter!" Emmie remarked as it whipped around her bare legs.

"Ah yes, winter. Does it actually exist?" Asked the iguana.

"It certainly does," answered Edward. "Winter is when most of our trees go to sleep and the weather can be icily cold or constantly raining. It's also a time when parents moan about the gas bills and go around the house turning the thermostat down so we all freeze."

"Well, bless my soul! It's always so hot on Malachite and Costa Rica too for that matter. I, personally have never experience excessive cold except of course when I visited the planet, Ice Leonard, but enough of that later. If we iguanas get too chilly we can't function. Low temperatures immobilise our brains making us lethargic and we've been known to fall out of trees because of it!" The lizardy beast told them.

"It's winter all the time in my house because we can't afford central heating!" Jack announced, forlornly. "Since dad died money has been so tight…"

"Jack, once the intergalactic war is over I promise you the Stanley family will never feel the cold again." Jack regarded the heap of hardcore that was once his home. Clearly, central heating would never be a concern because his house no longer existed!

Floss checked the time. Only one hour had elapsed since her ordeal had begun.

"My friends," began the iguana, "I've come here to recruit you five for a dangerous mission. Come with me and I promise you adventures that will take you into space, to ancient, exotic places, to dog eat dog war zones and chance meetings with charming creatures from distant planets." They were spellbound by the iguana's well-orchestrated oration and seeing this he jumped in and told them more.

"I've stopped all clocks in May Tree Close. We're sealed inside a time-bubble and I give you my word nothing bad will happen to your loved ones. So chill out," he repeated. "And, always believe that something wonderful is going to happen!" A tall order in their current situation.

Floss's hacking cough from the night before returned to annoy her. Her friends were worried and looked to Juan to use his cosmic magic to stop it. The iguana took the hint and with his eyes alighting on the rag doll lying trapped under the wheel of Miss Makepeace's car, he scuttled over to it, his tail bobbing from side to side. He pulled out the doll and blew into her face muttering a spell. Floss's cough left her instantly and as it did so they heard a faint cough coming from the little rag doll.

"Talk about transferable skills…" Lily whispered.

"Aw Jeez!" Whispered Jack to Edward, "That's amazing. I've only seen something similar once before. *Mogador the Manic and the Rescue of the Ancient City of Ivanich!*" Edward gave Jack a cranky look. "It's one of Harrison's video games. Part of the Super Mogador Saga," Jack explained, cool as a cucumber settling down on the cushions.

Juan with Floss's help piled up the pillows to give himself extra height and relax his four legs. Emmie frantically searched her pink satchel for a packet of jelly babies and finding them, handed them round.

"Floss, what's wrong now?" Emmie was bemused by Floss's stare.

"I was just wondering what else you might have in that vacuous pit of yours," she teased. The two best friends chuckled. Juan, meanwhile, curious about the sweets took a red jelly baby and violently bit its head clean off. It looked savage. The others watched, mesmerised.

"What?" Juan asked.

"It's the violent way you ate that jelly baby," Floss told him.

"Yeah, You're acting like a wild animal," Lily added.

"Hmm, technically I am a wild animal," the iguana replied whilst muttering under his breath, "they told me never to work with people-lets!"

Chapter 5

An Iguana's Tale

The fourteen year old posse settled, waiting expectantly to hear Juan's tale.

"Ani was the name of my soul mate. It's a lovely name, don't you think?" Juan asked.

"My grandmother's name is Molly Anne Groombridge and she's the best granny in the world. When you love someone lots you tend to like their name as well," Floss reasoned. Lily and Emmie nodded.

"Interesting. One day I'd like to meet your Grandmother Molly," Juan told her. "What about you Jack - how do you feel about the name, Ani?"

"I hate the name Annie with a vengeance! The man who killed my dad was married to an Annie. She lied to the police; said my dad fell asleep at the wheel. Luckily, a witness came forward and told the truth." Jack was emotional once again.

The iguana knew Jack was suffering.

"Jack, I understand how you must feel. My Ani's name is spelt A.N.I. as in groove billed Ani, a Costa Rican bird. The last time I saw Ani she was sitting on a telegraph wire above a dirt road swinging and singing in the breeze. I'll never forget that precious memory. She looked so beautiful," Juan sighed wistfully.

"I'd like a bird," Edward joked.

"How do you mean, you'd like a bird?" Juan was ignorant of English colloquialisms. Edward looked sheepish. Lily intervened.

"Just Ignore him," she snapped, "he's just a chauvinistic pig. Some childish men refer to their girlfriend as their *bird*. It's all rather tedious and sexist," Lily said. No one dared contradict her. Edward's chops flushed red and she hadn't finished yet. "In any case Edward Kimber, you only need look around to see there's a very nice *bird* in our midst who'd love to hang out with you," Lily ribbed him. She'd said too much. Floss blushed feeling perplexed, blew her wayward hair away from her face to cool her cheeks.

Juan flicked his long fingers and bobbed his head agitatedly, unable to finish his tale. Floss sensed his unrest.

"Please go on. Tell us more about Ani," she begged.

"Ani and I grew up together in neighbouring pods," Juan resurrected his yarn.

"Pods?" Lily repeated. "Peas grow in pods not people!" She exclaimed.

"We're not people. We are Malachitians and for the first ten years of our lives we are larvae with arms, legs, and good brains. We're fed by tube on a nutritionally balanced diet that nourishes our cerebrum – that's brain to you, and this builds our wisdom quickly. Three times a year we're allowed out of our pods to network with other youngsters and that's when I met my Ani in person. During our pod years she wasn't called Ani. She was Wormsical 2239. I know, not very inspiring! I was Wormsical 2240 because I'd emerged just after her. I suppose I'm, how do you Earthlings say it, her toy boy?" The teenagers sniggered.

Lily was still contemplating the hideous pod idea.

"Juan, why pods? They sound horrendous. So confining, like prison. If your fellow citizens are so clever, able to dash about space at a moment's notice how come they couldn't come up with something a bit more sociable?" Lily had a real bee in her bonnet on this topic.

"Thousands of years ago there was a virus that was so contagious that one virtually had only to look at someone else to catch it. Creatures were dying in their hoards on so many planets. The young of many nations were almost wiped out. So, our Malachitian engineers designed the pod system, isolating our babies from even their parents. It worked! And, we found that our bairns grew up and became respectable, caring creatures and well educated too. We kept the system and later discovered that the deadly virus was not a natural phenomenon but a man-made disease. Yes indeed! The virus was artificially manufactured by outer space's most destructive, merciless despot ever, Exitum Magnus, the forefather of our present enemy, Gregor, whom you've yet to meet. They say that silence is golden but in this instance it served only to mask the uneasiness they all felt as they pondered the iguana's unbelievable chronicle of childhood. Bewildered bafflement did not cover it!

The iguana's neck was hurting, giving him gyp from staring up at the teenagers. He wanted to move on quickly but Edward wanted to know about Juan's traumatized childhood.

"What about having fun with wormsicals your own age? Weren't you lonely? Didn't you miss reading books?" Edward was intrigued. He couldn't imagine a life without his books.

"Not a bit if it. We used telepathy. It's like sending a text message but directly to the recipient's brain. Ani was on my wavelength and we'd often discuss books telepathically via the cosmic star energy system - that's much like your cloud data storage but naturally, far more sophisticated." The iguana's priggish streak was showing through.

There just seemed to be no end to the inquisitive nature of these moody adolescents but the iguana reminded himself that this was why he'd come to Carshalton to enlist their help.

"What about learning to trust and be kind to one another?" Floss asked.

"Ah Yes! Trusting and holding the faith are two especially important concepts. On Malachite we trust our pod engineers and we have exceptional faith in our parents to make the right decisions for us, even though we don't actually meet them until after the pod stage when we're around your age, fourteen or fifteen years old. We spend a year acquainting ourselves with our mater and pater and then leave for finishing school, usually on another planet. After that we are free to explore our galaxy on a kind of Grand Tour that lasts until we're thirty-seven years old. It's then that the Mantle of Adulthood is awarded us." The iguana's childhood sounded incredibly grim.

The teenagers looked sad. The iguana's family life sounded nothing like their own.

"What about your parents. Do you ever see them again?" Floss asked, concerned.

"Oh sure. On our return from the Grand Tour we lodge with them for a while before we set out on our life's journey. During this brief sojourn we also make the important decision as to whether we want to amalgamate with another adult or stay single forever." Floss looked downcast. How could life on Malachite be so pre-ordained. And, a life without her family wasn't one she'd ever wish to contemplate. The iguana noted her solemn face. "What I forgot to say," he added, at the risk of harping on and on, "is that we're always in touch with our families. Modern communication eh! It's difficult not to be." It was the iguana's attempt at being funny. "I'm in regular contact with my mum, dad and my brother Maharg. They send me regular intercranial updates on things happening back home." He wanted them to understand that Malachite was a caring planet.

"Mind reading, living in a pod…all sounds gibberish to me. Even I know real life isn't remotely like that," Jack was having serious doubts about Juan's legitimacy. "You suggest you can probe people's brains. I bet you can't read mine?" Jack was pushing for proof. "What am I thinking right now?" Jack urged.

"You're contemplating joining the police force but doubting that you'll make the grade," Juan began. Jack's jaw dropped. "Jack, have faith in yourself! You've a bright future ahead of you. Get rid of your angst and enjoy life and don't copy your classmate Ollie's homework! You are talented enough. You can do it! And Jack, don't take his fruit gums without asking him first!" Jack hung his head in shame.

"Can we stop you knowing what we're thinking?" Floss asked.

"Oh certainly! Concentrate on blocking all incoming electro-magnetic fields, presenting an impenetrable wall to the likes of me," Juan divulged and then showed them how to do it.

Learning how to repel electro-magnetic waves was more difficult than it sounded.

"Emmie's there. I sense a complete black-out. Lily's struggling. I detect that Mrs Gibson has a special birthday approaching and Lily's hoping she'll like the silver brooch she's bought her. Jack and Ed are fighting me but they are making progress and, yes they're winning. I can feel no thought-pulses coming through. Well done, boys!" Finally, he came to Floss. "Floss stop fussing. It's still only 10 am. Trust me, please!" Juan implored. Her dental appointment was at 10 am. "Nevermind the dentist. I've taken the liberty of postponing your appointment. You can see him when you return," he told her. Return from where? Floss was flummoxed. Meeting a magical iguana was one thing but gallivanting around outer space with him, quite another.

Juan was fully engaged teaching his students the art of passing subliminal messages to one another. A skill that would be absolutely crucial to the success of their mission, he told them. Jack was wrestling more with linguistics. What did the word, 'subliminal' mean? Emmie gladly explained.

"Subliminal means to be below the threshold of consciousness. It came up at my Psychology of Code-Breaking course last Christmas." Juan nodded approvingly. Emmeline was exactly right for the task he had in mind for her.

Juan requested Emmie's satchel, a difficult decision for Emmie to make as she guarded her bag fiercely. The iguana thrust his clawed hand down inside the bag and fished out five pairs of rose-tinted spectacles.

"Where on Earth did they come from?" Emmie screeched. She couldn't for the life of her remember ever putting them in there. Juan gave them each a pair of the spectacles.

"These eyeglasses are little celestial wonders," he gushed.

"Here we go again," muttered Jack. "Everything to do with you is out of this world."

"These optical lenses have a binocular feature and together with the rose tints they'll paint the world a better place. We use them a lot on Malachite. They keep out harmful rays and detect if someone is lying. They're simply out of your world! They've so many benefits. I think you people-lets, ah sorry, young adults, would describe them as, Must Haves." They fiddled with their new toys. "Put them on. Try them out!" Wearing the glasses they were transported into a sea of tranquillity. Even Jack's sullenness evaporated. "It'll take a little time for your eyes to adjust. Keep the specs safe," Juan insisted.

Juan's neck was aching more. He desired a different, taller perspective requiring drastic changes to his shape and a great deal of magic.

"I'm thinking I should germinate into something bigger," he told them, "but what?"

"I think you mean metamorphosis rather than germination?" Edward was just being his normally pedantic self. "Germination is what seeds do. Metamorphosis is what caterpillars do when they're turning into butterflies and that sounds to me more likely in your case." With a loud sigh Juan accepted that he was more akin to a larva than a seed vessel. A pause followed Juan's exchange with know-it-all Edward. Floss came to the rescue.

"What about becoming a Malachitian?" She suggested.

"That's an interesting idea. Malachitians are a varied bunch but after being an iguana for sixty-eight years I can't quite recall how I looked before that."

"Sixty-eight years!" Lily exclaimed, "that's older than my granny."

"And mine," added Floss.

"Well my dears," began the iguana, "sixty-eight is nothing for Malachitians. I come from, Malowapham, Malachite's northern province where lifespans can be thousands of years!"

The iguana put his thinking cap on. It was bright red with question marks all over it and was tied with a knot at each corner resembling a large handkerchief, the kind people used to wear on the beach when they didn't have a hat.

"No! You're kidding us! You've actually got a thinking cap!" Jack exclaimed. The iguana ignored the impudent teenager and concentrated harder.

"I'm inclined towards being a pop star. The one that comes immediately to mind is, Valentine Stars. Lily's thinking about him right now," Juan revealed. Lily hastened to block out the iguana's prying brainwaves. She'd let her guard down. "It's the rose-tinted glasses," Juan laughed. "They've calmed you. You'll soon get used to the magic specs!" Lily hoped he was right. Meeting this reptile had completely unsettled her.

The iguana continued with his machinations, lolling his head from side to side trying to come up with an appropriate subject to transform into. He was torn between showing solidarity with his new human friends and choosing something more exuberant or going the other way entirely and selecting an animal that was more practical.

"I might go for the non-binary, neutral approach. Neither male nor female," he muttered, steadily drifting into a trance as he delved deeper into his memory looking for a suitable creature to metamorphose into. Lily was stuck on the iguana's phraseology.

"Neutral?" She was astonished that anyone would contemplate such a condition. Juan was mentally elsewhere and did not respond.

As if a talking iguana wasn't enough a giant green cricket alighted on the remains of a buddleia bush nearby. It's weight was too much for the weakened shrub and it swayed wildly up and down making it difficult for the insect to keep its balance.

"Pardon me for interrupting," the cricket answered for Juan. "May I throw some light on the neutral gender notion?" The teenagers nodded trying not to let the crickety thing see their fright. "Malachitian neutrals are earmarked to become highly trained engineers and the like. They choose the state of being genderless because it means they don't have to waste time on all the family stuff. They devote their centuries of life to serving their communities. We'd be lost without them," he explained. Five pairs of teenage eyes were unswervingly trained on the winged insect with Lily still grappling with the idea of people *amalgamating*. Malachite must surely be devoid of love and romance!

Juan was away in a dreamworld so the cricket took the opportunity to enlighten them further himself.

"At our thirty-seventh birthday party we can opt to be sprinkled with the pollen of the grimble flower, an enchanted plant that allows us to fall in love. This coming of age ceremony is always held on 31st June each year," the cricket explained.

"There isn't a 31st June," Emmie corrected.

"Oh really!" Irritated, the cricket's wings began to whistle as he beat them together making an awful din. "On Malachite we most certainly do have a 31st June!" The cricket announced defiantly. "And by the way, I'm Rodrigo, son of Rodriguez of the Honourable Gryllidae Family," Rodrigo bowed his head politely in greeting.

Everything was happening so fast. May Tree Close was in a state of collapse and a speaking wizard of an iguana had walked in on their lives, changing them forever, and now they found themselves talking lucidly to a cricket!

"Are you from Costa Rica too?" Jack asked the cricket.

"Yes indeed. I'm from that wonderful place where the bird song never stops filling the sky with beautiful music." The cricket was a hopeless romantic and had obviously opted for the pollen of the gimble flower. "Costa Rica is where Juan and I became re-acquainted many long years ago whilst on our Grand Tour," Rodrigo recollected. In the background the iguana's bones were creaking, making a real hubbub as his lizardy shape disappeared and a giant-sized something was forming in its place.

Rodrigo's wings began whistling again even louder than before.

"Stop that high-pitched row at once!" Edward ordered. It was doing his head in.

"It's my way of communicating with Juan," the cricket retorted. "He understands my musical notes and he's told me to stick around and not allow myself to be intimidated by you lot. Apparently, you're not a bad bunch of kids even though you don't look intelligent. Even funnier, he says you're going to be his new military commanders so you should be treated with respect!" The cricket swivelled his antennae as the teenagers digested his words, raising their eyebrows at the laughable suggestion that they, schoolkids from Sanders High were about to become military top brass! It was totally unbelievable.

"The cheek of it! Not intelligent!" Blasted Edward.

The cricket's inflammatory remark about their level of intelligence stung the teenagers. They were truly narked. A bad atmosphere was brewing so Floss stepped into the fray, diverting the conversation onto a less provocative topic.

"Rodrigo, what did you do in Costa Rica?"

"I helped others. Crickets are famed for bringing good luck and looking back I can honestly say that I did some good," Rodrigo reminisced. "I don't suppose in this tiny, sleepy backwater you heard about Gordon the Agouti falling into the Panama Canal?" He was doing it again, making derogatory remarks about where they lived this time. No one had heard or cared about an agouti falling into the Panama Canal. To show how cross they were they remained silent, returning blank stares, hoping the rude insect would disappear back to where he'd come from. Undeterred, the cricket continued. "Well, for the record, I pulled Gordon out of the water to safety!"

The pompous cricket rested his eyes on Lily's striped lizardy legs.

"Lily, would it be right to assume you're a member of the orthoptera order…" It was an innocent question.

"No! I most certainly am not an orthoptera thingy. I'm wearing stripy jeggings that's all!!" She bellowed at the insect. Rodrigo remained calm. He was used to living in the Costa Rican rain forest with monkeys howling all day long so wasn't put off by Lily's outburst, although he was starting to consider these cheeky individuals rather tedious. Hunger was getting the better of him. Flying across the Atlantic Ocean had worn him out and his need for nourishment was overwhelming. Losing interest in what seemed a fruitless task trying to befriend stubborn adolescents, he hopped onto the piles of rubble and searched for something to eat.

Chapter 6

Rabbits

Juan completed his transformation and the teenagers found themselves gazing up at a giant seventeenth century Cavalier. Standing at seven feet tall he towered above them. He had grown a moustache and was wearing a Jacobean cloak and breeches in purple, the royal colour. Underneath his cloak he wore a voluminous white shirt with a delicate lace collar. Shiny black shoes with gold buckles and lots of gold jewellery denoting his high rank and an odd choice – a pair of dark shades over his eyes completed the picture. The flies in the ointment were his great height and his facial features, the latter bearing a striking resemblance to a tousled haired pop star.

The iguana's new look was incongruous! He didn't exactly blend in and the teenagers weren't sure what to make of him.

"What do you all think?" The ex-reptile asked them wondering why they were so quiet.

"I think you could say you've over egged the pudding..." Jack returned.

"Jack, don't be so rude!" Floss snapped. Turning to the Cavalier she added, "we think you look great. It's just difficult for us to find the right words." Floss was ever the diplomat.

"Oh! That good eh?" Juan chuckled unable to understand the nuances of human speech.

"I think you're trying to be Valentine Stars, aren't you?" Lily asked.

"Well yes, of course I am!" Juan returned sharply. "Isn't it obvious?" The iguana was surprised that they felt the need to ask. Lily shook her head in disbelief.

"Juan, sorry to be the bearer of bad news but they didn't have pop singers in the days of King Charles II!" Jack sounded gleeful, enjoying this little episode.

"Yes of course. I knew that!" The swash buckling aristocrat fiddled with the gold necklaces hanging around his neck. "I just wanted to be a pop star for a while and I just love Valentine's latest album, don't you?" Juan croakily hummed the pop singer's latest song.

Floss drew her friends around for a group huddle to discuss the situation.

"A rapping Cavalier? I don't think so!" Emmie stammered.

"He'll take some feeding..." Jack said looking at the colossus standing nearby.

"Feeding him isn't going to be the problem. We know he can rustle up a whole barbequed ox using his magical powers if needs be," Lily reasoned.

"I'll speak to him man to man!" Edward insisted. Floss nodded, wondering what Edward's manly dialogue might entail. Meanwhile, the Cavalier's look had been enhanced by a ceremonial sword hanging down by his side and a large floppy, ostrich feathered, Cavalier hat on his head. The ex-iguana attempted to fasten his cloak with a large brass button. It wasn't easy. Buttons were a new experience for an Iguana!

The friends agreed unanimously that Juan should be shorter and it would work better if his clothes were more twenty-first century. A face change was an absolute must. Looking like a famous pop star was simply too distracting. Edward was given the unenviable task of explaining this to him.

"I was thinking along the same lines," he readily admitted. "These buttons are useless. Too fiddly by half and I've already bumped my head because I'm too tall," he said grumpily, rubbing his noddle and pointing at a wooden beam hanging precariously from what had been a house. "I'd still like to be a famous pop star?"

"NO!" The teenagers were unshakable on this point.

Juan reduced his height to a more modest five feet ten and then changed his clothes in favour of a smart pin stripped suit, regular white shirt and a necktie covered in pictures of tiny iguanas. Black leather lace-ups and a bowler hat completed the city gent look.

"I really dig the bowler," Edward chortled before noticing a flash of flesh that were the iguana's feet. "We normally wear socks…!" He advised. A pair of black woollen socks immediately appeared on the city gent's tootsies. The girls inspected the iguana's creation closely from every angle.

"Quite satisfactory!" Floss praised him. The pop star's head had been replaced with his old iguana bonce because he said it fitted better and moving everything from inside one head to another is a bit like changing handbags. There's always the fear that one might inadvertently leave something behind. The girls empathised.

Wearing clothes after spending so many years in Costa Rica felt a bit strange and confining and in particular the city gent found his necktie constricted his throat.

"I'm not liking this thing you call a tie," Juan said, tugging at the one that had come with his new outfit.

"Here, have my paisley cravat," Jack surprised everyone by pulling a red silky scarf from his trouser pocket. "Undo the top button of your shirt and stick it round your neck. It'll make you look dapper and be far more comfortable," Jack said smiling, handing him his most treasured possession.

"A CRAVAT!" Edward shouted. "Who wears a cravat these days and Jack, why do you just happen to have one in your pocket?"

"It was my dad's," Jack explained. Edward gritted his teeth. Why couldn't he have just kept his big mouth shut! Juan sensed Jack's grief and gladly took the cravat, thanking him for his kind gesture.

Floss noticed that Juan's hands, like his head, hadn't changed. They were still iguana-like with one long clawed finger on each hand.

"Dearie me! A mere hick-up, that's all," the reptile reassured her muttering some mumbo jumbo to make his claws vanish and two six-fingered hands appear.

"Six fingers?" Emmie smirked.

"What's wrong with six fingers may I ask? Six fingers can be extremely useful." Juan defended his new hands. He counted the fingers on Floss's hands. "I see. It should be five fingers." In the blink of an eye the extra appendage was gone.

"Actually, its four fingers and a thumb," Emmie told him.

"I knew that!" The iguana's obstinate streak was coming to the fore. "And, I'm keeping my long fingers, so there!"

The teenagers thought Juan's Spanish name didn't fit well with the English city gent image.

"Maybe you should change it?" Edward asked. The others provided some suggestions.

"What about William?" Floss pondered. The others pooh-pooed her idea. "What's wrong with William? It's a popular name. Don't forget Prince William!" The Roberts' household was truly royalist. The iguana was not impressed.

"I'm drawn towards the name John. I believe it's the English equivalent of Juan and the most common boys name of all time. Johnathon, Johannes, Ioannes, Jan, Hans, Evan, Gianni, Chon and even Jack..." The teenagers were reaching their boredom threshold.

"It was a silly idea. Lets' just forget it," Floss decided.

"I'm with you," Jack backed her. They agreed that Juan should remain simply, Juan.

Rodrigo was casually flitting from one pile of rubble to the next in search of a tasty morsel. He was already looking decidedly fatter. Juan called his friend over.

"Ah Rodrigo, my dear old mate! Come and join us. I want you to meet the most delectable company this side of Malachite." The insect was munching a nettle leaf to settle his tummy.

"Hi, Iggy, me old amigo!" The insect acknowledged his best friend. "We've already met," he called out, leaping across the rubble to be beside them. "Oops! Sorry," he berated himself. "I should've addressed you as, Sir Juan in present company," the saucy cricket admonished himself. "I do most sincerely apologise," he said, making a low bow.

"Sir!" Edward exclaimed. The others were equally surprised to discover that their new acquaintance was not just any old iguana but an ennobled one.

"Rodrigo, did you have to...?" Juan asked the leggy insect. He would now be forced into an explanation.

The iguana-ish city gent took a moment to reflect before explaining the curious family ancestries on Malachite.

"My parents are both from virtuous and highly esteemed families and like your dukes and earls such offspring have honourable titles. On Malachite we address our nobility as sir or lady until they reach three hundred years of age," Juan explained.

"What happens then?" Jack enquired.

"Our titles are withdrawn unless we've been lucky enough to earn a *Golden Reputation*. If so we may be awarded another titled three hundred years of celebrity status. Speaking for myself, if I fail to gain the coveted golden accolade I'll just become another all-so-ran, a dead duck or an old fuddy-duddy! Que Sera, Sera. Whatever will be, will be..." Juan appeared downcast.

"That's never going to happen. We'll make sure of it!" Lily cried out. As the school's official Equalities Representative she felt duty bound to offer solace even to an iguana.

The skies above May Tree Close darkened, becoming dull and overcast with clouds about to release a deluge of water.

"I feel rain," Floss said, wiping a drip from her forehead.

"Oh No, No! I can't believe this is happening to me," Emmie screeched. "My mini-skirt is brand new and I do not want to get it wet! It'll ruin the fabric. It's dry clean only!" The boys sniggered. It wasn't a problem they had ever had to deal with.

"Just take it off," Jack laughed.

"Trust you two to come up with a stupid suggestion like that!" Emmie's fashion faux pas was causing her great unhappiness.

"It's not such a silly idea," Floss murmured, turning to Juan. "You could use your magic to provide Emmie with a new rain-proofed outfit!" Anything to keep the peace. He didn't understand this fashion thing but was prepared to go with the flow.

Malachitian females, Juan told the teenagers, wore the same outfit for a whole year before taking it apart and remaking the pieces into a new creation. Putting this to one side, in the interests of maintaining a friendly atmosphere he chanted a few foreign sounding words and Emmie's mini-skirt was instantly replaced with an outfit to die for from the trendy, *Girl About Town* fashion emporium. She now sported pink trousers with a matching sparkly jumper and was more than satisfied with her new look. Her lurid orange designer trainers were still on her feet and looked at odds with the new pink outfit but she didn't care.

"Juan, thanks for my wonderful new outfit, but please note, I want my mini-skirt back in good condition at your earliest convenience!" Emmie's carping left the iguana wondering why mortals had to be so prickly.

The rain hurled itself down in buckets and was made worse by a wind that had mysteriously turned up too. Juan moved fast to provide a large tent for them all to shelter under. They hurriedly collected up their cushions and flung them into the tent. Whilst doing this a black and white flash caught their eyes. Whatever it was, it was now in the front garden of Mr and Mrs Becks at 73 May Tree Close.

"What was that?" Edward squawked, peeping out whilst trying to keep his head dry at the same time.

"That was Rosie, my rabbit!" Jack yelled. Edward nodded, remembering Jack's affection for his pet. "Rosie's been made homeless by this mess," Jack sighed, looking at the ruin that was once his home. "My lovely rabbit was my dad's pet originally. She's incredibly special to me and my mum." They now understood the reason for the depth of Jack's fondness.

Rosie had done a runner. Rodrigo, sheltering beneath masonry to keep his membranous cricket wings dry watched from afar. He pondered, could this Rosie thing be edible?

"Don't even think about it!" Juan shouted, reading his mind. "Crickets only eat plants!"

"Shucks Iggy! I guess you're right," Rodrigo used his friend's nick name. No amount of calling Rosie helped. Jack glared menacingly at the cricket.

"Listen up, bug. Rosie's mine! You stay away from her! Do you hear?" Jack loved Rosie to bits. "She'll drown in all this rain." Jack was distraught. Throwing caution to the wind he belted across the Becks' front garden to search for her. Guilt overcame his friends who were safe and dry in the tent whilst Jack stumbled about on the rubble, getting drenched through and blown around in the wind. Their loyalty to Jack got the better of them and they joined him in pursuit of the bunny. Not so for the iguana who remained inside the tent.

Juan watched his new friends carefully lifting bricks and fallen branches, avoiding as best they could, causing a rubble avalanche that might inadvertently squash Rosie. Muck from the wet debris coated their hands and the rain made them feel wretched. Floss noted Juan's reluctance to set foot outside the tent. It made her cross.

"Are you just going to stand there and do nothing?" She shouted, rivulets of water dripping from her face and hair and feeling horribly uncomfortable. "At the very least you could use your magical powers to stop this infernal storm," she bawled, trying to be heard over the lashing rain.

Did the iguana's powers stretch to controlling the weather? Probably not, but Floss was angry. The quietly unassuming schoolgirl had disappeared and in her place was a strong, confident young woman, ready to take on the world, and although she didn't know it yet, the Universe!

"You mean I shouldn't play the fiddle whilst Rome burns?" The city gent mused, his claws tucked casually in his pockets and looking unlike any city worker Floss had ever seen before.

"Another homily about Rome! That's all we need," Jack shouted, his clothes soggy and sticking intolerably to his torso.

"Rome does seem to feature highly in his repertoire," Edward agreed. Juan took the hint and sauntered over to the scene of the crime. The rain appeared to go round his body rather than on it - as if it knew better than to land on him. They were impressed. This Malachitian mystery could actually control the weather. They resumed their frantic search for the rabbit until Juan stopped them in their tracks.

"Cease!" He commanded. They were not sure whether he was speaking to the rain or to them. They stood still and interestingly the rain stopped too. All was quiet. "I'm listening for Rosie's breathing. I need more space. Please move further away from me," he told them. They did as requested, clearing an area close to the last sighting of the rabbit.

There was much about Juan they just couldn't get their heads around. He had magic for one thing and he appeared to have highly sensitive senses.

"You mean you can actually hear her breathing?" Jack asked incredulously.

"Naturalmente!" The city gent replied. Getting to grips with the English language was quite a challenge and he decided to give them the benefit of his new learning. "Did you know the word SPACE has a double meaning?" The iguana's students were nonplussed. "The word can mean the *space* where we're standing right now or up there in the cosmos." This creature from outer *space* was losing them. So far he hadn't told them anything they didn't know already. "Through hemispheres, past planetary nebulae, around star clusters, constellations, galaxies and universes and way up into the unknown...The concept of outer space began over three and a half billion years ago! Did you know that?" Before they had time to answer he'd moved on. "But enough about that. I want you to prepare yourselves for the trip of a lifetime. I'm taking you to the edge of beyond!" This was fascinating talk but Jack was impatient to find his rabbit.

With Juan's wittering on about space, the Finding Rosie Mission had ground to a halt. Floss brought the city gent back to reality but she needn't have worried because it seemed the iguana had kept his ear to the ground all the time.

"Rosie's telling me she prefers her freedom and absolutely doesn't want to go back to her hutch if it means continuing with her lonely existence, and who can blame her for that?" Juan understood what made the animal tick.

"But what about me?" Jack sulked.

"What about you, Jack? Would you like be cooped up in a wooden box? It can be arranged." Juan lost no time in muttering a spell. Jack shrunk to the size of a rabbit and became – a rabbit! The rabbit presented a miserable, forlorn expression to the world. He was stuck in a hutch peering out from behind a chicken wire window. A bunch of fresh kale hung nearby for his dinner. Juan tittered, not yet fully understanding the emotional upset he'd caused his sensitive new human friends.

They were shocked to see their friend turned into a bunny rabbit. They sensed life might be very uncertain with this odd creature around. Edward, however, couldn't resist seeing the funny side of this latest turn of events.

"I suppose Jack's a Jack Rabbit now is he?"

"Oh you're so funny!" The rabbit could speak. "Jack Rabbits are hares, stupid!!" Jack rebuffed his best friend.

"Return Jack to his previous self at once," Floss insisted. Juan's antics worried them. What might he do next? "I thought you cared about us. I fear we're seeing another side to you." Floss was livid. Juan didn't like being scolded.

"Florence, my brightest star, you have my unreserved apology. I stand contrite."

"So, do something about our Jack because he's still STANDING in that ruddy rabbit hutch!" Lily reprimanded the iguana sharply. Jack, with his long ears and twitching nose stared miserably out from his prison cell. His little black face was still instantly recognisable as Jack's. Juan reversed the spell. It was a while before Jack was able to stop scratching himself and give the fleas their marching orders. They say every cloud has a silver lining and Rodrigo, being partial to fleas enjoyed gobbling them up, one by one as they jumped ship, vacating Jack's body. Infuriatingly, Rosie's whereabouts where still unknown.

"Jack, don't fret. Rosie will be just fine. Leave her be for now," Juan reassured him.

Rodrigo was slowly recovering from his trip across the Atlantic. His tummy felt fuller but he was fatigued, needing something to cheer himself up, brighten what he saw now as his monotonous lifestyle. It had been fifteen years since he'd actively engaged in an exciting intergalactic tussle where the good people battle it out against evil oppressors. Juan's next mission sounded right up his street but he didn't fancy getting involved as a cricket. He wanted a change. Juan's new body had given him a new lease of life and if a transformation was good enough for his old chum then it was good enough for him, Rodrigo, Son of Rodrigues of the Honourable Gryllidae Family.

The fidgety cricket was looking off colour. His bright green hue had faded a touch. He felt down at heel.

"I do like being a giant cricket but sometimes it's not quite what it's cracked up to be," he bemoaned. "I happen to like marsupials and I'm thinking, thylacine. What do any of you think?" Regretfully, having been born after the last thylacine had allegedly died they had never heard of this beast. Of one thing they were all agreed. The thylacine sounded prehistoric. Rodrigo had the bit between his teeth and wouldn't let go of his idea.

"What do thylacines look like?" Edward tried to sound interested.

"It's a type of meat eating marsupial wolf. Some say it's extinct. The last one officially died in a zoo in 1936. I'm one of the few who still believe they exist," Rodrigo told them.

"Quite right too!" Juan interrupted.

"Why is that?" Floss asked.

"In 2009 I was sent on a cosmic assignment to North Queensland and whilst I was there I chatted to many a thylacine. They're pleasant enough animals just incredibly shy and a bit like Rosie - they just don't want to be found."

Rodrigo snarled thylacine-like. It was an unpleasant experience. Tiger-like stripes appeared along his back as he turned into a realistic looking thylacine.

"Thylacines have tummy pouches like kangaroos for carrying their young around in. Neat eh!" Rodrigo told them, stretching out his new hindlegs and looking ever more ferocious.

"I don't like the idea of a thylacine being so close to us," Emmie whimpered. Floss and Lily concurred. Juan drew Rodrigo to one side for a friendly chat and before it was over the wolf-like creature had disappeared and in his place appeared a black, fluffy, buck, angora rabbit like Rosie. Jack was spellbound.

"Oh dear, Jack!" Edward was teasing his mate again. "I think Rodrigo fancies your Rosie." His joke fell on deaf ears.

Chapter 7

Dicing with Death on the New York Subway

The city gent was suddenly impatient.

"We need to get moving. We've a long way to go," he said, looking at a strange clock he found in a pocket on his torso.

"Moving! Where to?" The five chorused together. Lily was also concerned about time as her ladies' football team had a game at 4.30 pm that afternoon and she was meant to be playing. Floss checked the time again even though Juan insisted they had nothing to worry about. Time was moving inexplicably at a snail's pace. Only a quarter of an hour in real time had passed so they reasoned there was plenty of time to go wherever it was Juan was taking them as long as it wasn't somewhere absurd like outer space! They laughed at the very idea.

"We're going to New York City. Didn't I mention that? Oh dear! How remiss of me." Juan drew gasps from them all.

"New York! Absolute lunacy," Floss said, shocked. "What about our parents?"

"Great. Bring it on!" Sung Emmie. "Bloomingdales, Macey's. Oh Yes Please! Can we have some spending money and fly first class?" Emmie was on cloud nine at the prospect of a free trip to the USA. The others were more circumspect. They needed more information.

The fashion conscious, code-breaking supremo, Emmeline Taylor was ready to believe anything. That particular morning had already turned out to be surprisingly earth-shattering so to hear they were flying, she presumed they would be flying, to New York, sounded entirely feasible. For whatever reason they were bound for that city, she hoped that a shopping spree would feature within their schedule!

"Floss, you never know you might be reunited with your heroine, Jackie Ambrose. She might be flying our plane!" Emmie was totally fired up and ready to go.

"Unlikely. Jackie covers Europe," Floss returned. "I can see you're happy Emmie but I'm concerned our parents won't know where we are. They'll worry!"

"You weren't listening to our new friend. He's taken care of everything. Anyway, you said your parents were out for the count!" Emmie could at times be indelicate. Why was this once scaly, beguiling creature taking them on such an adventurous trip? Stressing about it led to Floss lowering her mental guard and Juan read her mind.

"Floss, I'm getting that you have doubts?" He cooed. "Have faith!" Floss hurriedly shut her mind to the iguana's marauding, magnetic impulses.

Rodrigo rabbit stood with his head cocked, listening intently to an approaching roar that was growing louder by the second.

"Sir Juan, I may look like a cuddly rabbit but I was careful to keep my aural powers during my transformation and I think I'm right in surmising that our termite friends have landed in Wallington, just down the road from here and will be with us shortly." Rodrigo clasped his little paws together in delight.

"UP TWO, THREE, FOUR; UP TWO, THREE, FOUR," the chanting was disturbingly coupled with the almighty crash of boots on the ground. A force to be reckoned with was marching, unstoppably towards them. An army of termites no less; each insect having six feet and each of those feet clad in army issue boots.

The ground shook with every step the termites took causing the piles of rubble to destabilise and jump with the rhythm of their stamping feet. Juan saw this and ordered their sergeant major to break-step, putting an end to the thunderous row they were making.

"There must be millions of them," Jack remarked.

"More like billions," Edward corrected.

"Trillions," whispered Emmie.

"Hurrah!" Bellowed Rodrigo. "You're here at last!" He called out hopping onto a mound of rubble to get a better view and avoid becoming an accident statistic as more termites became visible, marching fearlessly and treading down anything in their way. The new Rodrigo rabbit twitched his nose, smelled the air, and detected a scent he loved. It was the fragrance of happiness! His old termite comrades had arrived. He waved his paws like mad in greeting and hopped excitedly after the first brigade to arrive in May Tree Close, coming to a clamorous halt outside Floss's house.

The intrepid insects stood tall in their ranks just metres from Juan and the teenagers. The brownie-red coloured arthropods were only a smidgeon taller than Rodrigo in rabbit form but daunting never-the-less.

"At ease, gentlemen," Juan ordered. The termites were exhausted but tried to relax still clutching their weapons, miniature cross bows and swords. Many of the fatigued insects collapsed where they stood. It had been a long, embattled flight in strong winds from their meeting point, Costa Rica. They had come together there from all the hot climates across our globe to fight for justice under the intergalactic banner and outwit the Universe's greatest adversary. The eagle-eyed sergeant major, for whom butter wouldn't melt in his mouth, insisted on disciplined troops and was not prone to tolerating any obvious lack of stamina. He navigated the lines of his dishevelled, lack lustre troops, nudging those hunched up over their weapons back into an upright position. They complied, looking all in and wondering when they would be allowed to eat and restore their depleted fat stores.

The termites' uniforms were turquoise in colour with a unique blue and yellow check beret otherwise looking pretty much like British squaddies. Their commanders arrived wearing the same blue uniforms but with stripes and bars full of regimental medals pinned to their chests. They shook hands with Juan and Rodrigo.

"Good to see you again, Sir Juan!" One of the high-ranking commanders whom they later learnt to be General Felipe, greeted the iguana. "You look a bit different to when I last saw you," the general added bluntly surveying the city gent.

"Well yes. You see human people-lets aren't that keen on iguanas," he fibbed. "We make them feel edgy, if you know what I mean?" General Felipe fixed a gimlet eye on what he made up his mind to be a bunch of ignoramuses.

"And how do they feel about rabbits and termites?" The general was regarding Rodrigo's velvety, rabbity appearance with scepticism. With all that rabbit fur hanging over his eyes he'd be a liability to any fighting force!

"Let's not go there at this precise moment," Juan requested, sensing General Felipe's disquiet. "Allow me to introduce you to my new friends..."

Juan presented his apprentices individually to the termite commanders.

"Florence, known as Floss to her friends, readily answered my call for help. Such a gifted young woman with a wonderful sense of duty that is sadly so often missing in the youth of today, don't you think?" Juan philosophised. General Felipe nodded. Floss hardly recognised herself from Juan's description. Lily came next. "Ah, Lily!" He paused. General Felipe saw her stripy legs.

"Is Lily part human, part iguana?" An innocent enough question. Lily regarded General Felipe like a python might look at its prey, ready to crush the life out it! She was preparing a rude reply when Juan blocked her ability to speak by sending magnetic waves intracranially, temporarily halting her thought processes. Lily was suddenly tongue-tied. Edward, Jack, and Emmie had worried looks on their faces. What would Juan say about them? Juan gave up and introduced the termite top brass instead.

"These extraordinary insects are my front line, my big cheeses, my rocks and my dependable war cabinet," Juan began. "General Felipe is my five-star general and my Minister for Subterranean Warfare. He usually works hand in hand with General Gonzalez, another subterranean termite who knows everything there is to know about subway tunnels. Admiral Mathias is my most experienced sailor and one of our most celebrated damp wood termites coming from your own Pacific shores. Generals Alvaro, Joaquin and of course Gonzalez are all my exemplary four-star generals..." General Joaquin interrupted Juan's flow.

"Sir Juan, I'd like to correct you on one small point if I may. I'm a damp wood too! I would also add for the benefit of these people-lets that my name is spelt J-o-a-q-u-i-n, but pronounced, Wah-Keen. I like everyone to get it right. Thank you!" The punctilious termite stepped back into line. Juan sighed loudly. At times, his generals could be too precise. It was time for General Gonzalez to take his leave and accompany a brigade of military engineers to reconnoitre the New York subway scene and put together an up-to-the minute intelligence report on enemy forces for when the other generals arrived.

The rank and file termites were seriously jaded and looked bedraggled. They struggled to stand in line as their weariness and hunger overcame them. They desperately needed sustenance. The sergeant major finally relented and considered the best options for feeding his famished troops.

"They need plenty of vegetation and wood to gnaw through," the sergeant major stated matter-of-factly, glumly surveying the scene in May Tree Close. Juan had certainly done a good job of destroying the plant life as well as the buildings. Not a single tree remained standing. A large spider ran out from under a brick causing the lower ranks to yell out, petrified. Spiders and termites are not the best of friends especially when termites are too tired to stop themselves being eaten alive. A wave of terror rippled through the ranks.

"What's going on?" Floss shouted, just as the spider realised he was vastly outnumbered and scuttled away.

General Felipe, the five star general and the highest ranking saw the food situation as urgent. The exhausted termites must be fed immediately or the mission would be jeopardised. Admiral Mathias was asked to assist.

"I seemed to recall troop feeding is one of your areas of expertise!" General Felipe addressed the old sea farer reminding everyone of the Battle of Deep Lake, a dreadfully bloody conflict occurring centuries before on Titan, one of Saturn's moons. On that occasion the admiral had excelled himself by providing mountains of well-rotted wet wood for the termites to munch through and therein had secured victory.

"Under control, sir," replied the naval arthropod. "The men will eat any kind of cellulose and in this Carshalton backwater there'll be masses of the stuff stashed away in bookcases and cupboards. The troops adore eating paper of any kind. If they forage in the ruins I've no doubt they'll find volumes of tasty old books, newspapers, computer paper, magazines, cardboard, blank or printed, it's all the same to our guys" he declared confidently.

Floss was still finding the arrival of Juan, Rodrigo, and the termites fantastically bizarre. Juan explained that the termites original home, before they spread out around the world was the Tropics of Pruna, a distant planet. The Pruna tribe were staunchly aggressive combatants, prepared to fight to the death. Their tooth-and-nail commitment to fighting power hungry tyrants meant they were often called up to fight for the Universe. Over the course of time many of them had been captured and banished by evil dictators to places such as Costa Rica, Spain, and California. It's why today, termites are found in hot countries all over the world. Floss studied the insects closely. Termites with moustaches! It was mind blowing but then she'd never seen termites wearing military uniforms before either. Life had suddenly become much more interesting and even allowing for all the magic going on around her something was bothering her. The termites appeared to be blind.

"Yes indeed, my dear Floss," Juan began. "Most of them are as blind as a bat! They have composite eyes but largely feel their way around. Living in their termite mounds underneath the ground in the pitch dark they really don't need sight. However, my generals and the admiral always have good clear vision. When it comes to the crunch and we're facing our enemies the commanders have the executive authority to issue each soldier with exemplary vision. It's just a matter of feeding them a magical serum." Floss was struck dumb. He had an answer for everything!

Emmie was excited about their approaching adventure and could hardly contain herself.

"Come on everyone. I'm itching to go!" She urged her friends, hopping from one leg to the other in anticipation.

"You look like you've got the heebie-jeebies," Edward teased.

"Time waits for no man or iguana come to that!" Juan quipped. "Emmie's right. We need to be on our way. Follow me, please." Juan struck out across a narrow slip road to the little green island passing through the heaving mass of insects scurrying, searching for food. The termites dutifully cleared a path for their Malachitian field marshal and his entourage. The most extraordinary adventure beckoned.

Juan checked his clock once more explaining that it was a space chronometer, a very precise watch-like piece of equipment giving wind speeds and planetary alignments.

"Gather round. Come close. I won't bite," Juan gestured for them all to come nearer. They did, expecting a rallying chat but instead found themselves having to listen to a heartfelt apology. "I'm afraid I've slipped up. Our fleet of air passenger transporters are all fully booked and I must improvise to get us to New York in time. I'm so embarrassed by my lack of planning; such an important trip as well. I took my eye off the ball. No worries! Where there's a will, there's a way! Isn't that what you Earthlings say?" The teenagers were sceptical. "Pay strict attention and do exactly what I tell you to do. I'll be our air limo! Just follow my instructions and we'll all be safely delivered to New York City."

The boys were uncharacteristically worried about the non-existence of an aeroplane.

"Ed, I don't like the sound of this one little bit," Jack whispered.

"I agree. Heath Robinson springs to mind," Edward replied.

"Who's Heath Robinson?" Lily asked. Jack and Edward glanced at each other, sighing.

"It's an idiom," Edward replied. Emmie, the lover of languages, elaborated.

"If something's Heath Robinson it's usually impractical, ineffectual or strangely funny," she explained. Lily shivered. Their situation suddenly appeared more dangerous than they had at first thought.

Juan's travel arrangements sounded wacky, worrying, and downright senseless.

"Floss, put your arms around my waist from behind me." She tried stretching her arms around the iguana's ample girth but they were just too short. "I see, I'm too fat. Oh well, try putting your hands in my jacket pockets and clinging on." If the truth be known, even Juan wasn't sure this would work. "Ed, come round to my front and hang on to my braces. Lily and Emmie, the latter's satchel still strapped to her back, were told to hang on to the iguana's arms, one on each side. He stretched them out t-shirt style so they could get a good grip. Jack was holding back, thoroughly disconcerted by this less than scientific means of travel. "Jack, be brave. Trust Me! Please hold on to my bowler hat if you will." Juan crouched down, allowing Jack to get into position. He had to really reach out over Florence to get to the hat's brim. The idea was absolutely bonkers. Jack's insides felt like jelly.

The unorthodox flying machine rose slowly into the sky, its passengers scared and euphorically joyful all rolled into one. Being so peculiar, their method of flight just had to be illegal. Someone would surely report them to the British Society for the Reporting of Unidentified Flying Objects. From sixty feet up, about the height of a medium sized sycamore tree they saw the full extent of the damage to May Tree Close and how massive the termite army truly was. It spread out beyond the junction with Wallington Park Road, where the traffic was still being turned away.

"Hell!" Spluttered Edward. "Look at that swarm of creepy crawlies down there."

"So weird!" Added Lily. It's like they must be invisible to all those people walking along Wallington Park Road."

"And yet, WE can see them…so we must be special!" Emmie managed to utter as they headed into the breeze.

Rosie rabbit and Rodrigo the cricket had only just met but were curiously standing arms entwined, waving madly with their free paws as the airborne travellers floated higher into the clouds.

"Isn't Rodrigo coming with us?" Floss yelled, as they drifted aloft.

"Rodrigo's staying here. He'll let us know if the enemy tries to make a surprise attack on Carshalton," Juan replied guardedly and not wanting to worry Jack at this point kept schtum that the rabbits had fallen spontaneously head over heels in love. The teenagers continued their ascent until the whirring sound of termites flying behind them filled the air.

"General Felipe's band of specialised troops will accompany us part way. They'll leave us before we get near the war zone," Juan told them. War zone! News that they were bound for a war zone with a load of blind termites sounded delusional. The teenagers were supposed to be in school studying for their exams not war mongering. Emmie's dream of a carefree shopping extravaganza sounded like it was just that, a dream.

With Juan they were learning fast that life never ran smoothy for long.

"I'm afraid I'll have to leave you to your own devices as we near John F Kennedy airport. The radar ruins my sensory nerves and renders my magic useless," Juan told them, humbly. "I'll accompany you as far as I can depending on the latest intelligence reports." Barely audible over the wind he did his best to continue. "The first thing I'm going to do when I get home is get this radar problem fixed. It's quite ridiculous for a man of my standing not to be radar proofed."

"What about us?" Lily demanded, hoping she would have the strength to cling on to Juan's arm for the whole three thousand miles to New York. Jack was feeling stressed out too. A couple of times the bowler hat had almost flipped off. Luckily, Floss had somehow managed to catch hold of him and save his skin.

Juan's elementary flying machine was surrounded by at least a hundred large termites. The flying insects were led by General Felipe's flag bearer carrying the regimental colours, an image of a brown termite surrounded by the motto, *To Do or Die*, on a light blue background. General Felipe's Special Subterranean Service troops, known as the SSS were being deployed in the subway tunnels to act on intelligence supplied by General Gonzalez. Their adopted policy was a simple one. Shoot to kill and then Eat. Admiral Mathias had cadged a lift across the Atlantic Ocean to his naval headquarters on Bermuda. The two commanding officers sat comfortably chatting in plush armchairs as they flew. Their transport was cleverly designed to resemble a bald eagle to deter insect eating birds from swallowing them up mid-air.

The din of so many termite wings beating in unison was deafening as they drifted over the streets of Croydon and then Sevenoaks in Kent where they enjoyed the pleasant sighting of deer in Knole Park.

"KENT!" Floss exclaimed. "We're going the wrong way. Geography is one of my best subjects and I know that Kent is too far to the east. We need to go west like the Pilgrim Fathers on their epic seventeenth century voyage," she yelled. Juan thought differently. The mention of the New England settlers, however, reminded him of a previous adventure.

"The Pilgrim Fathers left Plymouth on a ship called The Mayflower. Do you see the connection?" The iguana asked, shouting over the wind.

"Yeah, we get it! But May Tree Close or The Mayflower - who cares?" Jack yelped, and then, "OMG, my hand is slipping..." Luckily General Felipe's carriage was alongside and the termite caught him, instructing his aide to tie the silly boy to the field marshal with a mysterious gold twine.

Their flying contraption flew over Canterbury and from above it didn't look like a twenty-first century city. No high-rise blocks of flats, no lorries belching out fumes and the streets were strewn with straw and animal poo. They had gone back in time to the Canterbury of 1381. Wat Tyler, leader of the medieval Peasants' Revolt was marching through the streets to persuade King Richard II to make life better for the poor. Wat looked up and gave Juan a cheery wave just as a vicious fight broke out between Wat's followers and the king's men. Lily's natural inclination was to help the underdogs.

"We must rescue Wat before he's cut to shreds!" She screeched.

"We cannot change the course of history," Juan told her, "we simply mustn't intervene. To do so would change the world as we know it today. The consequences would be dire," he explained, leaving Lily feeling wretched.

"But what happened to Wat and the peasants?" Lily nagged.

"Alas, Wat was murdered by the king and the peasants went back to their homes. The march achieved nothing at all." Lily felt sad. If only human rights lawyers had existed in the middle ages!

Juan descended to the seashore at the white cliffs of Dover landing on the shingle.

"Short stop for a brief assignation with my friend Eva and maybe a snack," Juan heard Edward's stomach rumbling.

"I'm assuming Eva's another one of your wacky friends?" Edward mocked.

"Indeed. Eva is my Aussie red necked avocet colleague. An avocet is a wading bird with a cute upturned bill and as you might expect, Eva's no ordinary wading bird. She's the intergalactic community's Spy Extraordinaire!" He told them proudly. "Eva's an expert in cloak and dagger intelligence and not to be trifled with…the criminal underworld quake in their boots when they hear Eva's on their case!" Juan looked along the beach for the femme fatale. "There she is!" Juan shouted joyfully. "Eva, we're over here. Come and meet my new friends."

At the sound of Juan's voice the bird stopped swishing her bill in the water. General Felipe and his military escort had slowed down over Romney Marsh but having now caught up were flying directly overhead. His crack troops were needed in position in New York ASAP so there was no time to stop for a chat. They all watched as the insects made a flypast just like the RAF's Red Arrows and then flew on, becoming just dots on the horizon before totally disappearing from view.

"What's the difference between termites and ants?" Edward was testing Juan again.

"Well..." Juan had to think for a moment. "As I recall, ants have a cinched in waist and antennae with kinks in them, a bit like an elbow shape. Their wings are different too. My termite friends have two sets of wings the same length whereas ants mostly have no wings at all unless of course they happen to be flying ants!" It wasn't the clearest of explanations. "Termites and ants really don't like each other. Ants are nasty little blighters where termites are concerned, always forming raiding parties and destroying termite nests."

The avocet tottered over. Was it possible that this scrawny little clump of feathers was so highly regarded by the international community?

"Hi, Juan. You're on time for once!" Eva cackled.

"We got lucky! Pushed along by a north wind," Juan explained. "I hope we haven't interrupted your search for lunch?"

"You're joking aren't yer? It's useless here. I can't find a decent crab or worm anywhere. A freshwater muddy creek at low tide is more my cup of tea or a burger bar!" She squawked, laughing at her own joke.

"I hope we're not expected to eat worms?" Lily sulked.

"Worms! Of course not! I was thinking more like pan fried beetles," Eva replied, causing them all to wince. Lily rolled her eyes and grunted.

"Lily, look at it this way - worms and beetles are gluten free!" Emmie told her.

"You're not getting worms for your victuals!" Eva chortled. "I was just pulling your leg." The bird winked at Juan who was busy conjuring up some comfortable seats.

Five white plastic garden chairs appeared on the beach along with a matching table piled high with appetising food. There were plump beef burgers in buns, hot sausage rolls and bowls of steaming chips covered in tomato ketchup. For those with a sweet tooth, which was all of them, there were fluffy pink meringues sandwiched together with thick cream, strawberries dipped in white chocolate and a passion fruit cheesecake. Lily's faddy diet hadn't been forgotten. A dish of natural, fat free plain yoghurt floated in, landing right in front of her. Plenty of lemonade in old fashioned glass jugs was provided to wash down the sumptuous banquet.

"Right then, bottoms up!" Edward declared, pouring himself a tumbler of soda. They dived in, whilst the iguana and Eva talked tactics further along the beach.

With the speed at which the teenagers packed the food away snack-time didn't last long. Juan turned the chairs into a six seater flying machines propelled by rotating blades and a mysterious energy supply. The chairs were engulfed in a transparent bubble to keep the wind at bay. They climbed in.

"It'll be like travelling in a hot and stuffy greenhouse!" Emmie feared.

"Beggars can't be choosers! It's just got to be an improvement on hanging on to Juan for dear life. I've never felt so scared!" Jack admitted. Juan ignored their comments.

"Floss, come sit up front with me. You can operate the controls," the iguana suggested. Edward sat next to Emmie and Lily and Jack sat in the backrow. Eva scratched her head as she watched them rise up into the sky, wondering if Juan had finally lost it!

"See you all there then...! The scrawny clump of feathers screeched after them.

Chapter 8

The Story at Last

Juan's flying machine rose above a turbulent ocean where giant waves were crashing, hurling spray so high it hit the sides of the bubble. The expanse of grey-green, gruesome water below seemed to go on forever. At times, the teenagers were forced to grip the arms of their chairs with all their might to stop themselves falling out. Emmie released a worried squeal each time they hit a thermal. She couldn't swim. Should the worst happen and she came a cropper she would drown before they ever reached New York City. She couldn't decide which would be worse - dying by drowning or missing the New York shops!

"Juan won't allow any of us to drown," Edward reassured her. Lily was feeling nervous too and contemplating whether Juan had undertaken a risk assessment before leaving Carshalton. They were the latest craze at school. Each time Lily's sports teams played away from home her teachers considered every type of pitfall before they were allowed to put a single foot on the bus.

Hitting calmer weather the iguana-cum-city gent took the opportunity to give his students some background information on their approaching mission.

"It all started in London's Hyde Park in May 1882," he began. "The park was always at its best in springtime before the black soot of Victorian factories and the smoke from coal fires smothered the new leaves on the trees, causing them to wither and die.

"The Clean Air Act of 1956 stopped all that," Edward butted in, distracting Juan.

"Rotten Row is a sandy track on the south side of Hyde Park. The Route Du Roi or The King's Road is what it should have been called but in Victorian times it had become Rotten Row. This famous pathway was always full of notable people riding in their carriages. The ladies wore their finest silk gowns and matching bonnets and sat proudly in their carriages for all to admire. They were usually accompanied by princes, lords, diplomats, bankers, high-ranking military personnel, and anyone who was anyone. It was a sight to behold and it was just so on the morning of Wednesday 31st May 1882..." Juan had grabbed their attention.

The bubble was doing an excellent job at keeping out the wind - you could have heard a pin drop. The iguana continued his yarn.

"A carriage carrying Princess Beatrice, the youngest daughter of Queen Victoria passed along Rotten Row with Count Abdul from Alexandria in Egypt by her side. The princess waved happily at those she knew. She enjoyed her morning drives as she had little other time for herself. Her mother relied on her one remaining unmarried daughter to act as her consort for official events. Visiting heads of state from abroad, princes, princesses, and nobility from across the world were often seen in the tender care of Princess Beatrice rather than the Queen who became a bit of a recluse after the death of her husband, Prince Albert. She preferred to keep herself busy signing Acts of Parliament or holding meetings with Mr Gladstone, her prime minister," Juan related.

Juan amazingly revealed he had spent time at Buckingham Palace in the guise of a footman during Queen Victoria's reign whilst searching the world for the worst intergalactic pirate the outer space community had ever seen. This monster was Gregor Magnus and along with his side kick, Effria, had been the intergalactic security force's main targets since time immemorial. Both were hardened criminals, interstellar fugitives, and the enemies of the Universe. Effria was an escapee from Malactron, the prison planet where he'd been serving a long hundred and ninety year sentence for bribery and corruption when fifteen years before he'd broken out. From that time onwards he'd roamed the galaxies, hitching lifts on passing spaceships by using different aliases and being an absolute master of disguise, tricking young astronauts who were too young to have read about him in the outer space newspapers, and hence ignorant of his dastardly acts. Prison had strengthened Effria's resolve for revenge and he was prepared to work his evil wherever necessary if it earned him pots of money as a mercenary. Gregor Magnus had engineered Effria's escape knowing that, as long as he stayed on the megalomaniac's payroll his loyalty would be assured and the greedy creature would always do his bidding.

Count Abdul had come to the Big Smoke, a term referring to late Victorian London, which was also the richest city in the world, to discuss with Her Majesty the difficult and tense situation in Egypt. The British ruled Egypt in the 1880's and the Egyptians living in Alexandria, the Egyptian capital then, were angry about their low wages. Tensions were running high and an uprising looked likely. Abdul wanted to discuss options for averting a rebellion before thousands were killed.

"Princess Beatrice wanted to help Count Abdul's cause and the two royals discussed the impending riots as they rode along Rotten Row. Her Royal Highness was totally unaware that the Count's mind had been infiltrated by

Effria who was definitely not striving for world peace. Princess Beatrice was conversing with an imposter and one that would do everything in his power to undermine any good that Count Abdul hoped to achieve."

"I don't understand how Count Abdul's Egyptian problems would have a bearing on an appalling creature like Gregor Magnus' plans for universal domination?" Edward liked to have all the facts.

"Small steps, Ed. Revolution in Egypt could have brought down the British government and therein its empire. Such events have a habit of ricocheting around the world, bringing down states one after another like a row of dominos," Juan told them.

"What you're suggesting is that once this despicable bully, whose name I refuse to say, had Earth within his grasp he would look further afield and find a way of undermining elsewhere such as your planet, Malachite," Floss summarised.

The teenagers were concentrating fully, listening to Juan's tale and because of this they no longer felt every little bump in the thermals as they flew through them.

"Where does this, *mister high and mighty bogey man*, Gregor Magnus, live when he's at home?" Emmie asked.

"We know he has a powerbase on Ice Leonard, a cold glacial dwarf planet that few seek to visit. It's the most distant planet in the Solar System, a wasteland of frozen water. Civil engineers have cleverly constructed centrally heated cities beneath the planet's crust otherwise it would be totally inhospitable. The Ice Leonard population is in any case low in number and as a result of the terrible climate tend to be pale faced through lack of sunshine and very miserable and open to persuasion by scallywags like Gregor Magnus.

"Why don't you just go to Ice Leonard and arrest him!" It all looked so easy to Jack.

"Ah yes, well we think he leaves Ice Leonard for long periods of time and especially when there's something important brewing like a full scale assault on a nation, state, star or planet. And, I forgot to tell you that he has powerful magical qualities. We need to take great care when approaching him." Juan painted a chilling picture.

Edward had an urgent call of nature. He fidgeted, definitely feeling uncomfortable.

"Sorry everyone. I need to pee!"

"Ed, please, too much information," Floss giggled.

"Just go. We won't look," Lily shouted.

"Yes Ed, we can't stop now." Emmie's sights were still firmly fixed on New York.

"I'd like a bit of privacy! And, what if I fall out of this bubble, midstream?" Edward cast his eye on the swirling water below. Jack, being a bloke could see his mate's point.

"He's right! And guess what's gonna happen if he pees into the wind?" Jack laughed. Without further ado Juan turned left intending to make a comfort stop in Bermuda, an island lying five hundred miles from New York. As soon as they landed Edward ran off to find a big rock to hide behind.

"This stop will give me a chance to tie-up with Admiral Mathias and you can all take a toilet break. There are beach bathrooms just over there," Juan told the girls, pointing to a path leading to a small brick building. "There's a power shower with copious hot water and soap for Floss!" Juan had read her mind. The awful shock Juan had given her that morning had meant she'd missed taking a shower.

"Of course there is!" Lily muttered sarcastically.

The girls walked briskly towards the rest rooms with Emmie removing a comb from her pink satchel in anticipation of a decent mirror. Juan had thought of everything so she wasn't disappointed.

"If we're going to be leading lights in Juan's intergalactic war, facing new terrors on a daily basis shouldn't we have a catchy name?" Floss asked, smiling. "What do you think about the *Fantastic Five*?"

"Sounds a bit like, The Famous Five," Emmie said, not feeling enthusiastic about Floss's suggestion.

"I agree," Lily added, "I'm a bit too old for Enid Blyton too."

"I used to love Enid Blyton's stories," Floss recollected. "I adored all of them, Famous Five, Secret Seven…"

"And Noddy!" Emmie added, making them all laugh. Lily, as usual, had the last word on the subject.

"No way Jose!" She exclaimed "I'm finding this whole experience difficult enough to handle as it is without a silly name tag!"

Jack did his own thing, clambering over a rocky outcrop and looking into the next bay where he spotted an official-looking naval dockyard and a harbour full of ships. The vessels were small by naval standards but they were definitely ships with their pennants flying high. He could make out the outline of a termite on the flags. Retracing his steps back to Juan, enjoying an impromptu bun of squirming sand worms, he told him what he'd seen.

"Yes. Quite! That'll be Admiral Mathias' fleet. We've been in communication. He'll be joining us shortly for a seafood snack," Juan mumbled, finishing his bun.

Bermuda was flooded with cheerful sunshine and golden sandy beaches and the soon to be military commanders and intergalactic big wigs were having doubts. Bermuda was beautiful and they felt like they had arrived in paradise.

"I'm just gonna stay here. I'm not cut out for hair-brained schemes like the one the iguana's hatching. I'll just lie on this beach and soak up the sun. Pick me up on your way home!" Lily said, guessing her request would fall on stony ground. The iguana had a fight on his hands with Lily in particular, so he appealed to her sense of justice and fair play.

"Lily, I really need your help. I chose you for your caring nature. You're going to be absolutely vital to my strategy. Please don't let me down." Lily knew it was hopeless to hold out. She gave him one of her grunts and became resigned to flying on to New York.

Admiral Mathias arrived as if by magic. He certainly didn't climb over the rocks in his cripplingly knee-high leather boots, heavy dark blue naval coat and his overhanging stomach, the latter being the resting place of many slap-up tropical wood banquets.

"Hello, Sea Salt! Good to see you again," Juan shook the admiral's stick thin hand. "What's the lie of the land?" Juan enquired.

"Sir, we're ready to set sail. My armada is anchored in the next bay." The admiral glanced at Juan's attire. The city suit looked inappropriate for engaging in an all-out battle.

"I have it in hand," Juan acknowledged, noticing his investigative eye. The city gent set to work straight away. The pinstripe suit was replaced by camouflaged combat gear topped by a khaki baseball cap.

Edward was still mulling over the Count Abdul story.

"Juan, this Effria, the one who inveigled himself into Count Abdul's brain," Edward was stifling a grin, not fully convinced of the authenticity of Juan's account. "What's to stop this geezer getting inside our heads too?"

"Errrr!" Lily grunted again, "This Effria's giving me the creeps! Keep him out of my head!"

"Indeed, Lily. There's far too much going on inside your head already," Juan jested. "Trust me! You'll all be quite safe. That monster won't ever infiltrate your brains."

"But if YOU can do it…It's all so disconcerting," Lily said, feeling emotionally drained.

"The intergalactic space agency has already taken steps to prevent Effria from invading your minds. Blocks are in place. I promise. You'll be as safe as houses!" The iguana reassured them although he probably hadn't chosen the best metaphor with their memories of May Tree Close still so fresh. The new team shot suspicious looks at each other. They were not convinced by Juan's words.

Once in New York City their mission was to rid the Universe of a power grabbing autocrat and his right hand man. Failure to do so was not an option. Life just couldn't get any better!

"So, Juan," Floss began, "if we're to annihilate these wicked adversaries we need to know the minutiae." Florence loved mysteries but this one sounded a bit too far-fetched and well outside her comfort zone.

"Hmm," Juan muttered, "You're going to make a wonderful airline pilot." Floss's cheeks blushed red. How did he know about her ambition? "Gregor Magnus is a megalomaniac who has defiled the concept of goodness. All will shortly be revealed," Juan sighed, thinking about the vast number of atrocities this vicious and savage aggressor had committed.

Juan was briefly emotionally drained by the recollection of Gregor Magnus' many sins against the Universe. Admiral Mathias stepped forward, giving his old ally time to recover.

"Our intel suggests that fiend, Magnus, will be in New York tomorrow but where he'll he hiding, we just don't know. We have everyone working on it. It's one reason why we need Emmie at her new post, like yesterday!" Emmie looked stunned. There wasn't time for questions because the admiral had more to say. "My fleet's setting sail in the next hour and we'll arrive in New York's East River at dawn tomorrow ready for the big push for freedom." Every time Juan opened his mouth a new and perplexing situation confronted them.

"Admiral, why would Magnus go to New York? Isn't he more likely to be captured there? And another thing, why do we need a fleet of ships when this warmongering idiot will be slap bang in the middle of a city? Surely, a land army is more appropriate?" Floss asked.

The answer to Floss's question was somewhat complicated, which she kind of half expected. Nothing was logical in Juan's world. The admiral tried to explain.

"Inferior dwarf planets such as Ice Leonard, Magnus' true home, are more easily travelled to and from when they're furthest from the sun. This window of opportunity will occur in the next few days. He will travel covertly to Manhattan because he needs to plan his next major assault with Effria and pay that terrible side kick his blood money. Effria insists on getting his cash on time! With regard to your second question, Sir Juan's strategy is based on a two-pronged attack. Your skills will come into play commanding our land armies but there'll also be some heroic action on the East River and in other watery locations, which will be my forte," the veteran damp wood naval expert explained proudly.

The admiral's theory suggested they would be commanding armies! Floss knew nothing about such things and neither did her friends. The admiral interrupted their thoughts.

"On the question of land versus water my damp wood sailors are familiar with living in swampy conditions and are, therefore, well equipped to fight in New York's sewers. I have the best trained commandos. They'll squirm through watery tunnels and won't flinch at wriggling along squishy, smelly, rat infested city pipes to catch these heinous criminals."

It was all so mind boggling. If the admiral had set out to put their minds at rest he'd achieved exactly the opposite. Rat infested tunnels! Emmie was already mentally packing her bags and Lily and Floss were not far behind.

"I'm hearing a lot of talk about sewers," Edward began. Even he thought he must be having a nightmare. "First we're told that General Gonzalez is investigating the subways, which in my book is a euphemism for sewers.

Then, General Felipe actually went to reconnoitre the city's sewers and now you're telling us that you damp woods are deft at swishing through them in tiny boats! What is it about stinking sewers? Does the main chance of defeating our enemies lie beneath the streets of the Big Apple?" Silence followed.

Admiral Mathias was flummoxed by Edward's outburst. Juan was back with them in spirit and stepped in, not wanting Edward to get cold feet before their mission had even started.

"All sewers are full of rats and smell like rotten eggs! New York's are no different. Sewers have another thing in common – they are full of water and hidey holes where nasty things can secrete themselves away. They're simply wonderful places in which unscrupulous creatures can build command centres and remain totally undetected by law enforcement organisations. More importantly, they provide effective transport links and escape routes across the city. The reprobates in all our societies use them all the time. They're using them right now in London. The sewers underneath Westminster are full of notorious rats!" Sewers, therefore, are the ideal place for unprincipled rogues to use for their own moronic ends." They thoughtfully digested Juan's words and Edward nodded, understanding the logic employed by the iguana and his comrades.

Jack's concentration had waned. All this talk about sewers was boring. He liked a bit of noise and fast action and his wayward streak drove him to mimic a sniper with an automatic rifle. He made a terrible racket. Floss glowered at him, shushing him up.

"I'm still tempted to agree with Floss," Jack said defiantly. "Don't mess around. A couple of grenades would do the trick! Indulge in a bit of guerrilla warfare and the show's over! Much more exciting in my book." Juan stoically patted Jack on the back.

"I do think, Jack, you might have spent too much time watching computer games. Our ongoing battle with that outrageous, blood and guts antagonist, Gregor Magnus will be a real life experience and not one to be taken lightly. Perhaps you're missing Rosie? Feeling a little down in the dumps eh?" Jack felt fittingly chastised and calmed down but not before he'd let one of his main concerns be known.

"I'd like to be sure that Rodrigo hasn't turned himself into a fox and eaten my Rosie," Jack admitted. Juan borrowed Floss's mobile phone and dialled the rabbit.

"Here, speak to Rosie. I won't have an unhappy rabbit owner in my band of intelligentsia," he said, handing Jack the phone.

"Rabbits can't speak! Jack crowed, taking the phone just in case and self-consciously holding it to his ear. Anything was possible with this iguana so just to be on the safe side he uttered a few well-meaning words to whatever might be at the other end of the line.

Feeling rather stupid Jack spoke hesitantly to the phone, hoping that he'd be right and no soft rabbit's voice would reply.

"Hello Rosie?" He whispered, trying to avoid attracting the mirth of his friends but failing miserably. They sniggered at his discomfort and he blushed, wishing the ground would swallow him up - and then it happened, his beloved pet rabbit answered. There it was. A squeaky voice was clearly speaking to him on Floss's mobile phone!

"Hi Jack! How are you?" The dulcet tones of an angora rabbit were asking him how he was feeling! Jack was in shock. "It's Rosie. Can you hear me, Jack?" The rabbit was concerned by Jack's silence. "Now Jack, please don't worry about me. I'm fine. Rodrigo's doing a grand job of looking after me." The doe sounded so excited. "Oh, Jack! I think I'm in love! I've been alone for far too long. Rodrigo bought me a whole bunch of kale for my dinner last night and then he proposed." Rosie started giggling.

"That doesn't sound proper to me," Jack replied, shaking his head, wondering what the hell he was saying. He was conversing with his pet rabbit!

"Oh Jack dear, it was quite proper. Rodrigo went down on his front paws and asked me to marry him. It was so beautiful!" Rosie sounded deliriously happy. "You've been a good master to me and I'll never forget that. Roddy and I will live together in my hutch so in a sense you'll have more bucks for your money! Did you see what I did just then… more bucks!" Rosie was in her element.

Jack wanted Rosie to be happy, of course he did, but he felt he was losing a good friend. Once married to Rodrigo she would belong to another's heart and one that brought her expensive bunches of leafy vegetables well out of his price bracket. All Jack could afford were cut price, out of date carrots or free dandelions from his garden. Jack did the honourable thing and wished them well trying to sound happy for the loved up couple.

"Rosie, take care. I'll look forward to your wedding on my return," he said, putting a brave face on it all and handing the phone back trying to imagine what a rabbit wedding might look like. Edward was just waiting for the chance to poke fun at his friend.

"Oh dear!" He twittered, "by the time you get back your garden will be overrun by tiny bunnies!" Edward was pulling his leg but he caused Jack to frown, the truth of the matter hitting home.

The dispassionate Admiral Mathias became impatient because like all termites he didn't truly understand the emotions of human beings. It was time to go and feeling bored with listening to the romantic inclinations of rabbits he saluted and made to leave. Lily stopped him.

"Admiral, sir, something's bugging me..." It was Lily's turn to be funny - termites, bugs, bugging! "Termites, I believe eat wood. So how do you stop them munching your wooden ships?" The admiral glared at Lily. He didn't like being challenged by an adolescent girl. The experience mariner knew how to behave in public so he treated her question respectfully and humouring her gave a brief but sensible answer.

"Well said, my gel! Termite sailors are wood eaters and to keep them fit we feed them up on their favourite tree bark before we leave port." The admiral didn't get to where he was today after three centuries of naval battles by not knowing how to manage his navy.

Admiral Mathias hovered above the ground for a few seconds powered by an energy source strapped to his back and after another salute flew away to his ship, the Golden Isopteran. The teenagers watched him disappear into the distance using the binocular feature on their rose tinted glasses.

"Isopteran is the scientific word for termites," Emmie informed them all.

"Well said!" Juan congratulated her. "And, by the way, deep down inside Mathias is just a pussy cat," he chuckled.

Chapter 9

Let Battle Commence

Operation Lizard, the name of Juan's imminent offensive was coming together. It was absolutely critical that Juan's newly appointed military leaders be placed at their command posts urgently and before the enemy had time to unleash its dreaded forces upon the world. Urged again by Juan to make themselves comfortable in their impromptu flying machine he prepared for take-off. A sudden change in the weather caused the sky to darken and the wind to howl, sweeping the sea up into gigantic tsunami-like waves, bigger than they had seen so far.

"Such dreadful meteorological conditions," Juan noted, nervously. "I fear Effria is on to us. This uncharted weather will be his doing for sure." The iguana's companions were worried. "Have no fear! Our bubble will protect us from the elements," Juan told them seemingly occupied elsewhere. Eva was beaming intelligence reports directly into his brain.

"I take it that was the red necked avocet, Spy Extraordinaire was it?" Jack asked caustically, noticing Juan deep in thought and muttering to himself.

"Jack, trust and faith! Do let's try to be friends," Juan retaliated. Jack shut up.

Juan peered at his apprentices. Their attire was quite inappropriate for military action.

"I suggest something along the lines of a smart navy boiler suit and fast-trainers for now with military uniforms for the boys later on," he said, waving his arms about and procuring the necessary changes to their dress. "I'm sure Floss will be pleased to have a decent pair of trousers for a change without gaping holes around the knees," he added. Floss liked her slashed jeans but didn't argue.

"What are fast-trainers?" Emmie wanted to know, worrying about having to forsake her expensive designer orange footwear.

"Fast-trainers are gym shoes with hidden wings. Just say the little word *PRESTIDIGITATION* and lo and behold, wings will sprout at your heels and transport you wherever you need to go. Far more comfortable than those high-heeled stilettos Emmie wore to the high school disco last term. Why would anyone want to wear daggers on their feet?" Emmie was shocked to hear that she'd been under surveillance for so long.

The winged shoes looked fun and had to be tried out immediately. Since they hadn't yet lifted off Juan could see the sense in letting his apprentices practice their flying before being thrown into the thick of things. Jack was the first one out of the bubble.

"Prestidi-whats-it…?" He must learn to pronounce this word. If Juan's interpretation of coming events was accurate these magic trainers would be vital in getting them out of dangerous scrapes.

"I wouldn't exactly call it a little word," Edward remarked.

"Latin I think," piped up Emmie.

"Yes, indeed," Juan confirmed, "It's a fancy word for magic. I'm a prestidigitator, a magician. It's from the Latin for a juggler!" Juan told them smugly. Without wasting time they practiced saying the word, prestidigitation until they were word perfect and able to fly, whizzing over the rocks and sand dunes. They were having so much fun Juan temporarily lost control but eventually managed to call them back to the bubble to start the final leg of their journey. They rose up into the bright blue yonder and on towards the USA, flying over several islands on their approach to New York. Long Island, Brooklyn, Governor and the famous Ellis Island known to the world as the gateway to a better life. Back in the day Ellis Island was where immigrants first set foot in the USA. The island's history and Operation Lizard were about the same thing - freedom. Gregor Magnus must be stopped.

Just a hop and a skip further and they were at their destination, Staten Island. They flew to the far end and put down on a sandy beach in Wolfe Pond Park.

"I hope there aren't any wolves still prowling around!" Lily shrieked plaintively, remembering Rodrigo and the thylacine episode.

"I can assure you there are no wolves here!" Juan said. "However, if you look out to sea you'll see many graceful yellow-headed gannets flying over the water looking for food to sustain them before going north to breed in Canada. They look like normal birds but they are in fact spies, working for the intergalactic space agency, the Parallel Universe Peace Association, usually referred to as PUPA. Whilst looking for food the gannets are also watching out for unusual activity below the waves. If they detect anything sinister they pass on their suspicions to our more than capable spy, Eva." Juan was deadly serious.

"I bet the gannets speak English too!" Edward was being his normal cynical self again.

"Why of course not!" Juan exclaimed, getting his own back. "They speak Gannetish!"

The iguana clasped his temple, concentrating hard as another message came in from Eva.

"Bad news! Many of General Felipe's termites have been sucked into a passing jet engine. Our first casualties of war! Felipe's troops were the best. He'll have to re-group. Such a loss!" Juan shook his head in despair. As well as trying to avoid the disastrous effects of the airport's radar he'd now have to find the time to support General Felipe and console him on the sad loss of so many of his SSS. Most crucially, he needed confirmation that the general had enough able bodied termites for their next sortie. The teenagers would defintiely have to travel into Manhattan on their own.

Juan instructed his soon-to-be intergalactic warriors to catch the no. 78 bus to the Staten Island Ferry Terminal where they were to board the boat to Lower Manhattan. Once on the mainland they were to take the R Line train at Whitehall Street to 8th Street where they would meet Fabio, a Malachitian under-cover agent. Fabio would be standing beneath a mosaic spelling out the station's name and wearing a grey hooded New York University sweatshirt with the NYU logo set against a purple background on the front. Fabio's hood would be pulled up over his head.

Juan gave each teenager a MetroCard for unlimited travel so they wouldn't have to juggle with dollar notes and small change. The MetroCard could also be used on the bus. The ferry was free. He handed geographer Floss an essential subway map.

"Before you go please check that you have your rose-tinted glasses safely tucked away and easily accessible," Juan wanted no slip-ups. The space community was depending on them.

"Are you sure you can't come with us?" Floss suddenly felt insecure.

"I have other eggs to fry," Juan said.

"I think you mean, fish to fry," corrected Lily.

"Ah! Quite right," he admitted his mistake. "I'll be taking mind readings every few minutes so if anything crops up or you need to get a message to me you know what to do. And by the way," he added, "you can also talk to each other that way too. When stressed your hormones will connect to the rose-tinted glasses and by pressing the little button on the ear-stems and uttering the name of the person you want to speak to, you'll be connected to that person. Does that make sense?" It didn't really but then nothing made sense where Juan was concerned so they nodded anyway.

Floss felt clueless but for the sake of universal peace she was willing to give Juan's mission a go. She led her friends towards the bus stop and amazingly a bus turned up as soon as they arrived. Juan's magic or just a coincidence? The ferry was fun. They sailed near to The Statue of Liberty and Ellis and Governor Islands finally docking at the South Ferry terminal. Masses of people were awaiting the next ferry back to Staten Island. The teenagers pushed their way through the crowds to the exit and found the subway station. A street seller selling cloche hats stood outside. This style of hat was Emmie's favourite and she veered off towards the hat stall. Floss tugged her back.

They were on a mission! Clutching their MetroCards they descended into the subway and boarded the R Train bound for 8th Street.

The train rattled along the track on its way uptown. The visitors from Carshalton regarded their fellow travellers who were checking their phones, reading their e-books or chatting. The teenagers felt anxious, wondering if they were all innocent New Yorkers or possibly Effrian sympathisers, transformed into people lookalikes and out to get them. Butterflies fluttered in their stomachs as 8th Street loomed. They exited the train and looked for Fabio. A man wearing a hoody was just where he was meant to be. He greeted them each with a firm handshake before swiftly ushering them through a secret doorway in the white tiled platform wall and thence into a tunnel lit by small flickering candles set in orange cups.

They had walked a fair distance when Edward asked the obvious question.

"Where are we?"

"We're beneath Washington Square Park. In a couple of minutes we'll climb up through the archway to the Retipus' Coordination Centre right at the top. Eva will brief you there on Operation Lizard. How are you with stairs?" Fabio smiled mischievously. The five had no idea what a Retipu Coordination Centre was and felt anxious about finding out! Fabio stood for a moment in the glow of the candlelight with his hood down giving them the opportunity to study his face. He was man-like but on closer scrutiny his eyes had a glassy quality and were purple, matching his eyebrows. Fabio was a curiosity but the teenagers were getting used to weird creatures and politely kept their views to themselves. The stairs leading to the top of the archway seemed endlessly exhausting and were making their leg muscles smart. They eventually reached an old wooden church-like door. Curious tapping sounds were coming from the other side of it. Fabio heaved the door open and they walked into a large room full of space-aged computers operated by ten bear-like creatures. This was the Retipu Coordination Centre.

The scene that greeted the teenagers sent goosebumps coursing up and down their spines.

"Fabio, who're these p-e-e-e-ople...?" Floss blurted, perturbed.

"These gentle creatures are the Retipu. They are from the planet of the same name. They're harmless cyber geeks mostly. There's nothing they like better than spending twenty-five years in intergalactic timescales in front of what you'd call a desktop," he whispered before waltzing across the room to shake hands with the IT savvy beings.

"Ahoy shipmates!" The red necked avocet yelled from the other end of the room. "So nice to see you again." An unpleasant odour of onions emanated from the Retipus' steaming bodies and the boys rudely pinched their nostrils to keep out the smell. Floss was not impressed and her sense of good manners came to the fore.

"Stop that. It's so impolite," she reprimanded them, quietly, so as not to upset the bears. Eva ignored the bickering to give them some facts about the creatures working so hard in front of them.

"Take a butchers at the Retipus' delicate fingers," she encouraged. "See those special black pads at the end of each digit? They're for tapping at transparent and virtually invisible keyboards, year in and year out! You'll also notice that each bear is a different colour. Don't read anything into that, they just happen to like bright colours. And, don't be alarmed by their lemony-green snake heads and darting tongues. They're not poisonous," she paused, "well, not that poisonous...," she joked. The Retipu bears, masters of all things computational banged away at their keyboards whilst scanning computer screens hanging in mid-air, closely monitoring activity on the subway and totally unfazed by their visitors.

The Retipus' screens revealed armies of giant termites wearing full military gear making their way along both sewers and shadowy subway train tracks. The subway good-guy termites were massing on several different lines unnoticed by all but the Retipu in the pervading darkness cloaking the tunnels. Unassuming New Yorkers hurtled past in their trains going about their business, going to work, taking children to school, visiting the dentist... The last thing on their minds was the likelihood that their subway was full of termites about to embark on a subterranean war involving a plethora of intergalactic characters from unheard of planets.

Jack was still being bad mannered, ogling the Retipu and thinking they'd make interesting characters for a video game.

"Jack, didn't your mother ever tell you it's rude to stare?" Eva scolded. "Xenophobia is not tolerated in our intergalactic armies! We accept everyone regardless of how they look. We're humbled by the skills of our friends from outer space and especially the art of the Retipu who analyse secret codes and help us to win intergalactic wars without expecting fame or fortune." Eva took a breath before elaborating, "Our goal is to make all worlds peaceful places where creatures can live in harmony." Lily liked what she was hearing. Her school equalities role fitted well with Eva's extra-terrestrial ideology.

It was the relative smallness of the termites that concerned Edward. Watching them on the screens they looked extremely vulnerable even accepting that they were larger than normal.

"Aren't they a tad on the short side for soldiers?" He asked Eva.

"Naturally, our termite heroes need to be smallish," Eva was miffed at Edward's criticism. "If they were bigger their movements on the subway would be hindered. Their smaller size means they can move freely and undetected. Can you imagine the chaos that would ensue if commuters saw that their transportation network had been infiltrated by creepy crawlies? Absolute mayhem, that's what!"

The fact that the Retipu were code-breaking geniuses struck a chord with Emmie. They were her kind of people.

"I can do code-breaking!" She enthused. It sounded a lot safer than running around in gloomy, termite infested tunnels or getting wet on the high seas courtesy of the admiral.

"Exactly Juan's view," Eva agreed de facto. "You'll stay here with the Retipu and keep things ticking over." The avocet lowered her voice. "The Retipu are absolute marvels at what they do but someone has to crack the whip, if you know what I mean! Emmie, that person is you." Emmie looked shocked. "Juan has studied your code-breaking skills in fine detail and he's convinced you're the woman for the job. Remember Mr. Cygnus at the MI6 Orbit Deciphering Symposium you attended?" Emmie nodded. "That was PUPA's intergalactic code-breaking guru, Cygnus Callisto. He selected you, Emmie, out of the fifty-nine other conference delegates. You should feel rightly proud of yourself!" The bird exclaimed.

Emmeline Taylor was unusually silenced. She had no idea she'd been under the eye of such an internationally renowned decipherer. Mr Callisto, she recalled, was an absolute wizard at solving mysteries and she'd thought at the time that he must be a top British spy.

"Wow!" It was all she could muster.

"Emmie, I'd like you to spend some time with your staff, build up a rapport," the bird suggested. Emmie smiled at her friends. Staff? At her age! Eva directed her to a desk labelled, Supreme Code-Breaker Taylor. Her appointment had been pre-ordained and clearly they hadn't expected her to reject their offer.

Whilst Eva was giving the others a bit of a pep talk Emmie wandered over to the one small window with a view over Washington Square Park below. Americans were sitting on benches eating brunch, chicken wraps, burgers and so on and slurping fizzy drinks and take-away coffees as they snatched a short break away from their desks. Nannies were pushing their charges in buggies through the trees or watching jugglers and giant bubble makers on the main square. Others were feeding the squirrels with breadcrumbs. The newly appointed Supreme Code-Breaker Taylor spotted a lonesome raccoon curled up asleep in the crook of a large tree oblivious to the activity below. It would stay there safe until nightfall when it would wake up and go forage, totally unaware that at the top of the arch top secret work was underway. Life was indeed strange.

It was time to move on. The rest of the teenagers needed jobs.

"I think we'll ride the elevator," Eva suggested, pleasing everyone. Their legs were still aching from walking up all those steep steps earlier. But where was the elevator? They looked around seeing only the wooden door they had come through. "Okay. Treah. Do the business if you will," Eva called out to the Retipu supervisor. Treah was a red bear with a blue line through her lemony green snake head denoting her seniority. Treah punched a few characters into her keyboard and after a bit of rumbling and rattling a rusty old elevator appeared looking on the outside like it could do with an upgrade. The creaky metal door slowly opened and inside it looked like it had recently housed sheep and bales of hay. Remnants of whiffy ovine droppings littered the floor. "Sorry about the mess," Eva apologised. "Looks like Treah's borrowed this one from one of the Amish farmers. I must have a word with her about that. It's just not right when we have guests. Tread carefully!" Eva advised. The door closed and they waved goodbye to Emmie who returned a mere cursory wave as she searched her satchel for a roll of soothing fruit gums.

"I've seen everything now," Edward said matter-of-factly. Eva pushed a button reading, Hospital.

"Ed, my boy, you've hardly seen anything at all yet," Eva replied. The elevator descended sluggishly, in its own good time. "The next stop's Lily's," she announced.

Chapter 10

Surgeon General Gibson

The elevator stopped outside what looked like a state-of-the-art medical centre. It was set up deep beneath Washington Square Park and had many wards filled with empty beds in anticipation of some future disastrous event. Eva ushered them into one of several emergency theatres kitted out with operating tables, bandages, sets of scalpels and other items of surgical equipment all laid out on trays ready for action. Nurses with grey, characterless faces scurried in and out of the wards carrying towels and bedsheets. Others were checking equipment, placing bed pans by beds or filling up jugs with fresh water. It was an absolute hive of industry.

"Lily, you'll find we've thought of everything," Eva said, flapping her wings excitedly as she made the announcement.

"Excuse me!" Lily exclaimed. "Why are you telling ME this?" Baffled and knowing nothing about medicine she suddenly felt unnerved.

"I see! Juan hasn't explained has he?" Eva said, noticing the sheer look of fright on Lily's face. "Lily, you'll be our surgeon general. You'll manage this field hospital efficiently. We're aware of your energetic nature and your determination to treat everyone equally. It'll be your task to ensure that all soldiers, regardless of rank or creature type receive the treatment they need. We're giving you the ability to operate on the injured and the know-how to prescribe the correct medicines. Don't fret. It'll all come naturally, you'll see."

Lily took several deep breaths to calm herself down.

"Do you have your rose tinted specs with you," Eva asked. Lily nodded.

"Good. In your case, the glasses will have an extra property. They'll enable you to amputate legs, remove bullets, sew up wounds or whatever other skills you may need to mend our injured troops and naturally, our enemies too. All you have to do is press the little green button on the stems and the specs will make sure you make the right decision. The same goes for medicines. Our system is linked to the cosmic Cornucopia of Pharmaceuticals and the correct drug will be prescribed every time you give it the symptoms. You won't be able to make a mistake and poison anyone!" Lily's head was reeling. Her first aid knowledge was limited to the application of sticking plasters!

Lily decided to trust the avocet and rely on the special specs to aid her confidence. She would rise to the challenge! Putting a white coat on she even looked the part. The bird relaxed. So far, so good! It was all going according to plan.

"Your nurses are from Star Kibas, a planet that's around seventy-five light years from Earth. Star Kibas nurses are noted for their exceptionally caring nature and ability to make everyone feel at ease. Incidentally, a curious quirk of theirs is the ability to change their faces so they resemble someone special. I believe, in your honour they're planning to adopt the facial features of a Carshalton nurse," the avocet squawked.

Two of the vague looking nurses appeared at Lily's side.

"Allow me to introduce you to Staff Nurses, Percina and Buttercup. They'll be at your service night and day," the avocet exclaimed. Jack was paying attention for once.

"My mum's a nurse at St. Helier Hospital. She deals with broken legs, knee replacements, sprained ankles and all that kind of stuff. I think she'd be a real asset to a hospital like this," It was an innocent remark. He was so proud of his mum.

"Good show, Jack," Eva acknowledged his suggestion but that was all. There was so much to do, so many jobs to dish out and not much time to do it in.

"Come along people-lets. Your armies await you!" She twittered to Floss, Edward, and Jack as she practically flew down the corridor to their next rendezvous.

The teens ran to keep up with Eva barely having time to wish Lily well in her new task.

"Lily, take care. Keep in touch and remember, in an emergency you can message me," Floss shouted, feeling guilty for getting her friends into such a predicament.

"I'll be okay!" Lily called back.

"Ed, I'm feeling edgy about all this. What about you?" Jack whispered.

"It's a bit late for that! We're in it up to our necks now," Edward retorted as they entered a tunnel similarly lit by candles sitting in orange cups. This tunnel had the added feature of water trickling down the walls suggesting they were deep underground. A large official sign on a door proclaimed they were entering, N42: Central Command Room, Grand Central Terminus. Inside they found another bank of humming computers operated by pink octopus-like cyber experts from the planet Kampujan, each of their tentacles controlling a different machine and being supervised by stickmen from the same planet.

The three friends stared around the room. Flashing and flickering lights along with beeps and squeaks from various bits of space-aged kit reminded Jack of Blackpool Illuminations.

"Why is this room called N42?" Floss asked Juan who had newly arrived from Roosevelt Island where he'd been commiserating with General Felipe and his SSS survivors following their bad luck on their flight over to the USA.

"The N is for Neptune, the Roman God of the Sea," he explained "The Central Command Room is our power hub and the air is full of energised particles that fuel our mindreading capabilities and provide the source of power for our time travel. With such a lot of energy circulating we needed to site the command room deep beneath the Earth's crust. It's closer to the sea than the railway terminus above us, hence the name, Neptune."

"So what does the forty-two refer to?" Jack asked.

"It's a Malachitian measurement. We're forty-two of them below the ground."

Walking further into N42 the friends were greeted by some familiar faces.

"Hail Generals!" Eva led the salute to Generals Joaquin and Alvaro as she danced about happily on her skinny pins evidently pleased to be there at this important time, right on the brink of war. Sir Juan was dressed in full military regalia, a look completed by a golden scabbard and ceremonial sword.

"An especially big welcome to our new Knight Commanders, Kimber and Stanley," Juan officially welcomed them. Edward and Jack glanced at each other wondering what a knight commander did. It wasn't a title they'd heard before. Dressed from neck to ankle in boiler suits they didn't feel like army grandees.

"I was thinking that too," Juan echoed their innermost thoughts. "You'll feel more the part in these…" he said, uttering a spell. The boys were shrouded in a red mist, which on clearing found each of them attired in the turquoise uniforms of the termite generals. A wall mirror gave them the opportunity to admire themselves. Jack smiled, wondering if the image he saw was really himself. His dad would've been so proud. He mustn't let him down.

A lull in proceedings gave Field Marshal Sir Juan of Malachite the chance to perform an important official task.

"Eva, please do me the honour of flying up onto the control desk," Sir Juan requested. The room went quiet. "Eva, Spy Extraordinaire, I confer upon you this day the title of Colonel-in-Chief." Juan pinned a shiny medal to a tiny sash and presented it to the dizzy bird who whizzed around the room showing it off to everyone. There was no time for celebrations; they had a war to fight. Eva bade everyone farewell and left for an assignment. They watched the avocet on the computer monitors flying along the subway tunnels, whistling with joy at her well-deserved promotion.

There was no time to sit around and dream. General Joaquin was eager to get started.

"Knight Commander Kimber," the general used Edward's new title, "you're being deployed to Cherry Hill in Central Park. Our intel is that Effria's First Army, The Crystal Riflemen, is camped in the Ramble. It's a hilly part of the park with lots of twists and turns for the enemy to hide in. They've been there for some time and the SCBT," he paused, seeing Edward's eyes glaze over. "SCBT, it stands for Supreme Code-Breaker Taylor, in other words your friend Emmie, sends word that the enemy has dug in. SCBT's Retipu team has intercepted communications that strongly suggest this to be true." The abbreviated forms of their new titles were real tongue twisters. Edward dwelt on them for a moment or two. If Emmie was the SCBT he must now be KCK or KCEK and Jack, KCJS! He stifled a laugh as he imagined getting tongue-tied or worse, referring to the wrong person in the heat of a bloody battle.

Edward's thoughts were interrupted by General Joaquin.

"KC Kimber, you've been assigned to our Termite Foot Regiment, code name Columbus. You'll meet them at 59th Street. Your adjutant, Major Gubby, will escort you through the subway via the Purple Line to its junction with the Red Line. I'll rendezvous with you there later." Major Gubby was surprisingly man-like if you ignored his pointy wood mouse ears. He approached, clicked his heels and stood ready to carry out his orders.

Edward dutifully followed Major Gubby into the bowels of Grand Central Terminus and in moments they were making their way through yet another secret doorway, awkwardly in Edward's case as he was unaccustomed to moving about in a stiff, restrictive uniform covered with gold braids. They found themselves standing beside a rarely used train track where they boarded the major's Malachitian oxygen fuelled jeep, rendered invisible from the eyes of the general public as it flew through the train station. The cathedral-like building hummed with commuters and shoppers and Edward noticed the appetising food stalls and wanted to stop and sample them. His adjutant was in control and he was to be sorely disappointed.

Floss and Jack waited for a task of their own, hoping they hadn't been forgotten.

"We've intercepted a coded message from Effria's East River Brigade in the Ramble," General Alvaro shouted. "He's preparing to attack!"

"At long last!" Sir Juan replied. "And now it begins! We'll shortly attain peace for the Universe," the field marshal relished the news. "In any case all this standing about isn't good for an army. We need to engage before they lose heart." Floss looked worried. In her book, conflict was nothing to get excited about. The result was always the same, lots of people dying needlessly.

"EVOMYLIHTLAETSSDRAWOTTSAEREVIRTAECNO," Slowly and with great difficulty Sir Juan read out this coded message to Floss and Jack.

"I'm not very good at puzzles," Floss confessed.

"Me neither," admitted Jack. General Alvaro took the piece of parchment on which the code was written from the field marshal.

"I'll get it over to the SCBT then shall I?" He grunted, disappointed that these supposedly intellectual go-getters weren't as capable as his leader had made out. General Alvaro was an action man. A.S.T.L., *Action Sooner Than Later*, was his modus operandi. His bravery on the battlefield had been noted intergalactically and had culminated in his appointment as a four-star general.

The intercepted message was sent on to Emmie and within five minutes her team had decoded it. She appeared in a photographic light field above N42's control desk.

"Deciphering this was like a walk in the park," she told them excitedly. "The message means as follows: '*Move my troops immediately and stealthily towards the East River Battlefield and engage with the enemy when opportune*', The message was signed GM." It was obviously a direct order from Gregor Magnus to Effria. Emmie had cracked her first code and at breakneck speed.

Juan left Floss and Jack alone for a few minutes with Generals Alvaro and Joaquin. The high and mighty termites decided to test these silly humans that had been foisted upon them.

"If we may, we'd like to speak to the two of you in camera on our likely attacking strategy?" Invited General Alvaro.

"We can't talk inside a camera!" Floss laughed nervously. She'd never heard the expression before. The experienced militia frowned, glancing at one another. General Joaquin took it upon himself to put her out of her misery.

"Madam, the term means, in private." The two generals wondered why Sir Juan had recruited such naive commanders. General Alvaro couldn't stop himself from tutting at Floss's lack of knowledge.

"Thank you gentlemen," Floss didn't like their attitude one little bit. "I'll only discuss tactics with Sir Juan," she told them curtly. Jack, meanwhile, had joined the computer operators and was watching the screens, ignoring the bust-up going on behind him.

A cyber geek supervisor, a tall thin stickman approached Jack.

"Knight Commander Jack Stanley?" He asked, as he approached. Jack looked up from studying the buzzers and bells on the control desk. "Sir, you're required to make your way to the East River Front where General Gonzalez, just returned from the sewers, awaits with your army. Admiral Mathias is putting down anchor in the East River at this very time." Where was the East River? Jack had trouble remembering left from right, let alone east from west. Trying times were ahead. He must hunker down and concentrate. General Gonzalez reported over the airwaves that the enemy was on the move and the termites were on red alert and ready to engage, adding diplomatically that he would, of course, be delighted to serve KC Stanley in whatever guise he felt appropriate. Jack was suddenly worried sick, realising that he was now in charge of so many lives.

Sir Juan returned to N42 and called to a female officer wearing the sage green uniform of the military police. The officer's ash blonde hair was wrapped in a bun at the nape of her neck. Jack thought she looked extremely smart. She kept her hands hidden behind her back as she strode over to Jack's side.

"Jack, allow me to introduce you to Captain Greta from the planet Graveny. Greta will take good care of you. She's a 10th dan and Malachitian Liatram Rainbow Belt. It's a form of judo," the iguana explained. Jack knew about martial arts. His friend Harrison had loads of computer games featuring karate, kung-fu, jujitsu, taekwando and so on. Jack smiled at Greta and extended his hand in greeting. Greta did the same. Jack faltered. Greta's hand was not a hand at all but a sharp clawed eagle's talon. Not wishing to seem unfriendly he shook her talon with the greatest of care. Greta returned his smile and Jack noted how pretty she was.

"This way please sir," Captain Greta invited Jack to follow her. Jack was smitten!

Emmie, Lily, Ed, and Jack were all now fully deployed on Operation Lizard so Floss was left alone with Juan at N42 - the security guards and computer minions were totally engrossed in their work and ignored them.

"Juan, surely you can find a way to deal with GM without launching a full scale, interplanetary war?" Floss sounded more like a mature adult every minute. "You're so clever. You must be able to think of something. In most fairy stories I've read there's a magic potion or a good witch that makes things right without the need for relentless death and destruction. Good always prevails over evil!" Floss made it all sound so easy.

"Like when the prince comes along and kisses Sleeping Beauty or the woodcutter rescues Little Red Riding Hood and chops up the wolf? Juan asked innocently.

"Something like that," Floss agreed, getting the impression that the iguana believed such tales were actually true. Finding a fairy godmother in the middle of their present plight might prove difficult but if anyone could do it, Juan was the one to do so.

Sir Juan's aide-de-camp, Lieutenant Clive Hawkins approached. Floss observed him closely. He too had the appearance of being normal the exception being a clutch of black shiny feathers substituted for hair. It seemed everyone associated with Sir Juan was a bit of an oddball. Lieutenant Hawkins was what is known in military circles as an enabler. He got things done. Anticipating his commanding officer's every need was his main responsibility. The lieutenant thought the iguana looked tired and brought him a glass of a sweetened, pink Malachitian elixir called marberry juice. The juice released square bubbles that played happy tunes as they burst forth at the top of the glass. Sir Juan drank it down in one gulp and felt immediately refreshed. Floss drank some of the juice too. It was a bit like drinking fizzy tropical fruit juice with a twist. The bubble music made her want to dance but with a battle looming she decided more decorum was needed.

Juan wasn't just a military commander. He had a softer side and he took the opportunity to put Floss at her ease by talking to her about her granny.

"Floss, what would your granny do in my position?" Sir Juan was in earnest. She was taken aback. It was ages since she'd given Granny Molly a single thought.

"Well," she began, hesitating, giving her think time, "my granny would insist that beating hell out of other galaxies was a totally uncivilised thing to do. In fact, she'd say it was rather childish. She'd lecture this Gregor Manus on how much better it is to live side by side, peaceably. She'd also point out that sovereign nations like to make their own decisions and not be lauded over by dictators from other planets." The reptile was listening intently. "My gran would also tell old mangy Magnus that if he didn't behave himself he'd be grounded…" Floss laughed, explaining that her granny had once stopped her going to a friend's house whilst her mum and dad were away because she'd been badly behaved.

Sir Juan liked the idea that his enemy might just need a good talking to.

"I appreciate your candour. I think a granny discussion with this foulest of tyrants might be the way forward."

"If, and it's a big if, you ever get the chance to talk to him, you should delve into his past. Granny says some people are bad because they've never been loved. They get chips on their shoulders making them do stupid things like trying to take control of the Universe as in Magnus' case."

"So, you're saying he likely bears a grudge because he was shunned as a child?"

"Yes. Every child should have plenty of love."

"Do you think renouncing his crimes publicly would be a good idea?" Juan asked.

"Well, it would be a start but he shouldn't get away scot-free. He should be sentenced to a long stint of intergalactic community service to teach him how to be kind to others!"

Juan was mightily impressed by Floss's mature attitude and knew that she would be the ideal candidate for the job he had in mind for her.

"Floss, my dear, you must be wondering what your role might be within Operation Lizard?" Floss was hanging on to every word, hoping it would be just as exciting as those handed out to her pals. "As I see it, your skill lies in your calm, sensible approach to life." Floss saw herself as often being angry and ill-mannered so didn't recognise the picture he was painting of her. Indeed, her mum often said, 'Bad Tempered', should have been her second name. Juan continued. "You've the right characteristics to make a great director of operations and I'm offering you the job. You'll report to me as the field marshal in overall control." Floss Roberts, Director of Operations. It must be a dream!

"Yes, yes! I would be thrilled to accept," the calm, sensible, teenager cried out.

"Good. I'm glad that's settled. Just remember this, always have faith in yourself and General Alvaro! I'm leaving Alvaro with you just in case you need his help."

Floss's head was buzzing with questions. Everything was happening so fast.

"This is probably a silly question but won't New Yorkers panic when they see battles raging around them?"

"Ah yes! I should have explained earlier. You've heard of time warps?" Juan asked. Floss nodded, although not particularly understanding the finer details of the term. "Our campaigns will take place within a no-mans-land time warp. All involved in the approaching conflicts will be invisible to the outside world. Joggers running through Central Park, friends heading to the Boat House restaurant, horse drawn carriages full of tourists, they'll be none the wiser, totally unaware of our mission to uphold universal democracy," Juan explained. The new director of operations was speechless.

Chapter 11

The East River

Captain Greta drove Knight Commander Stanley at top speed in her cosmic hovercraft through the many disused subway tunnels. Jack felt nothing but sheer exhilaration as they whizzed through the bendy underground passages. The captain, sensing her commander's sheer joy made a detour and extended their ride until they eventually arrived at a place where several tunnels converged, coming to a halt in a centrally vaulted cavern below the city. Column after column of termites ordered in strict rows with their guns standing erect by their sides greeted them. It was a sight to behold. General Gonzalez, four-foot tall and an expert in subterranean skirmishes was perched atop a white charger. He acknowledged Knight Commander Stanley's arrival with a salute. Captain Greta hovered away to find a safe parking space. It would be the Knight Commander's main means of escape should the enemy reach their base camp.

General Gonzalez dismounted and appraised Jack of their enemy's position.

"Effria is massing his Second Army on the Manhattan banks of the East River. Admiral Mathias is currently moored up on the Hudson River but will float his armada round to the East River within the next couple of hours where he'll await instruction from yourself. His submarines, should you need them, are already in place. What are your orders, sir?" Jack had no idea what Effria's armies even looked like so didn't have a clue how to fight them. Nevertheless, he had a war to win and a large scale disaster to avert. He must get his brain in gear and fast. Termites, he cogitated, weren't exactly known for their combat skills or so he thought. He recalled no mention of them in legends, fables, or fairy stories. It was laughable to think he was actually in charge of an army made up completely of six legged insects. His second-in-command would surely know how to proceed but asking General Gonzalez for advice brought another dilemma. Would he look down on his commanding officer when he realised how inexperienced he was?

Stuff was happening fast and Jack had no time to waste. He must swallow his pride and ask for advice.

"General Gonzalez what or who are we fighting - men, insects or animals?" It was a start. Any information gleaned would be helpful. Jack wondered if he should be wearing, Learner Plates like new drivers do at home. General Gonzalez was thinking along the same lines.

"Commander sir, our aggressive adversaries are neither insects nor animals. They are simple plants albeit with animal characteristics. They come from the planet Ailhad, a far-a-way place known as the Riviera Planet because of its balmy climate and oodles of sunshine." Jack's enemies were mere plants! His opponents would be a walk over, the battle a doddle!

General Gonzalez hadn't quite finished. Jack's hopes of a *walk over* were disappearing fast.

"The more temperate climate on Ailhad provides excellent conditions for sprouting lush green leaved tropical plants. The planet's mineral rich water and nourishing soil allows them to thrive. Luckily, they're not intellectual giants. The over fertile conditions has, over the years, changed their genotype so their already miniscule brains have become gullible, easily influenced by cruel, hypnotic tyrants such as our very own, Gregor Magnus. The Ailhad have provided the tyrant with an unending supply of stooges over millennia. Millions of these leaves have done his dirty work for him, allowing his ugly campaign for universal domination to continue."

General Gonzalez's exposition on the plants was scary and there was more to come.

"Sir, I should explain that the plants have great strength and are a dab hand at using weapons. They follow commands to the letter, never questioning why - and they fight to the end, come what may. Such is their tenacity!"

Jack closed his eyes. Momentarily he wished he could go home to May Tree Close! General Gonzalez was pressing ahead at full steam. "The only activity these damn botanics are bad at is swimming. They hate being totally immersed in water." The general sounded gleeful knowing that the battlefield was really close to the East River and unlimited litres of the ruinous wet stuff. Jack's stomach churned. Think! He told himself. What video games featured plants as the attackers? His brain was in melt down as he tried to recall some. He was clueless. His foe were simple biological specimens and yet he was in a quandary as to how to deal with them. His neck muscles felt like metal rods, so stiff and painful with the tension of the situation.

Ailhad was a new planet on Jack. Emmie and her odious band of Retipu code-breaking bear-snakes might be able to help. He needed to contact her secretly to avoid causing panic amongst the termites. It wouldn't be good for them to know that their commander was totally ignorant in the art of warfare. It would damage their trust in him and worse still, they might revolt, mutiny even. Turning aside from General Gonzalez he sent an intercranial message to Emmie. Jack's deputy commander gestured for him to climb the steps to a platform overlooking his troops. From here he was expected to address them all. He paced up and down, head bowed low as though deep in thought, praying that Emmie would respond soon. The Duke of Wellington, he considered, must have similarly contemplated his position before the Battle of Waterloo.

Jack felt his ears tingle. Emmie was coming through to him.

"Hello Jack. Are you receiving me?"

"Copy that. Please proceed," Jack replied.

"Ailhad is home to venomous and carnivorous plants that are partial to eating their prey."

"Magic!" Jack muttered under his breath. "Not only do I get the chance to outwit cyber crooks but I might get eaten by them too!" Jack was consumed with misgivings. How should he tackle these cabbages? It now occupied every corner of his mind. "What else do we know about them. Any chinks in their armour?" Jack was desperate.

"They communicate by thought processes rather like we're doing right now. They're not buoyant and therefore hate large bodies of water. Interestingly, if they make a whimpering sound it's because they're feeling miserable and depressed. Hear this and you'll know you've got them on the run." Good to know, Jack thought. "And, I almost forgot," Emmie came back, "They have long tentacle-like arms. Intergalactic reports suggest they've won many a confrontation just by whipping their opponents."

Jack recalled the novel he'd read in Year 9, *The Day of the Triffids.* It was about a strain of plants that sounded very much like the Ailhad but he couldn't remember how it all ended. He must think up a plan of action and fast. Emmie was still in communication with Jack.

"My dad uses *Wilson's Weed-is-Gone* on our garden weeds," Emmie advised. "The little horrors are dead in days."

"One tin of weed killer won't do the trick. I'll need a whole swimming pool full of the stuff to cope with the numbers I'm fighting," Jack lamented.

"They do have two other major weaknesses. Slugs and earwigs. These little garden pests absolutely love to feast on Ailhad plants," Emmie remembered.

"Great! Thanks Emmie," Jack said, feeling downcast. All he needed was a trillion slugs and earwigs miraculously transported to the East River and victory was in the can!

"I'm sensing you think slugs impractical so here's another suggestion. Why not look at adulterating their food supply? Their food to die for is alfalfa, another plant, which I guess makes them cannibals in a sense!" What was alfalfa? Jack's confidence was at a low ebb. Emmie had to get back to her code-breaking role so left him alone with his thoughts.

Jack despaired. Captain Greta returned from parking the hovercraft and noticed how crestfallen he appeared. Jack summarised Emmie's suggestions.

"Sir, I might be able to help. The New York Corporation has a depot below Central Park where they store their weed killer. We can check it out in minutes by flying there on my hovercraft?" Captain Greta was keen to leave immediately. Jack was hesitant. His troops awaited his pre-battle chat and even if large amounts of weed killer were a possibility the the logistics of getting gallons of the deadly liquid to the East River were challenging. For one thing, if the enemy were monitoring their movements and got wind of their plans they would be back to square one. Before making any snap decisions he put a radio call through to Edward on Cherry Hill.

Edward responded immediately sounding like he was in more control than Jack was.

"Hi, Jack. How's it going?" He asked, cheerfully.

"Big problem!" Jack gushed. "I need to erase the East River battlefront of a very large number of gargantuan killer plants."

"Sounds like *The Day of the Triffids*. We read it last year, remember?" Edward recollected.

"Yes, but how did it end?" Edward couldn't recall either. "Ed, immediately below your army base there's a depot full of weed killer. I need to get it here to my tunnel by the East River, sharpish. Any ideas?" A lull in the proceedings followed as the two commanding officers considered the weed killer issue. Floss listened in from N42 having received vital information that Effria's Crystal Riflemen were on the move. It would have been the ideal time to invite General Alvaro to advise her but General Felipe had apparently requested his help elsewhere so Floss was on her own at this crucial time.

Edward's adversaries were camped just beyond the Ramble and he knew they were preparing to attack. He must focus on his own manoeuvres to ensure success of the Cherry Hill campaign. His basecamp was a flurry of excitement as the Termite Foot Regiment stopped eating their gnat sandwiches and reappraised their weapons, regrouping into rank and file and readying themselves for their first assault on the aggressors. Floss needed more information so insisted that Edward stay in contact whilst she spoke to Jack and Lily. Recalling a lesson on genetically modified crops or GMC as it was better known, Floss spoke to Jack. Her idea was a long shot but worth investigating.

Jack's mind was elsewhere so Floss wanting to talk about farming methods surprised him.

"Jack, what do you remember about GMC?" She asked him.

"Hmm, not much!" He didn't want to think about it. Floss turned to a cyber geek.

"Get the surgeon general on the hologram thingamajig now!" She barked. The pink computer egghead stretched out a feeler and punched codewords into a machine.

"Lily, it's me, Floss."

"Of course it's you. I can see you clearly. You're hovering above my head!" Lily laughed.

Floss ignored her friend's merriment and plunged straight in.

"We need your help. Jack's facing a militia of termite eating plants."

"Yes, yes, I'm fully aware of that! I'm up to speed you know!" She sounded disgruntled.

"OK! I want you to think back to last term and genetically modified crops when we learnt that it's quite easy to change a crop's genome. They do it in the USA to increase yields and fight plant diseases, but, and this is a very big but, could it have the opposite effect? Could injecting the plants with poison slow them down or even kill them stone dead?"

"Probably, but where's this leading?" Lily had work to do.

"I want us to think about offering the plants a luscious food laced with herbicide they can't resist. The reason I'm discussing this with you in particular, Lily, is because you're the cleverest, most conscientious chemist I know and you'll make sure it works." Floss's flattery worked. Lily took the bait.

"OK, doctoring the alfalfa with weed killer will work. I'll do it, but I want the resulting product diluted to stun them instead of killing them outright." It was just so Lily Gibson to demand clauses preventing an infringement of human or in this case, botanical rights. Floss, however, was grateful for her support and offered up a prayer of thanks.

Knight Commander Kimber had one eye on his troops and the other on communications between N42 and Jack on the East River Front. Another workable solution had come to mind and Edward relayed this to the others whilst he still had a minute to spare.

"Listen up everyone. Blow ghrelin gas at the plants! Ghrelin is the hunger hormone and it'll make them feel absolutely ravenous. Once they've inhaled the gas they'll eat anything that crosses their path. They'll even eat old shoes!" He laughed. "Then, we pump water over them containing the genetically modified liquidised alfalfa legumes mixed with the weed killer. The alfalfa seeds have a soporific effect on the photosynthesizing monsters. It'll slow them down before the poison kills them." Luckily, Lily had signed off to take care of an urgent matter at the hospital so was kept in the dark as to the plants potential demise.

"What's a legume?" Jack asked.

"Think peas..." Edward gave him short shrift. His armed force was primed and ready to go.

The director of operations needed as much information from Edward as possible and would not let him off the hook that easily even knowing that he was chomping at the bit to lead his troops into their first offensive.

"So, you're saying the plants absorb the deadly alfalfa poison from the water, a bit like drinking soup through a straw?"

"Yes, that's right," Edward kept his answer brief. Floss demanded clarity. Jack's own idea to use weed killer was simplistic enough but there were practicalities to consider.

"Ed, any idea where we get the alfalfa seeds and the weed killer from?"

Anxiety was getting to Edward. His first battle approached and he was itching to give the nod to his troops to go forward and yet, here was his director of operations keeping him from doing his job, asking more and more questions. He was feeling tense and on top of it all he didn't have a clue where they might source the alfalfa. He rudely and abruptly shut down his communication channel, surprising Floss. Luckily, Jack was still transmitting and replied with a positive game plan. He set out his proposal.

"Captain Greta will deal with the acquisition mechanics. She's acquainted with a farmer growing alfalfa down south who also happens to be one of PUPA's undercover agents! Greta also knows a guy working at Central Park's maintenance depot where they store large volumes of weed killer." Jack sounded confident.

The quickly formulated plan sounded entirely workable providing Lily could mix up the required amount of weed *stunner*. Floss called the surgeon general back online.

"Lily, are you sure your laboratory can cope with mixing up such a large amount of solution?"

"Yes of course. I'm already researching it! Just to remind you, I'd like it put on record that I'm uncomfortable with the idea of totally annihilating a whole species of plant life. Stunning them, I'm happy with!"

"We'll dilute the poison so they fall asleep instead!" Jack confirmed.

"Great!" Lily was content. Floss and Jack felt a wave of relief sweep over them.

Jack now had an acceptable way forward. It wasn't fool proof but one which at least had Lily's approval. He still had to consider the subsequent fate of the plants that would, in spite of his kinder approach, end up lying around in a deep sleep. An *After Hostilities Strategy* was needed. Besides the sleepers there would also be millions of plants that had died during the affray. Jack weighed up the situation, his eyes wandering and alighting on his termites. He had an idea. It was such an obvious solution. The termites would get very hungry engaging in combat so they could eat the dead plants! It was such a brilliant idea and one he knew would make General Gonzalez happy, what with him being a military veteran eager to forget the niceties of overindulging prisoners of war - a modern idea he just couldn't get used to.

The final part of Jack's plan was to deal with the defeated and able-bodied plants making sure they couldn't remobilise. His idea was to smother them in oil rendering them incapable of moving and then, courtesy of Admiral Mathias, allow them to be ceremoniously dumped at sea. They'd have no more trouble from the Ailhad! Lily must never know the truth. Jack ran his cunning exit plan past his colleagues making sure the surgeon general was busy elsewhere and so out of the loop. They agreed to his strategy but Floss wanted absolute proof for the record that the plants were definitely fighting under the orders of Gregor Magnus and not some other outer space lunatic.

"You need to interrogate the survivors!" Floss told Jack.

"I don't think it's possible to interrogate the Ailhad," Emmie cut in. "From what I understand they're too simplistic. It would be like trying to get blood out of a stone."

"Anyway, Floss, how many megalomaniacs do you think there are out there?" Jack asked, wondering how on earth he would interrogate a bunch of weeds.

"Ask General Gonzalez or Admiral Mathias for advice. They'll know how to proceed," Floss demanded, knowing that the generals' feelings were at rock bottom; their noses had been put out of joint because a bunch of wet behind the ears teeny boppers had supplanted them in Juan's affections. If nothing else, including the generals in the decision making process would help them feel that at least they were still considered a vital part of the military machine and so reduce the feelings they'd been side-lined.

Jack took Floss's words to heart and looking at General Gonzalez sitting astride his horse tried to butter him up.

"General, I thought Sir Juan said you were a subterranean termite?"

"Indeed I am sir," the rotund insect replied.

"I have to ask then, why are you on a horse working as my second-in-command when you might be better employed in the subways?"

"Ah well sir, you see it's my tummy. Too much rich food. It's rather taken its toll on my physique. I'm getting too fat and less agile for running around in tunnels!"

"Well then general, I'm glad of it because I really need your expertise here on the battlefield." Jack had made himself a new friend. He was learning fast.

At N42 Floss was still alone, unsupported by other high-ranking personnel apart from Juan's aide, Lieutenant Hawkins. Unnervingly, evidence was coming in of enemy infiltration into PUPA's communication systems. It was becoming apparent that someone close to the nerve centre was passing vital information to their enemy. The nub of it all was that Gregor Magnus and Effria were always several steps ahead. They appeared to know what orders were being given out before the generals had had time to digest them. General Felipe's SSS, now re-established following the terrible incident enroute to the USA, had on several occasions almost arrived in the nick of time to catch the evil pair but sadly, were always just that little bit too late. They needed a clever tactic to unmask and net the perpetrator of the leaks and fourteen year old Floss found herself in charge of setting the trap.

The director of operations set about developing a strategy to oust the traitor but the HQ machines were buzzing non-stop and coupled with the shrill voices of the octopus-like computer operators and their stickmen supervisors who were chattering away to each other, she couldn't concentrate. The situation grew far worse when the most horrendous drilling started beyond the central command room. The Cyberians were frightened and stopped chatting, listening instead to the spine-chilling din above their secure bunker. N42's muscly termite security guards bolted the doors and stood ready with their lasers to defend Floss should the need arise.

The drilling continued, growing shriller. Several explosions followed. Everyone shook with fear. The noise sounded so close that it could have been just outside their door. Floss summoned Sir Juan via a hologram.

"Juan, where are you. Please speak to me," she pleaded.

"Hello there, Floss," Juan was as good as his word and replied immediately. "What's happening?" Just hearing his voice made her feel better.

"We're hearing explosions right outside N42! Security haven't a clue what's causing them. I think we're about to be opened up like can of sardines!" Floss trembled.

"Calm down. I've heard the New York Transit Corporation is putting in four more train tracks but I didn't think that was happening until the autumn. They must have brought their schedule forward. Don't be afraid. They won't find you. Carry on as usual," he urged.

Floss's nerves were not allayed. She still felt jittery and would have preferred the field marshal to return post haste. She tried to keep his attention for as long as possible.

"Juan, I need to bring you up to date with events," she yelled just so she could hear her own voice. "Jack and Edward are engaging the enemy as I speak. Jack's plan is to drug the Ailhad with poisoned alfalfa seeds and then hand the drowsy weeds over to Admiral Mathias for drowning at sea. What do you think?"

"Wow! That sounds like a good plan right enough. Alfalfa. Hmm, that old chestnut! Alfalfa used to be called the Father of Foods. The Ailhad will lap it up. They'll be dead ducks in no time!" Juan enthused.

The unbearable drilling racket continued and Floss struggled to put a sentence together.

"Juan, where are you right now? Can't you return to N42?"

"That's a bit difficult right now. You see I'm in Egypt, Alexandria to be exact. I'm meeting the Khedive, the Egyptian ruler. We're discussing how to quell the Egyptian uprising and I'm hoping that between us we can stop any future attempts by Effria to masquerade as someone like Count Abdul ever again." Juan was back in 1880's Egypt.

"I thought you said we couldn't change the course of history. Sounds like you're doing just that!" Floss had been paying attention to Juan's words.

"Absolutely correct!" Juan was pleased to know he was being taken seriously. "I can't stop what's already happened but I can hope for future peace." Floss couldn't argue with that.

The drilling stopped temporarily and Floss relaxed, engaging the iguana in a little bit of innocent banter whilst she still had his attention.

"What's it like in Egypt?"

"The place is full of Alexandrian parrots screeching from daybreak to dusk and it's stiflingly hot! We Malachitians can usually tolerate hot climates but being part human and wearing my field marshal's uniform I'm finding the heat unbearable. If I were still a fully-fledged iguana I'd be able to run up a tree and take a long nap in the cooler air!"

"Surely time travel and speaking to people from the past must be exciting?"

"It can be quite tedious having to learn new customs all the time..."

"Juan, please take me with you next time!" Floss implored.

"Okay. I'll give it some thought," he said, slipping away to parley with the Egyptians.

Chapter 12

Rumble in the Ramble

Knight Commander Kimber and his hardy termites were preparing for action. The thunder generated by the enemy's boots was ear-busting. General Joaquin stood with a stiff upper lip, his ear proverbially to the ground. The Cherry Hill birdlife such as the red cardinals, American robins, mockingbirds, blue jays, and chickadees had taken flight sensing imminent danger. Armageddon was coming. The smell of blood, sweat and tears seemed to be hanging in the air. Death was not far away. Edward assumed his new role as commander with a sense of foreboding but in the face of adversity his mental reflexes, foreseeing brutal clashes with his enemy just minutes away, triggered inner resources.

"Bring it on!" He screamed, marching his troops up to the front line where they would await the order to engage the enemy in no man's land.

Edward knew the fighting would result in a great many injured on each side. There was simply no way such a depressing outcome could be avoided. Even if he knew what his enemy looked like and what their capabilities were, no one could escape the fact that gallons of blood would be spilt! Being fully aware of this he told Major Gubby, his wood mouse ears bristling with trepidation, to warn Lily to expect casualties soon. This is all he could tell her at this stage. He'd liked to have been in a position to suggest the type of wounds she might expect. If, for instance, the enemy were human beings then broken bones would undoubtedly have featured highly on the list of injuries. He reassured himself that Lily and her team would be ready for anything that came their way.

General Joaquin saw how Edward's confidence was building and feeling that they were now presenting a more unified front, even though, unlike in Jack's case Edward hadn't yet found a way to befriend him wholeheartedly, he now felt able to offer him advice. After decades of being in the vanguard, leading armies in the pursuit of universal peace General Joaquin naturally, like the other generals, felt usurped and uninspired by kids with little or no idea of how to conduct a war. However, the idea of failure was not part of his make-up and being a professional soldier he rose to the challenge. He would do all in his power to assist his knight commander. Universal peace was at stake and that was far more important than any personal slights.

Edward readily acknowledged that his grasp of waging a war was pitiful. He also understood that his lack of mastery in this area was quite obvious to his elders and betters! He conceded he'd a lot to learn and this whole experience would be a sharp learning curve. So, when his old timer general willingly offered him the benefit of his experience KC Kimber jumped at the opportunity.

"General, I'd be delighted to hear your words of wisdom and really appreciate your help. You're the military veteran here, not me." The general smiled contentedly. Edward was at last learning the language of entente cordiale!

"Intel from Miss Floss confirms Effria's Cherry Hill Division of Crystal Riflemen consists of Triangular Midget Men from Optima," General Joaquin informed him.

"Optima?" It sounded like an opticians.

"Yes indeed, sir! Optima's a satellite planet to Ice Leonard. It's a secondary or some might say an inferior planet. We can safely suppose the powers that be on Optima are closely allied to Gregor Magnus and his evil power-seeking ambitions. No doubt he's promised the poor creatures much in return but we know they'll be just hollow promises. They'll receive nothing in return for their loyalty from that ugly dictator and I bet those suckers don't even know what fighting for!" General Joaquin sighed, contemplating the cruel extent to which their arch-rival would go to achieve his ends.

KC Kimber's stomach was heaving. A lot was riding on his handling of this offensive and he was still in the dark about his foe. He must quickly find out all he could about these Optima bodes, whom he now knew to be, Triangular Midget Men. There wasn't a moment to lose. He urged General Joaquin to tell him all he knew.

"The Triangular Midget Men are just over three feet tall so not much taller than our termite army. Their optical senses enable them to see in the dark and they're ferocious little things - prepared to fight to the end, that's for sure." The general surveyed their own six legged warriors. The termites were without a doubt, fearless, but definitely the more fragile of the two sides and they were largely blind!

Edward followed the general's eyes as they roamed over their troops.

"General, I may be inexperienced where war is concerned but I do know that an army needs to see where it's going!" Edward was feeling very sure of himself on this point. "We need to get their composite eyes to work tout de suite!"

"immediately, yes of course sir!" The general was wondering why he hadn't thought of this himself. Perhaps he was losing it, getting too old for such intense hostile campaigning. Maybe he should apply for a desk job when it was all over? "Sir, we need to give each termite a dose of marberry serum with an added special ingredient. I'll get the sergeant major to hand out cups of the stuff right now." The general paused. "And sir, thank you for being on the ball..." Edward quietly nodded but inside he was jubilant. The marberry serum was administered in record time and soon the termites' eyesight was better than Edward's and they now had a fighting chance. A wave of relief swept over Knight Commander Kimber as they prepared to engage.

The sound of pounding boots warned the regiment that their enemy was gaining ground and would soon enter the Ramble. Edward was steely faced.

"Well then general, we'll vanquish them before darkness falls!" KC Kimber was resolute adding, "Tell me, which part of these Optima creatures is triangular?" In his wildest dreams he hadn't considered a triangular shaped person before.

"It's their transparent glass heads, sir. It's an aid to camouflage. The light shines straight through them. As a matter of fact, you can see their brains whirring around inside. Somewhat gory but when you've fought in as many wars as I have over the past five hundred years you get to see a great many oddities," he pondered.

Edward felt sick and hoped he wouldn't throw up in front of his men as a second wave of anxiety swept over him. Stifling his need to puke he spoke to his deputy.

"General Joaquin, we need to consider tactics. What's the best opening gambit when engaging in a battle with Triangular Midget Men?"

"Sir, if I might make so bold, I would suggest taking a sabre-rattling approach and launching our attack at first sight of the enemy rather than waiting to be attacked."

The general's pearls of wisdom sounded sensible. "Taking the lead and becoming the attacking party is an axiom justified by hundreds of victories throughout the history of space. Getting the upper hand almost invariably brings success." Wise words from a military grandee. Edward pondered his general's advice. If attacking first had brought successful outcomes for myriad cosmic military strategies of yesteryear then it was good enough for him now.

"We strike first!" The KC shouted to his troops. A roar went up from the ranks mustered in front of him. Brandishing their artillery and waving their flags they marched forward in their columns with laser guns following each brigade. The mass of insects flowed like a river towards the Ramble's entrance leaving a silent base camp behind.

The softly spoken Major Gubby was seated on a chestnut horse and kept to his commanding officer's side. The major liked to be in the thick of things and wanted to do much more to help the cause.

"Sir, my large ears have many uses. I could, if you wish it, propel myself up above the trees and reconnoitre the enemy's position?"

"An excellent idea!" KC Kimber exclaimed. "Do so immediately but don't get shot down in the process. I need you here in one piece!"

"Quite, sir. I'll make myself invisible whilst airborne." The major dismounted and began twirling himself up into the sky like a sycamore seed in reverse, hovering over the Triangular Midget Men and recording what he saw.

The major returned with a full account of the Triangular Midget Men's numbers and descriptions of their old fashioned weapons.

"The midgets have one very good advantage over us, sir," Major Gubby reported. "Their glass eyes are set with strong lenses and they can see us before we see them, unless of course cleverly placed obstacles are put in their way thus obscuring their route and rendering the binocular function useless." The wood mouse man had done his job well. A division of engineers was sent forthwith headlong into no man's land to grub up bushes and replant them haphazardly at lightning speed, thwarting the enemy. Negotiating the shrubbery would slow them down considerably and their less than clear line of vision would give advantage to Edward's Columbus Regiment.

Major Gubby's intelligence helped too in the strategic placing of the regiment's laser guns to achieve maximum damage. Each battery flanked and supported the other to affect an efficient crossfire assault. With his own troops in place and the first midgets coming into sight around the decoy greenery Edward brought his arm down, signalling for the offensive to commence. The enemy was taken by surprise, faltering dazedly in their tracks, their antiquated guns unprepared for the attacking termites. Opening return fire at random in a hit and miss fashion they wasted bullets by firing everywhere else but at the termites. They wearied quickly. The confusion and sheer effort attached to constantly re-loading their historic firearms took its toll. They missed their targets again and again. They retreated. The brave termites moved swiftly forward to take up their newly gained ground and then embarked on hand-to-hand combat. The Triangular Midget Men fell at the feet of the Columbus Regiment.

With the first wave of Triangular Midget Men defeated their rear guard entered the affray. These were the flammenwerfers or flame throwers - a cruel weapon that could reduce the termites to charcoal in moments. Edward's guerrilla platoon quickly made it their goal to take out the flammenwerfers. Climbing high up into the trees overlooking their enemy they hit them hard from above quickly putting the flame throwers out of service. The termites had gained the upper hand and were stamping all over the injured and dying midgets. The ground was littered with crushed glass from smashed heads. The termites then used their bayonets to put an end to those midgets who were hanging on to life by a thread. Edward wanted to dismount and pitch in with the hand-to-hand combat but General Joaquin stopped him. Losing their leader would not be a clever move.

So many of the midgets were nursing massive cracks in their glassy craniums or were bleeding profusely. It was not a pretty sight. Lily would not be pleased to see the wholesale butchery taking place on Edward's watch.

"Major Gubby," KC Kimber barked, "put the body bearers to work now!" The body bearers were a group of military termites especially bred for their strength. Back in their colonies they guarded the termites' nests and presented the first line of defence against marauding ants. Here, they were equipped with stretchers and bandages and told to clear the battlefield of the injured and dead on both sides, friend and foe alike. Major Gubby used a megaphone to yell the order to their sergeant major. So far, so good. Edward turned his attention to his communications officer, waiting with bated breath for messages to send.

"Inform the surgeon general that at least a thousand injured midgets are on their way from the Cherry Hill Front many needing transfusions, amputations, strong sticking plasters and super glue for their cracked glass heads." Edward placed such faith in Lily. Her dextrous nature, he knew, would not allow her to rest until all the injured had been treated.

Feeling weary, the knight commander glanced at his timepiece, a gold pendant watch pinned to his military tunic. The battle had been all consuming and he'd lost track of time. It seemed like just a short while ago they'd been waiting for the off and it was now several hours later and the battle almost over. He remained on his horse allowing the reigns to hang loose whilst using his hands to sweep away perspiration effusing from his brow. He had won the first round. His situation seemed at odds with the green pastoral scenery of Central Park. It was the beginning of spring and the blossom on the many stands of trees around his base camp were coming into bloom. The tinges of pink and white looked so serene and peaceful and yet, just a short way from where his horse stood it looked like a bloodbath.

Major Gubby caught his commander gazing at the beautiful trees.

"Sir, if I might make so bold since the enemy is putty in our hands, would you allow me to spend a few moments telling you about this glorious park?"

"Oh yes, please do," Edward needed a diversion.

"This famous New York landmark, Central Park, was designed in 1858 by Fred Law Olmstead, the USA's answer to Capability Brown - the British eighteenth century landscape gardener..." Edward's parents had dragged him round so many of the National Trust's stately homes with umpteen sculptured lakes, rococo fountains, grottos, herbaceous borders and flower parterres.

"Poor old Fred," Edward muttered. "He must be turning in his grave, mortified at seeing his beautiful park turned upside down."

"Sir, we're hidden in a time-warp bubble, a parallel present if you like. As long as the bubble remains intact the damage will be temporary and only visible to those fighting our cause," Major Gubby reminded him, his nose twitching as it picked up the odious smell of an invisible, silent and obnoxious evil coming their way.

The air was suddenly filled with the raucous cries of the sergeant major.

"GAS!" He yelled. "GAS MASKS ON NOW!" He hollowed. A cloud of toxic fumes puffed towards the Columbus Regiment. Edward ordered his five turbo charged fans to be switched on. The fans whirred, blowing the gas back to where it had come from and saving the termites from an unpleasant death. Thanks to the fans the air quickly cleared on Edward's side of the Ramble and the Columbus Regiment breathed easy again. The respite was short lived as within minutes the Triangular Midget Men were regrouping, coming at them fast. Enemy soldiers were screaming, running straight into their opponents' base camp and the open arms of the termites. The midgets, now referred to in dispatches as the TMM were flourishing white surrender flags whilst others were turning on each other, using hatchets to violently chop off the heads, legs, and arms of their comrades. Mutiny?

KC Kimber and General Joaquin were speechless, unclear what was happening. Why were the TMM murdering each other? The new wave of slaughter was coupled with clouds of thick, black, smoke billowing from the enemy's camp seriously reducing visibility.

"The fans have saved our lives. Blowing the gas away from us and to the north meant it engulfed the glass heads instead. They weren't wearing masks so were totally unprepared for our reverse tactic. I'd hazard a guess that the gas has entered their bloodstream causing them to go berserk," General Joaquin conjectured. In their maddened state the TMM continued to attack even though their defective rifles back-fired resulting in home goals and the acrid smell of burning TMM flesh. Rivulets of blood from the fallen bespattered the still able bodied and blurred their vision, hampering their movements still further. The TMM's morale slumped. They yelled abuse at each other and were revolting in every sense of the word as they neared total collapse. The termites had gained the upper hand. Succumbing to a load of glass headed maniacs would have been such a travesty of justice!

The Columbus Regiment rounded up those of the TMM that could still be considered reasonably whole - with no cracks in their skulls and having two arms, two legs and in appearance at least, looking intact. They were temporarily imprisoned in a corral guarded by tough looking termite security police. The TMM's brains pulsated with anger and humiliation at having been beaten so easily by an army of termites. The glass heads were definitely not the sharpest tools in the box. Dejected and with their spirits broken, when questioned it turned out as General Joaquin had suggested, they no idea what they'd been fighting for.

Even if victory had gone their way their future fate would have been uncertain. Their evil tormentor would have had no further use for an army of glass miniatures, for sure.

"Effria would have ground their heads down to a powder and recycled them into glass bottles!" Major Gubby predicted.

Edward wanted to wind up his operation as efficiently as possible.

"So, what should we do with our TMM prisoners?" He asked his troops, hoping for some sensible suggestions. A termite corporal stepped forward.

"Sir, let's make windowpanes out of the lot of them!" His fellow squaddies cheered. It wasn't quite what Edward was expecting but he laughed politely. Major Gubby's intervened.

"Sir, the injured are already enroute to the field hospital but the fitter ones are saying they just want to go home, back to Optima as soon as possible." General Joaquin smirked. Pampering prisoners? If he'd been in charge he'd have wiped them out so they couldn't cause any more trouble. Edward couldn't agree to this. He called Floss for advice.

"The prisoners must be treated with respect according to the Geneva Convention. They must be kept safe until handed back to their own side," she told Edward unequivocally. Edward was praying the TMM's repatriation would not be his problem. This he anticipated, would rest firmly with the field marshal because by that time he and his friends would be on their way home to Carshalton.

Chapter 13

Winding Down

The injured from the Ramble combat zone were whisked away in space-aged ambulances kitted out with cushioning water beds to reduce the stress on their patients. Lily's team were ready and waiting at the hospital's doors with Lily herself directing patients to the most appropriate treatment rooms. The hospital was spotless. Whilst the battles had raged Lily had ordered the floors to be scrubbed until they shone. Freshly sterilised operating theatre instruments lay gleaming on trays. If Lily had anything to do with it, the hospital would run like a well-oiled military machine.

The wards filled up with whimpering, writhing soldiers with lacerated bodies and broken limbs waiting to be examined. The walking wounded hobbled up and down the corridor, moaning. Lily anguished over how to treat them quickly and sent the nurses scurrying from room to room keeping things moving swiftly along. No one was allowed to slacken. The nurses' featureless faces were featureless no more. They were now black with a familiar look about them although Lily couldn't remember who they reminded her of. Several doctors from planets she'd never heard of were assisting her on the surgical wards using technically advanced procedures. One doctor put his TMM patients to sleep by simply projecting a light straight through their glass heads!

The influx of bleeding soldiers quickly caused severe overcrowding. There wasn't even a broom cupboard to spare. Those needing complex procedures such as amputations had to patiently wait their turn. Cutting legs off required precision and took more time and in the case of the termites, removing six of them took even longer. The sight of the operating table made alarm bells ring, filling the injured with fear and foreboding and was more bone-chilling than fighting each other on the battlefield. Lily ordered cups of the marvellous marberry juice for all patients knowing that instilling in them a sense of calm before their treatments could only be a good move. It was the first time the TMM had tasted this wonderful pick-me-up and they loved it, gulping it down in seconds. Gallons of the delectable brew disappeared down their throats as they waited for their surgery. The unique marberry bubbles floated down the corridors playing soothing lullabies and brought peace to the overcrowded hospital.

Lily's next problem was what to do with the ever growing pile of amputated, putrefying limbs. As a start she tried spraying liquidised jasmine flowers into the air providing the scent of springtime blossoms to mask the stench of rotting flesh. The stink was so overpowering it was soon back again and causing everyone to retch. Lily contacted N42 and discussed the problem with Floss and Lieutenant Hawkins. Spiders were the unlikely answer! A team of giant, enchanted, weaving spiders! The arachnids were ordered to spin a huge furnace out of their indestructible silk; a furnace that could withstand extreme temperatures. The challenge was an easy one for them. It wasn't the first time that PUPA had called in their incredible skills after a battle. The furnace's blueprint had been used all over outer space and its shape resembled a weaver bird's nest but naturally on a far bigger scale. The oven was ready in no time and hefty porter termites bundled the defunct limbs inside and then incinerated them.

In the operating theatres surgeons were saving lives. They were removing bullets, sewing up wounds and using a special glue normally used to repair porcelain but on this occasion it was used to repair the cracks in the TMM's glass heads. A new procedure using garudian metal, an ore found on Malachite was used to replace knees and hips on the six legged termites. Garudian metal was known for its exceptionally flexible qualities and with joints made of this the recipient could literally fly several steps at a time. The termites were overjoyed. In future they'd be able to jump as far and as high as grasshoppers! As the recovering soldiers started to feel better they began to shout and sing at the tops of their voices causing an unacceptable din. Lily administered sleeping draughts, more marberry juice with an added secret ingredient to settle everyone down.

"Peace at last!" The surgeon general sighed, sitting down to take a short break.

The Star Kibas nurses were worth their weight in gold and one particular staff nurse had been by Lily's side throughout, understanding her needs before she'd even given the order. That nurse approached her now.

"Are you alright, mam?" The nurse asked politely.

"I'm fine, nurse. Thanks for asking." Lily was exhausted having constantly used the word, *prestidigitation* to activate the wings on her trainers enabling her to fly up and down the corridors. "Nurse, I've noted how hard you've worked," Lily said, scanning the nurse's name badge and noting her name was Barbara. "What's your surname? After all we've been through I should know more about you."

"Stanley, mam," she replied, putting a blanket around Lily's shoulders.

"Mrs Barbara Stanley?" Lily looked shocked, "Jack Stanley's mother?" This nurse was not from the astral Star Kibas planet but from Earth.

"Yes mam, Jack's my son. He's staying with a friend at the moment." Lily knew differently.

"Barbara, how did you get here?"

"Sir Juan approached me. He said life on Earth would be expunged if I ignored his plea to assist you. How could I refuse?"

Lily studied Staff Nurse Stanley's face. It was, of course, the same as all her other nurses' faces. She'd only seen Jack's mum in passing at the school but remembered him saying she worked in orthopaedics at their local hospital. The surgeon general then recalled Colonel Eva saying that, as a way of saying thank you, Lily's nurses' features would be modelled on a local Carshalton nurse. That local nurse was Jack's mum! How would Jack react when he found out his mum was working alongside them? He might not be best pleased. As soon as Lily had a moment she would let Floss know that Barbara Stanley was on their team.

At the East River Front Jack's Ailhad strategy was nicely moving along. Lily had delivered on her promise to provide as much of the sweet tasting fatal herbicide needed to bring down the wayward plants. Ghrelin gas, again the courtesy of Lily's chemistry acumen and a little bit of magic was pumped into the Ailhads' midst by General Gonzalez using a high speed water cannon requisitioned by Captain Greta. The gas, as expected, brought on excruciating hunger pangs making the plants desperate for food. They gulped down the toxic soup, their tentacles floating about in a state of ecstasy. The tasty poison worked like a dream. They were beside themselves with joy at the unexpectedly tantalising feast jettisoned their way.

"Well now, captain, it appears our botanical friends are even more stupid than we first thought. Just look at them lapping up that stuff like it's a milkshake!" Jack, Greta, and the termite army laughed out loud. The Ailhad heard them chortling but were so addicted to the moreish grog splashing around that they were compelled to ignore it and continued to knock back the poison with loud slurps.

The sound of weeds gurgling joyously was soon replaced by despair as plant after plant staggered and then dropped to the ground, totally immobilised in a giant muddy puddle of nasty liquor. Jack hoped that Lily was too busy at the hospital to see the true effects of the herbicide. He sent a platoon to check on the state of each plant. If they were still breathing but irrevocably damaged by the poison they were to be heaped up on one side for the termites' supper. Those merely stunned but otherwise fit were to be tied up in bundles according to their rank and piled high in mounds of wilting vegetation. They would be handed over to Admiral Mathias in due course for an ignominious death by deep water!

There were far too many dead plants for the termites to munch for their supper so cremation plans for the rest swung into action. It wasn't too long before smoke from the burning shrubbery covered the East River. Small boats navigating the waterway risked being totally engulfed by it. The Port Authority of New York and New Jersey had no idea where the smoke was coming from. The Authority's job was to keep waterborne craft and their crews safe from harm so it put out an urgent radio warning advising boatmen to avoid that stretch of water until the *all clear* was relayed to them. Those monitoring the smoke were doomed for disappointment because instead of thinning out, it grew thicker and continued pumping out across the river reeking of dead vegetation. Even the long-stayers working at the Port Authority were lost for words. They were witnessing a bush fire in the middle of the river! An impossible event and yet there it was, happening right there in front of their eyes!

Jack addressed his cock-a-hoop army.

"Great job! Well done, lads!" He congratulated them. The troops reciprocated by cheering their commander. Jack's wounded termites were a manageable number so Captain Greta patched them up at their base camp, avoiding clogging up Lily's hospital still further. Jack's termites for the most part had just small cuts and bruises that sticking plasters and antiseptic cream from the first aid chest were more than adequate for. "Extra marberry beer for everyone..." Jack ordered. The army catering corps sprang into action dishing out tankards of the termites' favourite tipple. Jack's next headache was wrestling with what to do with his army now that victory had been secured. Should they be disbanded? And if so, where would such a large number of giant termites be disbanded to? Floss would know what to do but right now it was time to relax with Captain Greta. A kitchen orderly brought them each a mug of coffee and with the smoke dying away they relaxed, drinking, watching the river swirl around the pier where only an hour before the Ailhad prisoners had sailed away on the admiral's ships. Jack felt happy sitting there with Greta, wondering if this was what true love felt like.

Chapter 14

Zebafe Adventure

Colonel Eva, the Spy Extrordinaire had been monitoring Queens, one of the five New York boroughs. It was absolutely clear now to Floss that a traitor to their cause was passing tactical information to the other side. Intelligence reports suggested that a closer look at a particular diner in Queens could prove prudent. The neighbourhood in question is at the end of the N subway line at Astoria, a place noted for its Greek cafes serving tasty Mediterranean food. Informers had reported suspicious behaviour at Konstantinos' Kitchen. This café had no star ratings so tended to draw in less affluent customers looking for a cheap plate of grub.

Being a wading bird at times proved rather difficult in the espionage trade. An avocet walking into a café would certainly have drawn attention, so the plan centred on a few regular sized termites that could run under the door and rummage around inconspicuously. The kitchen had not been inspected by the Public Health and Sanitation Department for years. A few additional insects scampering around wouldn't cause alarm. At the best of time the staff didn't bat an eyelid at mice or their droppings and congealed fat and cockroaches were an everyday occurrence.

After dark, the well-briefed termites searched drawers for paperwork that might give them clues as to what kind of misdemeanour was in train at this eatery. Nothing was found. During the daytime they scampered through the dining room listening in to customers' conversations with the owner, Konstantinos. The best they heard were comments about the weather or customers asking for their eggs to be fried sunny side up. It was all rather tedious. The bird patiently waited each night by the backyard dumpsters for the termites to come out and give her their findings. So far the information gleaned had been a bit thin on the ground.

Colonel Eva's big breakthrough came one night under a full moon. She was standing by the dumpsters when Konstantinos came out carrying a sack of food scraps labelled, Colchester Zoo. A tingle shot through her body because Colchester Zoo was also under investigation for a plausible link to the oppressor, Magnus, and his lynch pin, Effria. She ducked down under the bin. Someone with a familiar voice arrived and spoke to Konstantinos in English. They seemed to be discussing PUPA's plans. Unfortunately, from underneath the dumpster Eva couldn't see the face of the new person and in moments the rendezvous was over. The colonel honestly believed they had found the missing link. Secrets were being passed by someone close to N42 via the café owner and thence onto that most hated pair of losers! It had to be the answer. A few minutes after the rendezvous Konstantinos loaded his sack of food waste onto his truck and drove out of the yard.

General Felipe, his special troop numbers back to full strength following his fracas with a plane, had been searching frantically for Effria and Gregor Magnus. His searches had covered many locations in outer space and all of Earth's continents. Following a tip-off from General Felipe's SSS Emmie had ordered cyber searches of Alexandria in Egypt, London's thirty-two boroughs and Colchester Zoo in Essex where Effria had allegedly been caught on camera visiting a zebafe, a black and white striped creature with a zebra's head and giraffe neck, body and legs. The creature had mysteriously arrived at the zoo in inexplicable circumstances. No one had any idea where he'd come from. He was just there one morning when the zoo's managers arrived to open up and since he drew in the paying crowds and filled the coffers the zoo's owners were incredibly happy to have him there.

The zebafe's appearance aroused the interest of the intergalactic spy network and Colonel Eva was put in charge of the zebafe mission. PUPA closely monitored visitors to the zebafe's compound. Cameras captured an Effria look-a-like regularly turning up to speak to the creature and in his own language too. It so happened that each of these occasions coincided with battles and skirmishes in New York. The zoo would be the perfect hide-out for arch criminals such as Effria or even the big cheese himself, Gregor Magnus. Colchester Zoo's management was totally unaware of the intergalactic spy network's operation and continued to care for the zebafe with bales of fresh hay. This was the food they expected a grazing animal such as a zebra or giraffe to eat. PUPA's intelligence, gained from seeing the type of food scraps going into Konstantinos sacks, suggested that the zebafe felt differently. He preferred a richer diet of leftover eggs, bacon, and home fries. The paying crowds kept coming and the baffled zoo owners continued to be so grateful for the extra income and prayed he would stay around forever.

Colonel Eva and her spy network fixed up satellites and listening devices to watch the zebafe and record any conversations he might have. As the battles in New York raged on efforts to monitor the zebafe were redoubled. Juan's commanders had expected Effria, being Gregor's right hand man, to be present during the Ramble and East River assaults but his absence had been duly noted.

Masquerading as a zoo visitor would provide ingenious cover for Effria, keeping him safe from harm during the brutal fighting. And too, if GM were hiding INSIDE the zebafe and they managed to ensnare the two of them at the same time they would achieve a double whammy. The war would be over in a jiffy and all nations of the Universe could resume their peaceful existence.

The Bronx, Manhattan, Brooklyn, Queens, and Staten Island, all five of the New York boroughs had been electronically searched by the Retipu and physically by General Felipe's SSS to no avail. With the TMM defeated Edward had time to assist at N42 and he made his way there to help Floss.

"We know for sure that Konstantinos is taking food scraps to the zebafe without the zoo's knowledge, and we also think he's passing information from our traitorous leak to that philophobian pair, where one of them is disguised as the zebafe," Edward summarised.

"Philophobian?" Floss asked.

"It refers to someone who has a fear of caring or loving others," he explained.

"Oh!" Floss was thoughtful. Edward had never struck her as the most caring or romantic person himself. "There are just so many gaps in our knowledge," the director of operations lamented. "For one thing the diner's in New York and Colchester Zoo's in Essex! A small ergonomics problem springs to mind."

"You're forgetting these creatures can sprint across galaxies in a trice. Travelling across the Atlantic would be a joy ride," Edward reminded her. They decided the best course of action was to allow Konstantinos his sorties across the ocean whilst surveillance continued. It seemed a weak and feeble response but without more evidence it was all they could do.

Floss and Edward reappraised the situation when told that their target hadn't been seen at the zoo for some time. Emmie's reports suggested Effria was leading a band of ferocious winged dog mercenaries to hijack Admiral Mathias' fleet and free the Ailhad. The admiral's ships were the latest models with every space-age techno-gadget going. If Effria captured the fleet he would gain a hugely important asset enabling him to launch more attacks on PUPA's forces. The naval force was about to leave the East River and enter the North Atlantic Ocean so Floss knew she must re-take control quickly.

There was not a moment to lose and if there was ever a time for Juan's intercranial telepathy to work, it was now!

"Emergency! Jack and Lily, please come in!" Floss shrieked.

"Hi Floss. What's wrong?" Lily asked.

"Effria's on board the Golden Isopteran. We must stop him taking the fleet," Floss reported. Jack couldn't believe his ears.

"That's impossible! I've only just waved the admiral's fleet off carrying a thousand Ailhad prisoners. We carried out a thorough search for stowaways before they left. Floss, your information has to be wrong!" Jack sounded alarmed, adding, "if that pond life regains power over those gullible plants he'll reform his army and we'll be back to square one!" Jack sighed. The outcome sounded dire.

"You've got it in one!" Floss replied.

Emmie was pleased to be stuck at her Washington Square code-breaking centre. The East River was noted for its choppiness to say nothing of how rough the ocean could get beyond it. The whole *ships and boats thing* just wasn't for her. She was seasick just catching the Isle of Wight ferry and she couldn't swim. Juan was watching proceedings from afar and tuned in immediately.

"Termites can fly! Don't forget that people-lets. Is there any weed killer left?" Juan asked.

"Yes, I think there's a couple of drums still knocking about," Jack replied.

"Great. You have all you need to frighten off the flying dogs and stop Effria poaching the Ailhad." It sounded rather a tall order to Jack but he kept his thoughts to himself. "I'm still needed in Egypt. A settlement is close so I'll have to leave you all to deal with the situation yourselves," Juan told them.

Jack was still pondering the iguana's words when Floss took the decision to act decisively.

"Listen up everyone! We're gonna sort this one out ourselves. General Joaquin will fly to Admiral Mathias' ships and scare away those mad dingoes! He'll then douse the Ailhad with a diluted mixture of the weed killer. We'll drop it on them from a great height. At the very least it'll put them into a deep sleep rendering them useless to the likes of Effria." The director of operations made it sound effortless. Edward ordered General Joaquin to prepare a flying squad for action at sea warning him of the difficult labour ahead.

The sky was buzzing with termite wings beating one thousand times a second. The super-sonic hum filled the air as the amazingly strong insects lifted the drums of weed killer onto three wooden pallets along with the necessary spraying equipment. Everything was held in place by strong gold twine. Floss was glued to her screen as General Joaquin led his band of intrepid insects towards Admiral Mathias' ships. Everyone sat tight, anxiously anticipating a gruelling fight with the winged dogs. Termites against mad canines didn't bear thinking about. It would not be a cushy number!

Lily watched from the hospital saddened by what she was witnessing and realising that there would be more casualties as the defenceless plants were subjected to another dose of poison. She was still totally unaware that this would have been their fate in any case if Jack's original plan had seen the light of day. If Lily found out the truth they'd all be in for a savaging from her tongue. Fortuitously, Juan was keeping tabs, reading Lily's mind from his station in Egypt and taking steps to prevent his surgeon general from finding out the truth. At all costs he needed to prevent her becoming disillusioned with her intergalactic mission.

The iguana's travels through time had provided him with many friends. He had an idea.

"Have any of you Sassenachs heard of the Shetland Islands?" He asked the commanders.

"Of course we have!" Edward yelled, feeling indignant at being considered a blockhead. Juan ignored him.

"In the 1860s the Shetland fishermen believed in all kinds of apparitions and fairy tales. Witches, ghosts, pixies, and brownies. They were part of their everyday life," Juan explained.

"1860s! This is 2021. Get real! Those fishermen will be as dead as dodos. Modern people don't believe in that old codswallop," Edward wailed. Jack supported his friend. Despite having played hundreds of unreal video games he was actually a realist at heart. He laughed at Edward's pun, fishermen and codswallop. The joke was lost on Juan.

"2021! Is it really, Ed? Time just rushes by when you're so busy saving the Universe. I'd quite forgotten. 1860 seems like only yesterday and of course, for me it was!" Juan got his own back.

Floss insisted that everyone behave and allow Juan to continue.

"Today's Shetland fishermen still report sightings of apparitions, good and bad. The media pour cold water on their stories but I can tell you, truthfully, that these magical imps and fairies still exist on the islands. I spoke to a pixie only two days ago. They're nice, friendly little things," the iguana smiled.

"How can Shetland pixies help us?" Lily was inspired by Juan's words.

"I feel we should do what we can to preserve the Ailhad," The iguana said, making Lily smile. "If you all agree we'll fly them to Calders Geo. It's the largest cave on Shetland and actually, the largest cave in the British Isles. It has a swift flowing river and will be the perfect hideaway for us to keep the prisoners safe from, 'You Know Who'! Admiral Mathias has plenty of small boats he can drive deep into the cave. The pixies owe me a favour so they'll agree to guarding the Ailhad for a short period."

"It's a yay from me!" The humanitarian surgeon general cried out joyfully.

Juan's plan met with Lily's approval but General Joaquin was already on his way to douse the doomed plants with a deadly dose of the poison. It would probably be too late. Floss took the bull by the horns and gave the order to abort the mission.

"It's imperative that General Joaquin rescues the plants instead of killing them!" Floss commanded. Lieutenant Hawkins jumped into action yelling at the termite communications officer to pull his finger out and send the message to the general without delay. The teenagers waited anxiously for General Joaquin's response.

During the lull that followed Edward saw his opportunity to raise the subject of how and when the TMM prisoners would be repatriated to their home planet.

"Juan, we've a great number of recuperating glass heads. They just want to go home to Optima as soon as possible. What are your thoughts?"

"Knight Commander Kimber, I quite understand your haste but the TMM prisoners present the same problem as the Ailhad plants. I'm loath to send them back too early. With Effria on the prowl they could be intercepted and pressed back into his evil service. We should send them to the Shetlands with the Ailhad. However, I recognise that rock hard cave walls won't be a comfortable place for glass heads so I'm thinking we'll send them further back in time to the Iron Age settlers on the islands. My old pals who lived there two thousand years back will look after them well and keep them safe from being kidnapped. Their wooden huts will be ideal for the glass heads. Joaquin has his hands full with the Ailhad so we'll put Felipe in charge of getting the TMM to the islands."

"But Juan, the TMM will be broken hearted. They're so excited about going home!" Edward was showing that he did have the semblance of a caring side to him.

"I know and I promise you this, the TMM will be sent home as soon as is practicable just not immediately." The iguana was adamant.

Floss considered Juan's revised plan with misgivings.

"What's wrong?" the iguana prompted seeing her frown.

"Glass! I don't think it was invented two thousand years ago. When future archaeologists excavate the Shetlands and find bits of glass amongst the Iron Age artefacts they'll be mystified as to how they got there, won't they?"

"Hmm." Juan was thinking, his snout twitched. "Glass was being used in Egypt as long ago as 3000 BC, I saw it there myself, but I take your point. I'll send in the Intergalactic War Cleaning Squad. They'll remove even the smallest grains of glass. Satisfied?" Floss nodded, wondering what other cleaning jobs this squad might have undertaken over millennia.

Chapter 15

The End is Nigh

General Joaquin flew undaunted, battling high winds to reach the admiral's fleet before Effria could hijack the wayward plants. He was looking forward to finishing off the perverse lettuce leaves once and for all. Mollycoddling devilish foliage was not in his nature and he was delighted to have been put in charge of terminating them. Receiving Floss's message took the wind out of his sails. He was being ordered to make a complete about turn! He was NOT to kill the impish greenery after all! He was to save them instead! Bitter disappointment set in. He might be an aged termite but he was no fossil. He still had HIS marbles even if those in command had lost theirs! The headstrong herbage really did not deserve such good fortune but the general was a professional soldier and his personal preferences were not important. He must obey the director of operations.

Luckily, the canny general had a skein of robust neptunian hydrogen mesh with him. His nigh on impossible task was, without injuring the plants further, to lift them from the ships and return them to land in one piece. The mesh worked splendidly and the operation progressed well. Back and forth his team flew, touching down on the East Riverbank many times to unload the rescued sailors, returning again and again to the Atlantic to save more and more souls. General Joaquin's prompt response and military mastery saved a great many lives, however, the admiral stubbornly insisted on staying aboard his ship until his last mariner had been rescued. In spite of General Joaquin's pleading the old sea salt would not abandon his flag ship. Information from the Retipu metrology expert suggested that the current high winds would bring a turbulent storm and right enough the bad weather was soon upon them forcing the general to call a sudden halt to his mission. He couldn't risk putting his team's lives on the line and sadly, he was forced to forsake scores of plants and many sailors still on board the ships. Unless a miracle happened the storm would spell the end of any remaining seafarers and plants.

A miracle in the shape of five teenagers from Carshalton would save the day.

"Admiral Mathias and some of his sailors remain in peril," the general reported back, breathing heavily. His lungs and wings were showing signs of fatigue.

"What about Effria?" Floss needed to know the worst.

"He wasn't there. Mathias saw him jump ship just before we arrived. It was like he knew we were on our way!" He said, recovering his strength by resting on a plank lying on the riverbank. The commanders were gobsmacked. Yet again Effria had evaded them. General Joaquin was told to rest up before flying the rebellious plants to the Shetlands via Newfoundland and Greenland, the latter the largest island in the world, and then for safety reasons skirt Iceland before reaching The Shetlands. Flying direct would be nigh on impossible in the current freezing air temperatures. The storm was showing no sign of abating. Another worry was the cold air. This would render the general's termites' transmitters useless, reducing their blood flow to that of hibernating frogs. The only possibility was to wait until the squall eased off. It was suggested they take refuge on Prince Edward Island to the north until calmer weather arrived.

The sailors that had been lucky enough to be rescued lolled about happily in the East River's secret tunnels, thankful to be alive and praying that some kind of supernatural occurrence would save their mates still out there tossing around on the waves. The plants saved were locked away in makeshift prison cells for now while the director of operations considered suggestions for a rapid follow-up plan to bring Admiral Mathias and the remainder of his sailors safely back to port. Floss ordered an up-to-the minute weather report from Azure, a blue-bodied Retipu bear and a highly trained meteorologist who had been producing reports every hour throughout the New York affrays.

Azure was up to speed and able to report back immediately.

"This current turbulence is expected to become more violent than before and I detect an air mass bringing even angrier storms," he began, explaining that the USA's east coast regularly suffered hellish weather and the New York coastguard located at the offices of the Port Authority of New York and New Jersey had already put out a second red warning to nearby shipping. To be sure of his calculations Azure re-checked his figures using the International Metrological Code and confident that his predictions were accurate he reported his findings without delay.

"Prepare for hurricane force winds at around twelve on the Beaufort Scale with a probable wave height of forty-five feet to be quickly followed by snow!" Azure growled, bear-like. As predicted, drifting snow fell, followed swiftly by ice cold sleet. This weather pattern was unprecedented. Effria must certainly be at the heart of it. The whipping winds and ginormous up-surging breakers were rocking the admiral's flag ship. His other ships were also in trouble, disappearing below the water only to rise dramatically on the crest of the next wave all tattered and torn and with damaged rigging. The weather conditions were severely testing the damp wood nautical elite.

Next to befall the poor sailors and plants was the ocean freezing over, causing the admiral's ships to become stuck fast in the ice. The teenagers hatched a plan to fly out to the Atlantic Ocean themselves and rescue those marooned in the dangerous weather conditions.

"We must get to Admiral Mathias immediately!" Edward yelled.

"Agreed! Are we all wearing our winged trainers?" Floss asked. They were, but how could they carry the admiral and his sailors to safety?

"Bubble wrap!" Piped up Lieutenant Hawkins, his face glowing with pride.

"Bubble wrap?" Edward repeated looking doubtful.

"Yes sir. Bubble wrap. Sir Juan has a friend who invented the stuff. Not the cheap plastic bubble wrap you Earthlings use for parcels. Our bubble wrap is far superior and indestructible too. It's made from the strongest, most beautiful filaments of gold thread, inter-woven around bubbles of air by Malachitian gold worms. Take some with you. It's incredibly strong. Wrap it around the ships and you'll be able to drag them to safety," They had never heard Clive Hawkins sound so enthusiastic about anything before.

Lily had used the wonderful gold bubble wrap advocated by the lieutenant at her hospital. The nurses wrapped the injured in it to keep them warm whilst awaiting their treatment but the hospital only had limited supplies and the rescue operation would require several miles of it. Floss called Juan.

"Extraordinary! Quite extraordinary!" Repeated Juan. "Golden bubble wrap... What a splendid idea of old Hawkins. Give me a minute, I'll ask around," he said, momentarily disappearing from the visual field above their heads. He returned with good news.

"Thirty miles of best quality gold filigree bubble wrap is on its way to N42."

"We need it now! When's it likely to arrive?" Floss asked anxiously. The clock was ticking.

"In about ten minutes if you're using the Malachitian clock."

"How does that compare to British Summer Time?" Jack asked.

"I'd say that would be equivalent to about half a minute's time…." Another round of loud drilling occurred above them as the solid rock interface at Grand Central Terminus was blown up.

The youthful commanders steeled themselves. A messenger informed the admiral of the new plan and only just in time. The look-out perched in the rigging atop HMS Minotaur's mast, the admiral's second-best ship, perished, thrown forcefully onto the ice as the ship was squashed by it. HMS Seagull, another of Mathias' ships and its crew were not faring any better. The Seagull's Captain Elkington had ordered his crew below deck for safety when the ice had split open the starboard side sending many into the freezing water below the ship and to a certain death.

N42 was receiving frantic SOS messages. It wasn't just the Seagull that needed urgent assistance but the Morning Glory too. This was a ship equipped with Magnitude Sonar developed on Malachite for listening into enemy activity up to fifty-thousand space miles away. The ship listed as the ice crushed it. This futuristic vessel was certain to be lost. Even if the craft survived her delicate electronic systems would be ruined. The intergalactic community had invested megabucks in this state-of the-art ship. The teenagers had no time to think. Floss needed all shoulders to the wheel and so contacted Emmie, insisting she help them. Reluctantly, the non-swimmer agreed, arriving in moments at N42 via a PUPA intergalactic transporter machine.

The five indomitable young adults tied double knots in their shoelaces making sure their winged trainers didn't drop off in the river enroute to the frozen ocean. Emmie was naturally skittish about flying over the water so Floss looped some strong twine around her waist and hitched it to herself so her friend couldn't fall in. Flying out to the

Atlantic was the highest and longest trip any of them had undertaken in their magic trainers and it felt thrilling. As they neared the broken ships they each took a corner of the bubble wrap blanket and went first to rescue Admiral Mathias, the admiral finally conceding that if his commanders ordered him to leave his post, then he should do so. He would trust them to do their best for his crews. They then turned their attention to those who had fallen overboard. Emmie remained close to Floss as they flew low to reach the damp wood termites frantically trying to stay warm on the ice. Jack and Edward being the stronger pulled the sailors up to safety and laid them on the blanket, and only just in time as a shoal of hungry ice-cutting sawfish looking for lunch, chomped their way through the ice, racing towards the stranded sailors.

The rescuers pushed themselves to the limit risking their own lives fighting the cruel weather, returning again and again to save the remaining sailors and the dregs of the drooping plants. The temperature warmed up just as suddenly as it had dipped and the ice melted. Once all possible lives had been saved they turned their attention to HMS Seagull, dragging it out of danger and then hauling it all the way to the East River where they anchored it in a nearby dock. The Morning Glory came next. Using the twine they pulled the ship upright, cocooning it in the bubble wrap and likewise, heaved it back to port to join HMS Seagull, its state-of the-art equipment still miraculously intact. They had accomplished their mission!

Back on dry land Captain Elkington rallied the rescued termites by encouraging their scratchy voices to sing their woes away with choruses of, *Yo Ho Ho and a bottle of fizz!* They swigged nettle-pop laced with invigorating marberry juice and felt all the better for it. Captain Elkington had another surprise up his sleeve. He waited patiently for the right moment to introduce their favourite musical instrument, the bagpipes, played by one of the rescued sailors. The exhausted insects drank in the soulful music as they drifted off into a deep and relaxing sleep. Admiral Mathias was delighted to be reunited with his navy. He ordered a head count. One hundred and twenty casualties either dead or missing. The loss of his brave seamen saddened him but he was grateful for the three hundred that had survived. The admiral's reduced fleet could now only be described as a flotilla. A few empty ships had had to be left behind and they now drifted rudderless, like little wooden bath toys, bobbing about on the sea.

The teenagers were drenched through and ached all over. They had flown through heavy sleet at fifty miles an hour. It had been their sheer determination to do the right thing that had kept them going. Exhausted and their strength zapped they sank down onto the ground to rest until refreshments arrived courtesy of the catering corp., beetroot sandwiches!

"I'd rather have a bar of milk chocolate," Emmie protested, beetroot not being her favourite food.

"Beetroot, Emmie," Lily informed her, "is one of the new superfoods. It's full of antioxidants." It made no difference. Emmie was never munching her way through a beetroot sandwich, superfood or not! The rest tucked in with relish.

The rescued plants were securely caged in a separate tunnel on the East River and would be handed back into the charge of General Joaquin once he and his team were rested and able to set off on the first part of their journey to Prince Edward Island. Edward's TMM prisoners were marking time encamped on Cherry Hill. They were feeling lucky, cracking jokes, and engaging in friendly banter with their termite minders whilst awaiting General Felipe with General Alvaro's assistance, to repatriate them to Optima, still unaware that they would be spending an unspecified period in the Shetlands before that happened.

Colonel Eva was detailed to take over General Alvaro's current recognisance duties in the sewers allowing him to accompany General Felipe to the Scottish isles.

"Alvaro's not with me!" General Felipe told Floss sharply."

"Oh! Where will I find him then?" If the director of operations was honest with herself she hadn't missed the surly warrior at all.

"Not sure. I believe he's helping Fabio Lopez. There's some problem at Washington Square," General Felipe replied, sounding vague.

"Oh dear! I'm afraid General Felipe, you'll have to escort the TMM to the field marshal's Iron Age acquaintances alone," Floss advised the general.

Getting back to business Floss was still trying to uncover the identity of their traitor and asked Emmie to recheck thousands of coded messages received in the hour before the storm had broken. She was looking for any clue that might suggest the vile weather had been artificially induced by Effria and possibly also identify the traitor in their midst. Floss was back at N42 feeling tired but knowing she must stay alert. Stuck deep down in the bedrock under Midtown Manhattan she felt miserable and isolated. She wanted to stretch her legs, go for a walk in the sunshine but she couldn't do this. She must remain hidden away from the gaze of the public who were so far ignorant of the intergalactic tussle rampaging around them. The maniac responsible for all the spilt blood was still at large so Floss could not allow herself to be distracted.

Juan was still in Egypt but with Floss at a low ebb he did his best to revive her spirits.

"Hello, Floss! How are you?" He contacted her telepathically.

"Actually, I'm feeling a bit down in the dumps. I've discovered it takes a great deal of mental energy to run a war!"

"Physical energy too," Juan agreed. "Flying through such inclement weather on such an important rescue mission is exhausting for the best of us but for you humans, well, it just wipes you out! You'll be fine in a short while. I promise you." And then changing the subject. "So, what would your Granny Molly say if she knew you'd directed a war effort and had triumphantly prevailed against the enemy?" Floss brightened at the mention of her granny.

"Floss, she'd say, make tea not war! My gran doesn't approve of fighting. She thinks arguments should be settled quickly and before bedtime. Negotiation is key, is what she says. Then she puts the kettle on and we sit down with a brew and a digestive biscuit."

"Hmm, perhaps I should invite Gregor Magnus to tea and give him a good dressing down!" Juan laughed, knowing in his heart that a gentleman's agreement with this monster was never on the cards.

Chapter 16

The Fox's Den

PUPA's hunt for its enemies was relentless. All likely hiding places were searched leaving no stone unturned. Sooner or later Gregor Magnus and his side kick would err, revealing their whereabouts. Espionage supremo, Colonel Eva, was sure they were holed up somewhere on Earth rather than elsewhere in the galaxy, but in which country or century they had taken refuge, she didn't know.

Juan's mission in Egypt had been successful and he returned to New York clutching a contract guaranteeing that the sultan would, in future, do all in his power to prevent their common enemy from ever gaining a toe-hold in Alexandrian high-society again. The bonafide Count Abduls of this world would have nothing to fear in the future. However, before rejoining Floss at N42 the iguana made a speedy visit to nineteenth century Buckingham Palace to appraise Queen Victoria of the situation.

"One is not amused. Naturally, I'm grateful for your advice but feel it could have been timelier, thereby preventing my army from being discredited in the Egyptian uprising!" The Queen was known for speaking her mind. "However, as I said, I'm grateful to you Sir Juan, for alerting me and my parliament to the underhand tactics of Gregor Magnus! I would like to think of us as partners, friends even, who are willing to fight for the rights of our creatures whatever their shape or size in any future clashes with intergalactic hobgoblins of low intellect." The iguana could hardly disagree with her sentiment.

By way of thanks the Queen invited Juan to take tea with her. They chatted over cucumber sandwiches and sherry trifles. Her Majesty wanted to hear more about the iguana's planet, Malachite. It sounded so interesting. As Empress of India she was seriously contemplating whether her realm might be extended to planets further afield. Could her subjects benefit from stronger ties with Malachite? Knowledge of space travel and the cultivation of new food plants could only be good for the British economy. Juan promised to stay in touch. Whilst at the palace Juan made another important acquaintance. One of the Queen's leading military commanders, Colonel Ewart of the British Army had joined them for tea.

Colonel Ewart had just returned from the Egypt of 1882 and had mentioned a curious observation made whilst in the desert sands of Giza, near Cairo. According to Colonel Ewart the statue known as The Great Sphinx was covered in sand and often surrounded by an eerie blue mist. A very strange phenomenon. Swirling sand was a natural occurrence but a blue mist? Juan was intrigued and passed on this information to Colonel Eva who agreed it was well worth investigating. It became one of several strands of intelligence PUPA was pursuing in its search for Effria and his tyrannical boss.

Surveillance at Colchester Zoo was ongoing. There were longish periods when no interactions with the strange creature occurred and at such times the zebafe seemed more like an automaton, his movements becoming oddly robotic when previously they'd been lissom, graceful, giraffe-like and knowing. This great change in the creature's bearing always occurred shortly after he'd been fed by Konstantinos. Was the café owner passing vital information to the creature who might actually be Gregor Magnus himself? It would seem so. Eva had established that Konstantinos was indeed crossing the Atlantic with his sacks of leftover food by way of a magic teleport system. After each feeding the creature became animated, acting normally like a zebafe was expected to behave. Juan believed the animal's sometimes stiff and awkward movements could be due to a switch being flicked, turning him back into a robot when vacated by the despot. Data was coming in thick and fast and the team heartily agreed with Juan's theory but hard evidence was needed before any proposal to capture their arch-enemy could be put together.

Juan put his red thinking cap on. He needed a smart way to find out if the zebafe was, indeed, just another pawn in the hands of the diabolical Gregor Magnus or an innocent beast from a distant planet.

"I'm sending Hawkins to Colchester Zoo this instant. He's to ask the zebafe some pertinent questions."

"Hawkins speaks zebafe language?" Floss asked, sounding surprised.

"Yes indeed. Hawkins is exceptionally talented. I want him to show the animal the colours red, blue, green, and orange and ask him to indicate the colour red. Next, he's to persuade the zebafe to indicate the number five in the sequence, one to ten. Lastly, he's to ascertain the creature's mother's name." They seemed odd questions to ask a dumb animal. Juan explained his reasoning. "When presented with an array of colours a simple robot can't deduce red from blue and it's the same with numbers. Similarly, there's no way a robot would know the zebafe's mother's name." Juan's reasoning sounded plausible.

Hawkins was despatched forthwith arriving at the zoo after dark when it was shut to the public. The aid-de-camp's feathery head with its built-in torch lights were turned on helping him locate his subject in the darkness. On arrival the zebafe was snoring peacefully, lying comfortably on his ever-growing pile of uneaten hay. Hawkins rapidly and fearlessly assessed the situation. Tiny drone ants supplied by Emmie's department crawled up the walls of the zebafe's enclosure in thick black columns beaming live pictures back to Floss, coordinating the operation from N42. Edward and Jack worked alongside her. The tension inside N42 rose as the commanders watched Hawkins get to work.

"I have to say," began Jack, "Hawkins doesn't seem at all scared."

"Exactly what I was thinking," Edward concurred. They watched, their eyes glued to the transmitted images. Hawkins was standing just centimetres away from the beast's head. There were no records of a zebafe ever being a killer like one of the big cats but then no one apart from the café's Greek owner had ever ventured close enough to test out the theory. Hawkins gently stroked the creature's head speaking softly to him in his own language, a skill he'd picked up at linguistics school two hundred years before when Hawkins had been in his prime. The zebafe slowly opened his eyes.

The team watched the zebafe like hawks looking for signs that he might be an imposter.

"That animal's not real," Lily shrieked, arriving from the hospital and planting her bottom firmly on a chair in front of the computer screens. "The zebafe's reactions to Hawkins are just too wooden. You only need to look at his eyes. There's simply no emotion there."

"I tend to agree," Floss remarked, looking at Lily. "Anyway, what are you doing here? Who's looking after your patients?"

"Well, you see I've this splendid staff nurse called, Barbara Stanley, deputising for me..." Lily waited for the bomb to explode. Floss stared at Lily and then they both stared at Jack.

"You're having a laugh, aren't you?" Jack really believed they were pulling his leg but with the zebafe operation playing out there was no time for him to question Lily.

"Hawkins needs to get a move on," Edward remarked nervously.

"Yes Ed, I agree. I can't imagine how he'll get that blood sample without annoying the animal," Floss added.

"What blood sample?" Lily asked sharply, feeling left out.

"Juan's parting shot was that Hawkins should get a zebafe blood sample. He mentioned something to do with blood types and extra-terrestrials. I expect he'll fill us in later," Floss explained. They continued their vigil, a hush descending upon the room. Hawkins continued stroking the zebafe's head just as if he were patting a pet dog.

It was all taking far too long for the young commanders' liking. Hawkins hadn't even begun to ask the creature Juan's questions when suddenly the screens went black and the pictures stopped coming. Just moments later Hawkins was on his space phone speaking to them.

"All done here. I'm on my way back. Speak soon," he told them ending his call.

"Something's not right here! I don't understand how Hawkins could've completed his task in such a short time!" Edward exclaimed.

"I'm sure we're all of the same opinion," Floss reassured him. "Can we trust him do you think?" Floss had cast an element of doubt over the lieutenant's character. It was the first time Hawkin's loyalty had been called into question. He was Sir Juan's right hand man for heaven's sake and aide-de-camps were usually gallant knights, selected for their bravery, prepared to lay down their lives when necessary, for their lieges. The very notion that Hawkins might be anything less than squeaky clean was unthinkable.

An elevator sprung into life bringing Hawkins back to N42.

"Now remember, don't let on we suspect him of being our traitor," Floss whispered as the door swung open to reveal a smiling Hawkins.

"I have it all here," the flamboyant aide-de-camp called out, walking briskly to the main desk. He delved into a medieval leather pouch hanging from his waist and produced a phial of purple liquid. "The zebafe's blood!" Hawkins proclaimed, excitedly. "This wonderful glowing plasma is the food of life that runs through the creature's veins." The commanders congratulated him on his achievement. The blood would of course have to be analysed to make sure it was what the lieutenant claimed it to be.

"How did you manage to get the sample? We were watching right up until the power cut out and there didn't seem enough time for you to do the business," Edward confronted him.

"It was the blackout that played into my hands. The zebafe bolted cutting his flank on my boot spur. I reached down and using the tiny torches on my head as a source of light I managed to catch some of the blood spurting from his side." Hawkins parted the feathers on his head to show them the petite twinkling lights secured on his scalp, switching them on and off to demonstrate. "They provided just enough lumens for me to do the job," he explained. An analysis of the blood just might be enough for them to make an informed decision on the zebafe's authenticity, catch Gregor Magnus and even Effria and identify the traitor in their midst at the same time.

The Mh Negative blood group belonged to creatures evolving from Deep Sky communities such as nebulae from where plan-stars are created. Gregor Magnus' ancestors came from a plan-star, which is half star and half planet and formed following a nebula explosion around twenty thousand years ago. Its descendants, including Gregor Magnus still carry the same blood type. The phial was despatched to PUPA's laboratory. Hawkins was invited to get some rest whilst the commanders considered their options.

"Until we know the test results we shouldn't jump to conclusions," Floss insisted.

"Of course not," Edward began. "I happen to think that Hawkins is on our side. He's so pleased with himself I doubt he's our traitor. If he were working for the enemy he'd have returned without the sample because it just wouldn't be in his interests to help us."

"Ed, I disagree with you. I think the blood sample's fake. In the video game, Zombies and the King of Morocco, the king's blood sample is found to be tomato ketchup!"

"Oh really Jack! Wakey, wakey! A computer game? What we're dealing with here is real life," Edward teased his friend.

Floss summarised what they knew so far to be true.

"We know someone's passing information to our enemy because each time we get close to them they amazingly escape our clutches, literally disappearing off the face of the Earth!"

"We also know that the traitor is likely to be someone close to us," Emmie added.

"It's got to be someone we know and if we're discounting Hawkins at this point we should be considering everyone else in our close circle. It could well be one of your Retipu team, Emmie, although to be frank, my money's on Colonel Eva, our so-called Spy Extraordinaire."

"What about your generals?" Emmie countered. She'd built up a trusting relationship with her team and did not take kindly to them being disparaged. "They see the intelligence reports and battle plans and could easily relay information to our enemies!"

"What about Major Gubby or Captain Greta?" Lily considered, looking at the boys.

"Let's wait until the lab results are back!" Floss said, putting a stop to all their surmising.

Elsewhere, working in parallel with Operation Zebafe, General Felipe's TMM repatriation operation was now fully underway. A spaceship with seating for up to two thousand had been commissioned from Malachite for their Shetlands journey. Many of the TMM still had wafer thin cracks in their skulls and a bumpy ride through space necessitated seat belts and headrests to stop their glass craniums flopping around. General Felipe was expected to be away for a couple of days. The TMM were jubilant to be, they thought, on their way home. No one had yet had the heart to tell them they would be stopping at a half-way house in the Scottish isles for an extended period before heading home to Optima.

Chapter 17

The Noose Tightens

Colonel Eva was Intent on sniffing out her adversaries wherever they might be and flew around New York's skyscrapers peering down on the bustling city below whilst following up any leads, even the tiniest snippet of information coming her way. One piece of data reported some strange goings-on at Rikers Island, the notorious home of New York's main jail holding ten thousand men. If Effria was hiding out there it would be the devil of a job to find him. The prisoners at Rikers were not exactly known for their helpfulness. Effria was an absolute whiz kid in the art of disguise, merging into any background at the drop of a hat, fooling everyone. The Rikers' inmates would never grass on him even if they knew the extent of his brutality and monstrous crimes. They stuck together like glue.

Arriving on the island Colonel Eva perched on a handy flagpole. A white fluffy Persian cat leered up at her. This was not a place for a leisurely picnic. She would most likely end up as the picnic! The very thought made her shudder. She knew she must hold her nerve. The cat might know where she should begin her search. A long time ago Moggy language had been part of her cyber intelligence training because cats were considered an asset in the spying game. They roamed freely in and out of buildings, parks and wasteland. They knew all the nooks and crannies, all the open sheds and barns where criminals might hide. Felines were therefore, in a superb position to report unusual sightings or strangers they came across. No one notices when a cat walks by!

Colonel Eva thought a friendly approach might work best.

"Hi Tiddles!" She called out trying to sound happy and carefree.

"Who're you calling Tiddles?" The cat growled back in his New York twang.

"So sorry sir. Didn't mean to offend. What's your name? I'm Eva, the red necked avocet from Oz."

"I'm Rudy the prison cat," Rudy mocked her, licking his paw, his claws extended. "And before you ask," the cat added brusquely, "I was named after a New York mayor who, I'm told, successfully brought the city's crime rate down."

"Oh how sweet! That would be Mayor Giuliani," the avocet prided herself on keeping up with current affairs.

Colonel Eva had not set out to get the cat's life history but hey-ho, if it got him on side she was prepared to listen all day long if necessary!

"Yeah," the cat continued, "one of the mafia in C Block christened me Rudy. Before that I was just Puss to everyone." The Persian cat was keen to talk. "I'm famous hereabouts for being a good mouser. Oh boy, at times we've had a good few mice, I can tell yer!"

"How fascinating," Colonel Eva feigned interest. "Sounds to me like you're a vital part of the operation here. I bet you know your way round the blocks?" Eva turned on the charm.

"Right on! I know every inch of this god forsaken guardhouse," Rudy shot back whilst inspecting his fluffy tail for tangles. "Hey gel, where'd you say you come from?"

"I'm from the beautiful Australian outback." Tenacity was called for here. She dug her nails in, metaphorically speaking. Rudy was practically eating out of her hand, enjoying being the centre of attention. His aggressive nature was all bravado. Underneath his hardened exterior he was lonely, having no adorable She cat to love him. His mother had been the prison's only female feline in its whole history. Rudy was committed to a lifetime of loneliness.

Eva jumped in without thinking.

"I'm looking for a man..." She began, straight away regretting her choice of words.

"Well lady, you've come to the right place," Rudy told her. "We've a fair few thousand men here to choose from." The cat laughed out loud showing off his sharp teeth. Gnashers! Colonel Eva shuddered. His teeth must have sounded the death knell of many a poor mouse and a good few innocent birds as well. She decided she should stay put at the top of the flagpole even though squawking down at the cat was giving her a sore throat.

"The man I'm looking for is ..." she stopped to think for a second. What she was about to say was going to sound crazy. Why would an uneducated, unworldly prison cat understand intergalactic warfare, time travel, sorcery and the knowledge that there were evil tyrants from outer space on the loose and possibly hiding in his jail? The bird rejigged her address.

"The man I'm after may be pretending to be a prisoner when in reality, he's an hotshot, an international pirate working for a megalomaniac bent on taking over the Universe. It's imperative for the safety of Earth and the Solar System that this man is caught apace."

The colonel had the cat's undivided attention. With his fur standing on end, Rudy, the cantankerous, long-suffering penitentiary pussy cat was about to become a vital cog in an international stratagem to save the Universe.

"Blimey! When I got up this morning Block A's left-over herring bones and a saucer of milk from Prisoner

42539 was all I had to look forward to," he told her. Eva kept him talking and Rudy obliged by telling her more about the felons and Prisoner 42539 in particular.

"Wow, Prisoner 42539 sounds a nice person," the bird humoured her new fluffy chum. "So, thinking about your prisoners do any of them seem vacant at times, as though they have someone else hiding inside them?" She was pressing Rudy to think the unthinkable.

"Red neck, you listen to me. They're all a bit loopy in here. Think about it, gel. They got themselves banged up, know what I mean? Let's just say this, if burglary was their thing then they weren't very good at it, were they? They got caught didn't they!" The cat did have a point. The colonel was caressing her head with one of her wings to relieve the building tension. Discussions with a prickly cat was hard work.

Colonel Eva needed to change her approach, take the cat under her wing so to speak, and quickly before Rudy lost interest. She didn't want him to think that Prisoner 42539's saucer of milk was more appetising than a nonsense conversation with an Australian avocet.

"Tell me about your friend, the one who saves milk for you. What did he do wrong?"

"International swindler with links to organised gangs. Over the years he's been in and out of Rikers more times than I've eaten pigeon for my dinner!" Eva shuddered at the thought. The cat continued. "He gets a short sentence for embezzlement or duping some poor old lady out of her savings, serves his time, gets let out and does the same thing all over again. And, please don't ask me what embezzlement is because I haven't the foggiest...," A lot was at stake. Eva needed to hit it off with this cat.

"Embezzlement, puss, is the misappropriation of funds," the bird explained. Rudy wasn't sure he really wanted to know.

"The world we live in is a comical old place if you ask me," Rudy mused. "That gaffer I was just telling you about, Prisoner 42539, he's the funniest stick of them all. He gets lots of shifty visitors and if you ask me there's something weird about all of them but here in New York no one turns a hair." Rudy belched. "Sorry about that," he said, apologising for his bad manners. "I've eaten too many mice. They never fail to give me indigestion."

Colonel Eva tingled with exhilaration. Prisoner 42539 sounded like a person of interest to her. Could Effria be using a prisoner's body to evade capture? It was a distinct possibility. She needed assistance. Emmie's drone ants would be the perfect cover. With the zoo surveillance halted the spy drones would be available to use at Rikers. They were right now flying back across the Atlantic Ocean enroute for New York City. Emmie diverted them to Rikers Island. Rudy was warming to Eva and likewise she was feeling more comfortable about coming down from her flagpole, as long as she was able to keep a safe distance from those sharp claws. She'd tumbled that what the cat really wanted was to feel loved and coupled with this she needed to divert his attention to allow the surveillance drones to enter the building unheeded. The best way of killing two birds with one stone, an unfortunate analogy in Eva's case, was to feed the cat. She flew away on an urgent errand or at least that's what she told him. She was soon back with a beak crammed full of small fish. Rudy was ecstatic. Fresh fish on a weekday! He was so consumed with playing with his dinner, a trait in cats, that he was oblivious to the thick black columns of ants crawling across the tarmac and slipping quietly beneath the penitentiary's secure electronic door.

The ants poured in guided by sonar directed from afar by Treah, the Retipu supervisor from the Washington Square Park code-breaking centre. Once inside, they fanned out into smaller groups finding crevices to hide in until the opportunity presented itself to start gathering incriminating evidence, which they would then beam back to N42. The waiting was hard. Colonel Eva passed the time by preening her feathers, shaking out her wings, clipping her toenails and generally pampering herself in the hope that it wouldn't be too long before she received positive feedback. Seagulls circling the avocet were making her feel nervous. These aggressive bullies would make short work of a small defenceless bird like her. The sooner she could fly back to the mainland the better. In the meantime,

Prisoner 42539 was engaged on therapeutic craftwork making raffia baskets for a local charity in the remedial section of the prison. Colonel Eva deduced that this was the perfect cover for a mercenary biding his time.

At N42 the zebafe's blood test result was back from the lab. Elements of Mh Negative originating from extra-terrestrial lineages were found in the sample but were inconclusive. The sample mostly consisted of dinosaur blood. If Gregor Magnus had inhabited the zebafe earlier on he had certainly vacated it now and evaded capture yet again. The cold calculating sorcerer must have a tame informant!

"Disappointing but I guess at least we know where NOT to look," Edward speculated.

"Yes, and at least the poor old zebafe can rest in peace for now," Jack said. "I worry about what will happen to him. It won't be long before the scientists decide to pull him limb from limb in the name of scientific research." Jack was thinking about Rosie and Rodrigo and imagining the tabloid newspaper headline, *Pet Angora Rabbit Weds Bunny from Outer Space!* The academics would have a field day.

"We can't afford to dwell on the zebafe's welfare right now," Floss reminded him. "If it will help I'll ask Treah to assign one of her team to watch over him. Operation Rikers is in play and things are looking up." Floss pointed at the screen in front of them. Thousands of ants were marching in neat columns up prison walls and across cell floors, their progress monitored by tiny cameras hidden inside their eyes sockets.

Prisoner 42539 finished his raffia work and returned to his cell at 2.30 pm. At 3 pm a buzzer heralded the start of visiting time and remarkably, Prisoner 42539 had a visitor. The ants scurried over the pristine floors following their target to the reception area where he had to wait alongside all the other inmates to be searched before meeting his visitor. Armed Security Officer NY203 stood alert, guarding the entrance to the visitors' room. He was not an avid fan of wildlife. He also had a penchant for cleanliness having served most of his adult life in the military followed by the U.S. State Penitentiary Service, equivalent to the UK's Prison Service. In both walks of life his boots had been expected to shine brightly, always. He spotted the ants. They were marching with gusto in broad daylight around his steel capped boots on their way to Prisoner 42539's table.

Ants in the prison were not a good look. They suggested bad hygiene. The prison governor would not be pleased to hear about such an infestation. Additionally, the prisoners were sure to use them as an excuse to riot and a riot made the prisoners' day more interesting. Security Officer NY 203 was having none of that. Riots meant more work and he certainly had no intention of allowing the inmates' prison experience to be a happy one! Security Officer

NY203 furiously stamped on the ants breaking their miniscule transmitters in the process. The prison floor was littered with tiny bodies resembling squashed currants and sultanas in a bread pudding. The din of impassioned stamping caused belly-aching laughter from the prisoners. A dancing security officer was entertaining them whilst they waited for their relatives, an unexpected pleasure!

The ants stopped coming. NY203 had crushed them all. His senior officer ordered him to go and get a broom and sweep up the mess. Without question he did just that leaving the door to the visitors' room momentarily unguarded.

"Looks like my diversion ploy worked," Floss announced. The commanders were gobsmacked to hear that the ants' wanton destruction had been a deliberate plan. "Such a pity so many had to die though," she added wistfully. Edward backed her up.

"Floss, it was for a good cause. Don't worry about it."

"Millions of ants have breathed their last. What's to be pleased about?" Lily was cross.

"Dead drones won't send back too many live pictures!" Jack said gloomily, being realistic.

"Keep watching!" Floss advised. They kept their eyes peeled.

A white fluffy cat slunk into the room and made a bee line for Prisoner 42539. The free agent feline wandered without hindrance; the prison's psychiatric service believing that a cat was good for the prisoners' emotional wellbeing. The suspect was unaware that Rudy's left ear had been fitted with a camera that was so small it was almost impossible to see with the naked eye. The cat jumped up onto the table and nudging the prisoner's arm encouraged him to stroke the cat whilst allowing the camera to capture good clear shots of his face. The photographs were beamed back for analysis to N42 via the Retipu's Graphics And Optical Section. The avocet was unable to enter the prison herself so bit her tongue and waited anxiously for updates from the top of her flagpole.

The teenagers studied the images for features clearly showing a resemblance to Effria in his last known personification. Rudy was working overtime keeping his subject entertained. The cat rolled over to have his tummy tickled, purred and then licked the prisoner's face. When the opportunity presented itself the cat craftily attached an electronic device to the prisoner's wiry hair – should the operation go topsy turvey the team would be able to monitor his movements. So far so good! The bird demanded feedback from N42. In particular, she wanted to know if they were receiving good strong signals as sometimes the cameras malfunctioned and the whole process had to be gone through all over again. The situation was grippingly tense for both Eva and all those at N42.

The prisoners' families and friends passed through security and arrived at the visitors' room. A lady with pearl drop earrings and a bun at the back of her head made for Prisoner 42539. The mysterious visitor was wearing a smart blue two piece suit. She came up close to Prisoner 42539 and kissed him on the cheek and then sat down at his table. They seemed to chat like old friends. Rudy playfully nudged the lady and whilst doing so took shots of her too. Jack sensed something familiar about the lady and studied the screen closely. Her face was angled away from the camera so he couldn't get a good look of her features. The lady's white gloves caught his attention. The fingers were full of jagged holes. Jack was struck by a bolt of lightning. Sharp, spiky talons! The *lady* simply had to be his aide, Captain Greta! Oh why was life so cruel?

The others were similarly disgusted at Jack's discovery. Knowing their informant was one of them and one of the few people they had put their trust in made it worse, filling them with hopelessness. They felt sick inside.

"I'm always telling you to have faith in each other and to trust your own instincts but today my friends, it is indeed a sad day for such concepts!" Juan said dolefully.

"My gran says trust is hard to win but easy to lose," Floss added glumly.

"Your grandma's so right," Juan agreed. Jack was silent. He was trying to remain optimistic. He wanted to be wrong about Greta.

"I think we can all agree that Hawkins is in the clear," Edward said, satisfied that they had found the defector.

"What should be our next move?" Floss asked.

"Look on this set-back as an opportunity. We have the chance of catching two for the price of one, the despicable Effria and the disloyal Greta," Lily counselled.

"Are we totally sure that Prisoner 42539 is actually Effria?" Edward asked.

"They say the camera never lies!" Jack said morosely.

"Assuming that Prisoner 42539 is Effria we should be putting together a plan for his arrest." For Jack's sake Floss was steering the conversation away from Greta's desertion. They didn't have to wait long. The Retipu confirmed that Prisoner 42539 was indeed Effria.

The Retipu were receiving coded messages from Egypt using an unusual cipher made up of symbols, extinct birds and animals and looking similar to ancient Egyptian hieroglyphics. The messages appeared to be originating from inside the Great Sphinx at Giza and were being directed to Rikers Prison. It was another pointer to the fact that Prisoner 42539 just had to be Effria. It was the only logical conclusion. Effria's boss and paymaster, Gregor Magnus, was sending him encrypted orders via the prison advising him where to concentrate his next attack and, Gregor was sending these messages from the Sphinx, the very emblem of Egypt. The Sphinx must be his covert hideout. It had been sealed up from general public access for two thousand years with only a handful of archaeologists over that time being allowed to enter. As soon as Effria was under lock and key their quest to capture Gregor Magnus must move to ancient Egypt.

Colonel Eva was informed of the Rikers findings. It was now her responsibility to take Effria into custody and apprehend the traitorous captain so she could no longer endanger their lives. The avocet would need back-up. On Juan's advice Floss sent General Alvaro and his crack troops to Rikers insisting they must not arouse the suspicions of anyone at the penitentiary. The foray was top secret. Floss didn't want Prisoner 42539 or his visitor alerted to their presence. This was the one occasion when Effria would not elude them. Alvaro, however, had other ideas on his mind. It was true that since the start, Floss and General Alvaro had not hit it off, in fact she'd totally underestimated the depth of Alvaro's animosity towards her. He was feeling tossed aside, humiliated by mere juveniles who knew nothing about bearing arms. Unbeknown to Juan, General Alvaro had decided to retire from active service and this would be his last campaign.
General Alvaro had at first been fiercely loyal to his field marshal but a rare bitterness had crept in that Gregor Magnus had exploited. The general had fallen hook, line and sinker for the tyrant's false charms and being an easy target had accepted a lucrative back-hander in return for supplying information to the despot and assisting him

in evading capture. Alvaro was blind to the demon's lack of scruples believing wholeheartedly that he would honour his promises. Juan, the all-seeing and all-knowing Malachitian had an inkling of the general's capers and let the director of operations know what he had discovered about him.

Chapter 18

The Die is Cast

General Alvaro wore his military medals with pride for the last time. Mid-way across the East River on his way to Rikers Island from Manhattan the traitor was enjoying the moment, unaware that the game was up. Fabio, the odd bod with the purply glass eyes and brows the teenagers had met at 8th Street station was now Brigadier General Lopez with his own command. Fabio's original orders were to provide General Alvaro with a back-up force should it be needed. That was before the truth was known. Fabio's new instructions came through as he stationed his troops at the ready to assist General Alvaro on South Brother Island, just a hop and a skip away from Rikers and from where a rapid attack on Effrian sympathisers could be launched if the need arose. The plan changed and the brigadier was told to stay put until further notice.

Alvaro landed at the southern tip of Rikers Island just as a silent underwater tank driven by Hilton and Skelton, two expert sub-aqua mariners glided up the prison's boat ramp at the northern end. Alvaro's termite battalion felt peckish and being so close to the prison's vegetable garden they impudently helped themselves to a hearty meal followed by a nap. Meanwhile, Hilton and Skelton began their assault on a vulnerable Alvaro. With Fabio's back-up force no longer there to support General Alvaro and his own unit napping, the general was alone, isolated, a walk over for Hilton and Skelton. The sub-mariners from Spica, the brightest star in the Virgo constellation inched closer to their suspect until they were within touching distance. They sprang. Alvaro was netted. The miscreant was tied up in a bundle at top speed and rolled down to the water's edge to where the sub-aqua tank was anchored. With the task completed the underwater craft quietly sank down to the bottom of the East River and stayed there like a sleeping crocodile.

Events happened so quickly that Alvaro was prevented from forewarning Effria aka Prisoner 42539. Inside the building the quarry and his floosy, Captain Greta were on edge, constantly checking the clock. They had expected the back-stabbing Alvaro and his termites with Fabio in tow to attack the prison whilst visiting hour was in progress. With Alvaro's strike not forthcoming Effria's Plan B swung into action. This entailed Captain Greta insisting to the governor that Prisoner 42539 be escorted by herself, and without delay, to the United Nations building in Manhattan for interrogation on a trumped up charge of illegal arms trading. The captain had all the necessary paperwork, albeit forged. Greta rose from her seat and slipped unnoticed into a nearby room, speedily changing into her military police uniform she'd earlier concealed behind the central heating pipes. She calmly returned to collect Prisoner 42539 and the two of them enacted a sort of charade to make everything appear normal. Effria pretended to be difficult so Greta handcuffed him and with his refusal to move, rough-handled him, frogmarching him to the governor's suite.

The guard stationed at the entrance to the administration corridor was surprised to see Captain Greta and her prisoner turn up unannounced. Audiences with the governor had to be pre-booked. It was the rules!

"Well, I don't know about this," he said, unsure of this change in procedure. "If you ask me this place is going to the dogs! No one bothers to tell me anything anymore." The captain confidently showed him the paperwork making sure to point out the White House presidential stamp. What could he do? Reluctantly he complied. Captain Greta and her prisoner made their way to the governor's office where Greta opened the door with gusto shoving the six foot tall Effria inside and slamming the door shut behind him.

Effria, in spite of his size seemed suddenly defenceless. He was alone with the top man who was standing, gazing at the boats on the river with his back to the has-been troublemaker. This normally confidant skivvy of the most hated despot the galaxy had ever seen felt his remaining power draining away fast. He couldn't understand what was happening to him. It was after all just the prison governor standing in the room with him, a mere harmless human being! The governor turned to face Prisoner 42539, but it wasn't the governor. It was Juan! He was dressed in civvies and his extra-terrestrial magnetism was zapping the mercenary's strength directly from his heartless body. The trap had been sprung and Effria's freedom finally curtailed.

Brigadier General Lopez was summoned to restrain the busted flush that was Effria. Tying him up good and proper they used uncomfortable sticky tape to hold his eyes shut and then carried him unceremoniously to the riverbank. The sub-aqua tank was brought to the surface from the muddy bottom and the barbaric Effria thrown on board to join Gregor's other stooge, Alvaro. The teenage commanders watched it all on N42's screens. Effria would stand trial with his keeper, Gregor Magnus, once the latter had been apprehended. Their wicked campaign was almost at an end.

"I wonder what would've happened if Effria had reached Manhattan?" Floss asked.

"Once on dry land he'd have transformed back into his evil self, which would have been bad enough but on top of that he'd have regained his magical powers. An even more distasteful prospect," Juan informed her.

What was Captain Greta's part in Effria's capture? Jack was desperate for answers and wanting to hear that she was truly innocent as he'd always believed.

"I think I'm missing something crucial. If Alvaro's our traitor then Greta must be off the hook?" Jack asked, expectantly.

"Yes, indeed. There are a few loose ends to tie up but I can assure you Greta's in the clear," the iguana announced, going on to tell them he had tumbled Alvaro earlier but had wanted to give him a second chance to forsake Effria's bribe and return to the fold. To establish the facts he'd asked Greta to gain Effria's confidence, but when he discovered that Alvaro was still intent on using his military position to get Effria out of Rikers and that he was totally unrepentant and completely trusted Gregor Magnus, the iguana gave up all hope of saving his old comrade. It was at this point that he asked Greta to wrap things up as quickly as possible. "Alvaro forsook kind heartedness to become a ruthless renegade," the reptilian field marshal sadly concluded.

Alvaro's defection stunned the teenagers.

"Alvaro! I can't believe it. What a turn up for the books!" Edward exclaimed.

"King of the smokescreen that one," Jack added.

"Alvaro was too full of self-assured hubris," Emmie proffered. No one knew what *self-assured hubris* meant. Emmie was pleased to explain. "Alvaro suffered from an excess of pride and arrogance. It's like saying, *I'm the greatest*. Comes from the Greek."

"Perhaps we should all feel sorry for him?" Lily wondered. No one supported Lily's outlandish proposal for one moment.

Jack was holding his breath waiting to speak to his Greta. He absolutely needed to know the truth about her relationship with Effria and he wanted to hear it from her own lips. She'd kissed that lowlife on the cheek for goodness sake! Greta arrived at N42.

"Thank goodness you're here at last!" Jack shouted, animated.

"Calm down. Captain Greta's something to say to you…" Juan tailed off so Greta could explain herself.

"Jack, I'm on your side. I've always been on your side! Juan swore me to secrecy. I had to make everything look real even if it meant kissing him, yuck!" Greta pretended to be sick. "We had to find the mole, which meant playing everything close to our chests. Intelligence suggested that prior to Effria being imprisoned on Rikers he'd been stunned by a taser, distorting his magical powers. He'd become totally reliant on others to get him out jail, which was where Alvaro came into it. Gregor wanted his man back in Manhattan to rejuvenate as soon as possible."

"But you kissed him!" Jack yelled out again. Greta winced.

"A necessary evil. I had to let him think I'd gone over to the dark side!" Captain Greta smiled, giving Jack a big hug.

Jack delighted in reminding all that he'd never once believed that Greta was the bad egg.

"I'm perplexed," admitted Lily looking at Juan. "Why did you go on about …it being a bad day for trust…when you knew all along that Captain Greta's visit to Effria was a put up job?"

"I do apologise for misleading you all," Juan said humbly, bowing his head in penitence.

"What I can't understand is how Effria was able to dash here, there and everywhere even visiting the zebafe but couldn't get himself out of Rikers?" Edward asked.

"Effria was stronger then and could use Rikers as his sanctuary. His powers have been ebbing away for a considerable time; even he didn't realise how weak he'd become. My magnetism was the last straw. He crumpled at the ferocity of my alluring charisma!" The iguana laughed.

"What'll happen to Alvaro?" Jack asked.

"Alvaro is a silly old fool. No point in putting him in prison. He's had his day and to be frank, denying him his military rank is punishment enough. We'll allow him to cool his heels for a while and then let him spend the rest of his days building termite mounds in Central America. We'll hear no more from him," Juan said, sounding quite sure of himself.

Eva was mopping up at Rikers. Her cunning plan had turned the cat's dreary life into an exciting adventure. Without his help the plan would most definitely have failed. The cat strolled outside and laid down at the base of the flagpole. This gumshoe stuff was exhausting and he needed to rest. The avocet flew down from her high perch to thank him for his efforts. He opened one eye and gave her a soft, flabby even friendly kind of look.

"Rudy, baby," she began, "PUPA, that's the Parallel Universe Peace Association, is indebted to you and has asked me to convey its gratitude," she told him. "You, honey, are the hero of the moment!" She trilled, stretching out a wing and patting him on the shoulder. The cat was truly touched. His eyes moistened. No one had ever thanked him for anything before. More often he received a kick up the backside from one of Rikers' thugs. It had set him wondering. There just had to be more to a cat's life and he decided to throw himself on PUPA's mercy.

A sense of responsibility and adventure had awoken inside the moggy. The mission to catch the Universe's most hated criminals had been the most fun he'd ever had. He remembered Rikers crims often saying, '*there's no such thing as a free lunch*'. It was payback time. He'd helped PUPA and now he needed them to return the favour.

"Thanks for the compliments, old gel! Now then, there's something you can *doos* for me. You've got contacts on the outside. I was born here in one of them sheds over there," he said, pointing to a couple of dilapidated wooden structures. "I've no idea what Manhattan looks like on the inside. All I've ever seen is the New York skyline from Rikers. I've been a prisoner here my whole life just like the jailbirds and yet I haven't committed a crime. What *doos* you think about that, lady?" Colonel Eva was speechless. A rare experience for the avocet. "I just want to be like you and experience being as free as a bird. Sorry about the pun!" The cat said, his eyes welling up.

Dealing with weeping Tom cats wasn't something the colonel had been trained in.

"Speak up then. Let's hear it!" The bird encouraged the cat to get it off his chest.

"Take me home with you or find me a decent place to live my days out. I'm knocking on ten years old so I won't be a burden for long. I'd just like to die a free cat." Rudy was serious. Cat re-homing was an activity the avocet had little experience of. When not chasing tyrants from outer space it was the Australian rivers and creeks that were her more usual habitats and they might prove just as uncomfortable for a cat as Rikers prison had.

"Aw shucks, birdie! Rikers is in the middle of the river so I'm used to being surrounded by water. I know I'd be happy living in your Aussie mud creeks. Anyway, there's another reason I want to get off this rock. The governor of New York wants to shut down Rikers and when that happens it's an early death for an old, prickly, moggy like me. A quick injection in my rump by the veterinary and I'm a gonna. Comprehendy?" Rudy almost had his feathered friend in tears.

"OK, OK, I'll give it some thought," squawked the bird, hiding her emotions.

Colonel Eva's job at Rikers was finished. She flew back to the mainland and made her way through the disused tunnels of Grand Central, dodging track guards and engine drivers and arriving back at N42 where the team was preparing to search for Gregor Magnus in ancient Egypt. Begging a few minutes of the iguana's time Eva related Rudy's acts of bravery and the pickle he would shortly face when the prison was shut down making sure to pass on the cat's rehoming request.

"....so, you see field marshal, we owe this cat a decent future."

"I quite see your point. What a dilemma. I certainly don't want a pet cat myself. I can never be sure where I'll be," he said. "I've heard on my travels in Alexandria that thousands of cats have been made homeless during the bombardment so I'm absolutely sure none of my contacts there will be willing to take Rudy in. Food's in short supply as it is." Juan was thoughtful. If anyone could find an appropriate home for Rudy it must be him. "I've an idea. I've a favour to call in from an eminent person who I know adores animals." Colonel Eva clapped her wings in excitement. She knew Juan would come up trumps.

Juan was as good as his word and made arrangements to drop in on his old friend and ally, Queen Victoria and, having promised Floss a trip back in history decided now was the right time to honour that promise. Leading the way he took her to another room in the N42 complex and one that she hadn't seen before. Juan opened the door to find it filled with the most beautiful horse drawn, fairy tale, coach.

"Your carriage awaits..." The iguana invited Floss to step inside the golden coach. "We call this our Cinderella Spaceship although, it's official title is, Time Limo Mark One, but that doesn't sound nearly so romantic!" Two white horses were hitched up ready to transport them on their journey back in time to meet one of the most famous British monarchs ever. Juan passed Floss a blanket explaining that time travel could be a trifle chilly and then wasting no more time he cracked the whip and they flew through space back to the London of the 1880s, touching down on a plush red carpet in Buckingham Palace's State Ballroom.

Floss was amazed at the palace's grandeur.

"Follow me, princess," Juan beckoned. "We have an audience with an empress!" The field marshal's uniform looked apt for an audience with Queen Victoria. Floss on the other hand looked tatty in her boiler suit and trainers. Juan knew what she was thinking.

"What colour?" He asked.

"What colour what?" Floss replied, feeling dazed.

"What colour ball gown? You can't meet the Queen wearing workman's clothing."

"My favourite colour's lilac..." She'd hardly had time to utter the words before her rather inelegant, all-in-one boiler suit changed into the most beautiful lilac organza gown scattered with shiny sequins and jewels. Juan placed a small tiara studded with gemstones on her head. Floss looked at herself in one of the huge mirrors adorning the walls. She looked beautiful, like a true princess.

Juan and his princess walked regally along a richly decorated corridor, his bony fingers delicately placed on the top of her hand as they elegantly processed the length of the deep pile carpet and neared a set of richly decorated double doors leading into the Queen's private audience chamber. They were expected. A footman wearing a silvery-white powdered wig and a fine gold and red braided coat opened the door. The scene was awesome and they found themselves in the presence of *Her Most Gracious Majesty, Indiae Imperatrix, Empress of India, Her Majesty, Queen Victoria*. Floss curtsied to perfection.

"Your Majesty, we meet again," Juan spoke to the Queen as though they were old friends.

"We do indeed, and to what pleasure do I owe this unexpected visit?" The Queen asked, smiling at Floss and putting her at her ease as a servant poured the tea.

Juan broke the ice and started the conversation.

"Majesty, last time we met I had the unenviable task of filling you in on the devious goings-on committed by Effria disguised as Count Abdul."

"Ah yes, Sir Juan, I remember it well. I'm still so grateful to you for revealing the true identity of the imposter. You saved the Universe, my world and my monarchy on that occasion, I'm sure of it," the Queen sighed, thankfully. They drank their tea and chatted pleasantries until Juan decided it was time to come clean.

"Mam, I have a favour to ask."

"Ask away," her Majesty encouraged.

"It's about a cat. An intelligent fluffy Persian cat that, through no fault of his own has found himself homeless in the twenty-first century," Juan explained.

"He's not just any cat," Floss interrupted, feeling strongly about this issue, "he's a very brave cat that's played a vital part in stopping our Universe from falling into the clutches of that horrid dictator, Gregor Magnus..." The Queen was furnished with the full details of the Rikers operation and gladly considered their request. She already had several cats and dogs but one more wouldn't affect the palace's finances! Buckingham Palace was a big place and there were other royal residences such as Windsor Castle, Sandringham House and Balmoral, her Scottish bolt hole. Taking them all into consideration the Queen had plenty of room for another furry pet!

The Queen was clearly interested in providing a comfortable new home for the cat.

"Is this cat of yours good at catching vermin?" The Queen asked, interested.

"Oh Your Majesty! He's an excellent mouser," Floss enthused.

"I'm thinking more rats! My royal rat catcher, Jack Black is old and tired and the rats are regaining their strength and doubling in number in my cellars. I need a good rat killer so if you think he's up to catching rats I'll give your plucky cat a home," the Queen agreed.

"Oh Mam! He can catch both mice and rats!" Floss sung the animal's praises.

"A fluffy Persian you say?" The Queen was now sounding excited about the idea of owning both a useful and lively new playmate for her other more decorative cats.

"Yes, Your Majesty!" Floss answered expectantly, her hands nervously resting in her lap, "he's a white, fluffy, Persian."

"I'll call him, White Heather. He'll always remind me of Balmoral, my beloved home in Scotland."

Floss and Juan finished their tea and when the Queen asked a butler to clear the cups away they took it as their signal to leave. Floss was charged with arranging for White Heather's delivery to Buckingham Palace, which would of course require him to travel back in time to the 1880s. Juan would have to help her with that.

Chapter 19

Endgame

Juan remembered his previous visit to Buckingham Palace when Colonel Ewart had told him about his strange experience at the Great Sphinx - swirling sands and strange blue mists and so on, and with other intelligence reports confirming that the Sphinx was indeed the likely well thought out hiding place of their mark, and had been so for a considerably long time and especially during the nineteenth, twentieth and twenty-first centuries. Juan rapidly moved their campaign to ancient Egypt.

Juan's generals were scattered across the Atlantic either transporting prisoners-of-war to the Shetlands or wrapping up operations in and around New York. Being veterans of many campaigns involving the Magnus family they might have snippets of information that when put together would complete the jigsaw puzzle and hopefully provide additional support for Juan's Sphinx hypothesis. He called them all together by space phone for a video conference with himself and his commanders. He was right. The conference revealed what might normally be considered circumstantial evidence but when stitched together compounded Juan's belief that ancient Egypt was where they should converge. The Great Sphinx became their ultimate destination and the top termite military brass suggested pressing into service a gang of specialist Malachitian robotic miners to do any digging that might be needed.

Jack took great interest in the phone Juan used for his mini-airwaves forum. He liked electronic gadgets even though the Stanleys were not exactly flush with money.

"I haven't seen a phone like that before," Jack commented.

"We call it 20G. Our batteries are nuclear powered so they go on forever. Our phones are more like microchips than the physical plastic and glass paraphernalia you humans try stuffing into your back pockets," Juan snorted whilst studying a blueprint drawing of the inside of the Sphinx.

"If everything's stored on a tiny microchip how do you key in people's numbers?" Jack was looking at his own chubby fingers.

"Our brains are linked to the Malachite etherical telephone exchange. We send telepathic messages to the exchange and it dials the number for us. A bit like mind reading I suppose."

"A bit like driver-less cars then?"

"Indeed. We've had those on Malachite for yonks," Juan said nonchalantly, still poring over his architectural diagram.

Juan had been most fortunate experiencing many trips back in time and on one occasion had actually chatted with the architects of the pyramids and the Sphinx. During these tete-a-tetes he'd learnt much about the building techniques used to construct them. This knowledge, he told his commanders, would prove absolutely vital when they burrowed underneath the Sphinx. Edward was staggered by Juan's announcement. He was seriously unsure about digging a dirty great hole underneath this much revered relic especially as there was a good chance they would irrevocably damage it. He was also keen on ancient Egyptian history and knew that the Great Sphinx was a World Heritage Site.

"What if it crumbles and is reduced to a pile of bricks?" Edward vividly recalled the scene they'd left behind in May Tree Close.

"The Egyptian tourist industry will collapse…," Floss supported him.

"…and the world will lose an important piece of cultural history," Jack added.

"OMG!" Shrieked Lily. "It would all be down to us!" They directed their gaze at Emmie wondering if she too would be contributing to the debate.

"Don't look at me. I'm with Juan. I can't wait to get inside and take a squint at any ancient Egyptian hieroglyphics."

The iguana gritted his teeth hoping his commanders would come round and in the meantime offered them some sugar coated facts to soften their negativity.

"Our synthetic miners aren't part of the Malachitian military machine," he began. "They're exceptionally skilled in the latest digging techniques and are trained diplomats too. If it looks like the outcome will be tragic, and by that I mean the monument will collapse, they'll advise me in good time so we can avert such a catastrophe. My plan is merely for them to burrow below the main chamber using their larva track micro-machines. That's all!"

"Larva? I think you mean caterpillar track machines," Edward cheekily corrected him.

"Quite so," Juan didn't want to waste time arguing over a point of English vocabulary.

The young commanders were persuaded to adopt Juan's action plan but with a strict proviso that at the first sign of any damage to the structure all digging would stop immediately. A relieved reptile took a deep breath.

"At first our humanoid bots will make the tiniest opening for the delightful Starlight to fly through undetected by the

Sphinx's long-term resident, Gregor Magnus. On locating her target she'll render him defenceless. The bots will then excavate a bigger hole for the rest of us to squeeze through, allowing us to finish the job and get that Ice Leonard scumbag outside and exposed to the broad daylight, a fate he'll find intolerable. Ice Leonard residents hate being left to shrivel under the glare of the sun. Once the operation's completed the robots will, I promise you, expertly close up the apertures making sure no joins are visible. I can assure you there won't be the tiniest crack in the Sphinx. Trust Me! No one will ever know we've been there."

Floss racked her brains. She couldn't recall anyone called, *Starlight* being mentioned before.

"Starlight?" Floss asked.

"Oh my dears! I'm so sorry. I should've told you about Starlight, free spirit of the deep sky, a magical fairy with shiny wings and a crown of glittering moon dust."

"Very romantic but what does this Starlight have to do with the Sphinx?" Floss was in a huff. The talents of this, *free spirit of the deep sky* seemed too incredible for words.

"Starlight will enter the Sphinx and locate Magnus with her specialist sensors, injecting him with Malachitian harebell sap. It's poisonous to anyone born on Ice Leonard," the iguana explained. Lily tutted at the thought of more death and destruction. "Don't worry Lily! PUPA even treats despots respectfully! The sap will paralyse him. Killing him would rob the Universe of justice."

Like Edward, Floss was unsure about the iguana's proposed antics and wanted some background history.

"Why was the Sphinx built in the first place?" She knew little about this ancient monument that they were about to enter illegally. Juan did his best to explain.

"Legend has it that the Sphinx was originally a monster with a head made of worms, the body of a lioness, wings of an eagle and with a serpent headed tail. It was carved from the bedrock on the West Bank of the Nile River and has puzzled Egyptian scholars for centuries. People think it was probably built as a memorial to King Khafre of the 4th Dynasty, 2575 BC. His father, King Khufu, was the creator of the Great Pyramid at Giza. Both kings were cruel temperamental leaders so as soon as he could, the architect scarpered for a safer commission elsewhere. He told me this himself so I've no reason to doubt the information. He also mentioned a lack of planning regulations back in those days so the owners could build whatever and wherever they wanted. What might start out as a grain store one day could end up as a royal burial place the next! Even I don't know what we'll find inside." Juan was rubbing his hands together with glee, looking forward to rummaging around inside this hallowed icon.

Edward really did want to believe that Juan had fraternised with the ancient Egyptian jet set but it just seemed so improbable. Edward being Edward, wanted an answer.

"Where did you meet this illustrious architect of all things ancient?"

"I bumped into him at the coronation of King Khafre's successor, King Menkaure," Juan added casually, as though it was quite a natural thing for him to attend such events. Lily's brain cogs were turning, thirsting after justice and equality and pushing her to empathise with the ancient Egyptian pyramid builders.

"I've read that it was poor slave labour that built the pyramids and the Sphinx," she crowed. Juan frowned. Lily was sometimes like a dog with a bone.

"Lily, surprise, surprise! Oppressed Israelites were only the stuff of Hollywood films." Juan prayed he was right. "I heard the pyramids and the Sphinx were built by hard-working family men who carried hods of sand and bricks in return for a decent wage. So, Lily, not slaves at all!" Juan hit back, hoping she would now allow the subject drop.

Egypt was calling Juan to where the final theatre of war would be played out. Juan summoned Major Gubby, busy just at that moment cleaning out his furry, wood mouse ears using a soft toothbrush. Ignoring the major's preoccupation with his personal toilette Juan asked him to prepare the Crusader for their next voyage back to the Egypt of the 1880s. The Crusader was a Routemaster, an old fashioned London red double-decker bus with some space-age adjustments such as tightly fitting doors to keep the cold out whilst dashing through space. When not on

PUPA business the no. 25 bus was normally bound for London's Victoria train station via Bond Street carrying rush hour commuters to their West End offices. Today it would carry Juan and his team to the Egyptian desert.

"How long would it take to fly to Pluto in this contraption?" Jack asked, climbing aboard.

"By my calculation and in this supersonic chariot I'd say around forty-eight hours," Lieutenant Hawkins calculated.

"I'd go along with that," Major Gubby agreed. "In comparison, an ordinary aeroplane would take six or seven hundred years!"

"And what about an ordinary Routemaster?" Jack asked, chortling.

"I'd guess a thousand or more of your Earth years!" The major replied, laughing.

The cosmic bus trip was the smoothest of rides. They hardly knew they were hurtling through space. Whilst flying the boys took the opportunity to change out of their bulky military uniforms into lightweight cotton khaki jackets and shorts more suited to desert temperatures. In no time at all they were standing directly in front of the Sphinx, which was itself proudly standing tall discounting a missing nose.

"There are lots of theories as to how the Sphinx lost its nose. The one I particularly like is that it was blown off in !378," Juan told them. "Some power-crazed idiot didn't like people worshipping the Sphinx - thought they should worship him instead! The intergalactic community now think that crook was our very own freak, Gregor Magnus." They gazed in wonderment at the mystical nose-less shape standing majestically just a few metres away from them.

At the base of the Sphinx sat a group of life-like Malachitian robots surrounded by their drilling tools and eating what looked like fried egg rolls.

"Juan, if they're robots how come they're eating?" Jack asked.

"Mm! They're not actually egg rolls. They're specially coded tech packs that when swallowed will set in motion a chain of reactions that'll rejuvenate and upgrade their systems. Normally, this would be a home based sophisticated computer operation but since we're in a different time zone it needs to carried out by manual ingestion." The teenagers were agog.

A hundred metres away Egyptian police were patrolling a rope barrier that prevented sightseers from getting too close to the monument and touching it with their greasy hands. Juan's team froze.

"OMG!" Emmie muttered.

"I knew it! Making a hole in the Sphinx under the very noses of the Egyptian authorities was, as I predicted, a very bad idea," Edward whispered.

"Punishable by death, no doubt!" Lily added. Floss and Jack just stared at the throng ahead of them.

"No need to fret!" Juan reassured them. "You're all invisible to everyone on the twenty-first century side of the rope. The police and tourists you see are standing in 2021 whilst we're in 1882!" They were seeing into the future.

"I hope you're right, because if you're not..." Floss's voice trailed off.

"Mon Cheri, have faith! We'll be out of here in two shakes of a baby's tail." The teenagers had given up correcting Juan's inaccurate use of the English language.

The robots began drilling a fairy-sized aperture for Starlight and whilst they did that a heavy wind arrived blowing grains of sand into everyone's eyes. It was easy to imagine how terrible a desert sandstorm might be.

"What's to be done?" Floss asked, shaking sand out of her tangled hair. Emmie and Lily did likewise.

"So, where's this enchantress, Starlight?" Jack croaked, his throat full of sand.

"I'm right here, sweetie pie!" A twinkling light sweetly chirped in Jack's left ear. They were all startled. Starlight was indeed a dazzling fairy. The girls grinned broadly. A real, finger-sized fairy! It was the stuff of dreams. Edward, impatient as ever, ignored the flying virtuoso. Fairies just didn't cut it for him.

"Have the robots finished yet?" He was brusque, wanting to get on with the job. Juan cast his eyes over to the synthetic miners and a small pile of brick dust they had created.

"Yep," Juan replied, ignoring Edward's gruff manner. "Hawkins' is just getting the sap ready."

The bronze chested digging machines looked almost human with their ear-length blonde hair and well-honed arm muscles but that was where the similarities ended. Instead of skin they were covered with fish scales and they each had a pair of small wings attached to their shoulder blades.

"These extraordinary miners have another incredibly useful talent," Juan was biding his time before giving the order for Starlight to go in and get their man. "They have the ability to take temperature and vibration readings without any specialised external equipment. These qualities will tell us if Gregor's in residence. They have a kind of built in sensory gland that detects these things."

"That's good to know because mounting a guerrilla attack on the Sphinx only to find out that, 'You Know Who's' NOT actually at home would be a complete waste of our time!" Jack was being bombastic. Juan was not deterred.

"With our fiend, coming as he does from Ice Leonard where the climate rarely rises above - 200 centigrade, it means we can't rely on the more usual means of detection. This is why our robots are such wonderful assets," the iguana explained.

"You'll be telling us next that Magnus has antifreeze in his bloodstream!" Edward laughed.

"Why how clever of you, Ed! He certainly does!" Juan replied, tongue in cheek.

The bots finished their tests and reported that Magnus was indeed home. Juan's architectural plans of the Sphinx suggested a tunnel leading to several rooms and an inner sanctum, the Great Chamber. It was time for Juan to release his secret weapon, Starlight. This *Free Spirit of the Deep Sky,* as Juan had referred to her earlier darted in through the newly created opening and set about tracking down her prey. Everyone else waited outside with bated breath. The fairy was done in minutes, emerging triumphantly into the sunshine.

"Hi, puddings," she chirped. "Mission accomplished. That naughty little rascal is a bit tied up right now but I do believe he's open to receiving guests," she jested. Starlight had injected the tyrant with the harebell's immobilising juice and although he could still see, enveloping paralysis meant he couldn't use his sorcery to outwit them.

Juan instructed the miners to enlarge the portal so the rest of them could slip inside.

"Juan, before we go in I've a question for you. We've had to dig a hole to get inside so how did that maniac get in and out without doing the same?" Edward asked.

"A very good question! Colonel Eva heard on the grapevine that he's been making a nuisance of himself, nagging the Spirits of the Dead into assisting him. The spirits appear as elusive atmospheric ghostlike wisps and they have the power to turn Magnus into a temporary spectre like themselves thus allowing him to pass through the Sphinx's walls without injury. This has enabled him to flit around the Universe organising his vile and depraved campaigns and afterwards taking refuge in the safety of the Sphinx. According to my sources he's been pestering the spirits just a bit too much and incurred their wrath by asking them for too many favours. Their response has been to limit his movements to just six phantom Sphinx transfers a week!"

"So, there's likely to be one day each week when he has to stay inside?" Lily reasoned.

"Exactement!" Juan replied, "And, luckily for us, today appears to be that day!"

It was time to get the show on the road. With their target fast becoming immobilised they needed to get going. Torches in hand and led in by the chief bot with his vibration measuring pack on his back, they moved to the entrance.

"Rose-tinted spectacles on now please and then follow me," Juan insisted. They did as they were told, following Juan and the bot closely into the Sphinx, the latter picking up the sound waves emitted from the scoundrel's body. It was naturally pitch-black inside and they needed their torches to light their way. Creeping stealthily and edging ever closer to the source of the vibrations, the beating heart of the tyrant, they were privy to the sight of ornately painted chairs, gold bowls and strings of beads that glowed in their torchlight.

"What's all this stuff for?" Jack whispered, nearly tripping over a gold statue.

"They're priceless artefacts providing the dead kings with all they might need for their journey to the Afterlife," Juan whispered back.

"I thought you didn't know what the Sphinx was used for!" Floss remarked.

"Indeed. We're seeing things that the outside world knows nothing about! Archaeologists have been inside the Sphinx just a handful of times over the past two thousand years and never, ever, have they reported seeing any precious objects. Your rose-tinted spectacles are allowing you to see the full splendour of this snug treasure trove."

The teenagers' torchlight lit up a sacred Egyptian cat wall painting. Floss took a closer look.

"Would being a sacred cat worshipped by the ancient Egyptians be more interesting for Rudy?" She wondered out loud. Juan heard.

"Being locked up as a companion for a dead king wouldn't be a healthy lifestyle for your moggy! Rudy would be exchanging one prison for another and when it came to food he'd be living on slim pickings! He'll be far happier living with the Queen. Trust me!" They reached the Great Chamber and the chief bot left them to return to the entrance. The iguana and his team entered almost tripping over Gregor Magnus. The dupe was trussed up and writhing about on the sandy floor. The fairy had done a good job. The despot sensed their presence and spouted Ice Leonard gibberish. The word, diddum, was heard several times.

"Can you translate for us please?" Floss asked Juan.

"He's asking for his mummy!" Juan chuckled.

"His mummy!" They chorused.

"Quite so. He's referring to an ancient Egyptian mummy that was entombed in the Sphinx two thousand years ago. In Ice Leonard, the term for mother is, *diddum*."

"Diddum!" Emmie repeated. "It's a term we use to cheer someone up, as in, *Diddums hurt yourself*?"

"How interesting!" Juan exclaimed, searching Gregor's pockets for wizard paraphernalia.

Before the harebell sap fully took effect Juan had an important task to perform. The iguana didn't always follow protocol but in this particular instance PUPA expected the rulebook to be followed exactly; every T crossed and every I dotted.

"Gregor Magnus, descendant of Exitum Magnus, on behalf of PUPA I ask you this - are you deeply sorry for your crimes against all critters of the Universe?" Demonic eyes stared coldly back at Juan as the misfit cackled manically. Juan took this as a negative reply. The odorous megalomaniac was showing no signs of remorse. "Shame on you!" Juan's voice boomed around the chamber. "However, I'm pleased to say I was hoping that would be your answer. There'll be no special allowances for you. In fact, you'll be airbrushed from space's historical records. No one, you indescribably ugly, ne'er-do-well will ever hear from you again. You'll be a non-entity, a no one, an ignoramus, a cretinous buffoon... " Juan could have gone on and on.

The harebell juice had almost locked up Gregor's brain impairing his movements but Juan thought they should wait just a little bit longer until the paralyses was more complete. Juan had a glint in his eye. The operation was going his way. He felt relieved and while they waited a few more minutes until the tyrant was totally stiff he decided to tell the teenagers about the UK prime minister's intergalactic work.

"I bet you didn't know Mrs Murray's a member of PUPA? She makes top secret trips to other planets for talks and contributes public funds to help its finances. It's all hush, hush, naturally. No one in your Foreign Office would ever breathe a word about it." The teenagers were flabbergasted. "Do you remember recently when the newspapers said Mrs Murray was on a walking holiday in Italy?" They nodded. "Well, she wasn't in Italy. She was on Malachite with me! PUPA provides a military escort for her whenever she leaves the Earth's atmosphere on inter-planetary business and last summer it was my turn to do the honours," an enormously proud iguana revealed.

"Were you an iguana then too?" Floss asked incidentally.

"Why yes I was! Mrs Murray's very fond of Iguanas. We're good pals."

Gregor's irritating grumbling lessened as the sap strangled his senses but they could still catch the odd unintelligible piece of mumbo jumbo. Enough was enough and Juan began preparations for the despot's removal from his Sphinx hidey-hole.

"He's putty in our hands right now. We must work fast before the effects of the harebell sap wear off. We'll soon have him on his way to Malachite where the Supreme Court of Universal Justice will I'm sure, sentence him to centuries of penal servitude on an uncomfortably barren planet such as Malactron," Juan assured them. Floss suddenly had some unfinished business. She desperately wanted to see what this maggoty, quirk of nature looked like under his wraps. He was wearing an Arabian white tunic called a thawb that reached right down to his ankles and his head was covered in a keffiyeh, a red checked scarf-like headdress.

"Madam! Your wish is my command," Juan said, cheerfully agreeing to her request and removing Gregor's scarf. Despite the effects of the sap he still managed to vent his anger by screaming out a few Ice Leonard swear words.

"Mr Magnus, please refrain from using expletives in front of the children!" Juan mocked. The wraps came off.

Beneath his headdress the mutant, monstrous, enemy of the Universe was bald, barring a few straggly hairs. His nose was long and twiggy, his eyes like black shiny overcoat buttons and his lips were cold, thin and inky blue. His face was of a reddish hue and had exposed, spider-like, bulging, crimson veins that pulsated in his cheeks and pussy boils that made them want to throw up.

"Disgusting!" Floss exclaimed at the objectionable sight. Unveiled, he looked like a nightmare and then they saw his teeth! Glimpsing his three decaying biters shocked them even more. His yellow-black choppers consisting of two buck teeth in his top jaw and just one solitary, corroded, gnasher on the bottom were unsightly. They couldn't imagine an uglier creature.

The hideous fleshy mass on the sandy floor in front of them also had nauseatingly bad breath. It stunk to high heaven making his pursuers want to run away.

"I'm surprised we didn't smell the mucky pup when we were outside," Floss said, mustering the courage to open her mouth and speak whilst feeling sick at the same time.

"Alas, too many sour chockerlingos! They've ruined his teeth! The rot is making his already foul breath even more repulsive. My pod master refused to let us youngsters eat them but of course, Gregor was spawned not born. Parentless offspring emerging from the cold icy pools of Ice Leonard will gorge on anything sickly sweet for comfort. Dental hygiene isn't high on their list of priorities," Juan sighed.

"Chockerlingos?" Jack asked.

"Ah yes, sour chockerlingos!" Juan smiled at their memory. "They're to us what your chocolate bars are to you. Our taste buds are the reverse of yours. The sour taste makes our ears pop, which in turn makes us laugh. Kids love chockerlingos so much."

Gregor Magnus' drooling and grotesque demeanour was making them all want to throw-up more than ever. His lips and his left eye they thought were all he could still move and he kept the latter trained on his captors for as long as possible. The harebell's sap had infiltrated most of his brain and his vocal cords would soon be totally silenced. He was a heavy lump and they needed a stretcher to carry him outside on. Jack and Edward prepared an ancient bier stacked high with dusty old earthenware pots, carefully lifting them out so as not to crack them. The pots would once have contained grains, fruits and oils to sustain the deceased kings on their journey to the Afterlife. Some gold chains lying around were used to restrain Magnus just to be on the safe side before they heaved him up onto the bier and carried him out into the blinding sunshine.

Chapter 20

More Mummies

The fishy robots had to make a few speedy adjustments to the gap in the wall to get the bier and its worthless heap of dung out. The evil fortune hunter was then laid beneath the unrelenting sun's rays where his offensive body odour immediately attracted the flies. Large bluebottles massed on and above him. He tried hard to knock them away and shield himself from them and the penetrating rays of the sun but without success. His arms were paralysed. Equal opportunities and human rights sympathiser, Lily Gibson felt an urgent impulse to go to his aid. She moved towards the bier with her handkerchief at the ready.

"LILY, LEAVE HIM BE!" Jack shouted. "Ask yourself this: Would he help you if positions were reversed?" Lily stopped dead as she thought about Jack's words. He was right! She backed away from the charlatan.

"That bloke's nothing more than an intergalactic dirt-bag. Jack's right, we mustn't indulge him!" Edward agreed.

The bots sealed up the Sphinx and tidied up their tools neatly stacking them for Lieutenant Hawkins to arrange their return to Malachite. Their task was finished and no longer needed they plumped up their wings and flew up to meet the thermals. The teenagers inspected the place where the openings had been and to Juan's credit it was impossible to see where they had been. It was time for everyone to say farewell to Egyptian ancient civilisation. Juan summoned the Routemaster from its makeshift bus stop about fifty metres along the sand from the Sphinx and they climbed on board, settling into their seats ready for the off. Their crazy, con-artist detainee remained tied up under the glaring sun unable to squint and keep the sun out of his eyes. Shamefully, he managed one more act of defiance. He projected a cakehole of green, gobby slime onto Lily's window before finally succumbing to the sap. For this arch-criminal it was curtains at long last. The green gloop on Lily's window was an unpleasant sight. She watched it slowly slip down the pane leaving a sticky trail behind it.

"Charming!" She exclaimed as the muck reached the bottom.

"That's what you get for trying to be kind!" Jack reminded her. Juan asked Major Gubby to get rid of the stomach curdling mess at once.

"I hope he dies a nasty painful death!" Definitely an uncharacteristic remarked to come forth from Lily, seemingly no longer hell bent on lecturing everyone on civil liberties!

Their mission was at an end but Emmie had one last concern.

"We're not taking that idiotic apology for a living creature with us on the Crusader are we? I really don't want that maniac anywhere near me. He gives me the creeps!" She screeched, shivering. Their prisoner was still lying motionless in the heat outside.

"Indeed not!" Juan was unequivocal. "We've great plans for his lordship. Have no fear, his escort is on its way. He's being air-lifted to the confluence of the Nile at Khartoum. The White and Blue Nile Rivers meet there. It's an especially magical place, full of good fairies. It's where Starlight usually dwells. The fairies and a few goblins will keep our bogeyman entertained for as long as necessary, I'm certain of it." Juan double tapped the side of his nose and winked, knowing they'd understand. "He'll remain in Khartoum indisposed until Admiral Mathias and his 8th Flotilla arrive in Luxor from the Red Sea."

"Luxor! Isn't that in the Valley of the Kings? I believe it was discovered by Howard Carter in 1922. It's another burial place of the ancient pharaohs, and wasn't the boy pharaoh, Tutankhamun found buried there?" Edward asked.

"So he was!" Juan was impressed.

As director of operations Floss wanted to know what was supposed to happen next.

"After Luxor?" Floss asked.

"Once the admiral's taken charge of our surly and highly repugnant monstrosity he'll make full steam ahead to the Indian Ocean stopping at Flat Island off the coast of Mauritius. The intrepid PUPA space police in their unidentified flying object will be waiting there to rush him at top speed to Malachite for sentencing," Juan explained.

"Don't you need to present evidence at a trial before sentencing?" Lily was at it again.

"My dear Lily, we've been gathering evidence for centuries," Juan sighed, refusing to get into an argument. The Crusader started its ascent just as a platoon of flying termites arrived to transport the prisoner away. The insects attached handles to the bier and then dangling their infamous cargo over the hot desert sands causing him the maximum pain, they flew off in the direction of Luxor. The teenagers hoped they would never set eyes on the devilish oppressor again.

Lieutenant Hawkins handed round celebratory marberry juice drinks. Each glass was decorated with colourful miniature paper umbrellas and there were pretty marzipan snacks in the shapes of different fruits to eat too after which everyone dropped off to sleep with Hawkins, Major Gubby and Captain Greta dozing in the seats behind the teenagers. Juan was in the control room chin-wagging with Brigadier General Lopez, their driver. A mewing sound came from the top deck. Captain Greta being a light sleeper awoke and went to investigate. The moaning grew louder as she went up the steps. What could it be? Standing on the top step she gripped the handrail to steady herself. It looked distinctly like an Egyptian mummy reclining across the long back seat of the bus. The mummy's face was adorned with a pharaoh's beard and his whole body, except for his hands, was wrapped in swaddling clothes that were covered in a mouldy green fuzz suggesting he'd been dead for a long time. A crown of ostrich feathers sat on his head. At his side lay a crook and a nasty looking whip, called a flail.

Captain Greta wasn't sure what to do. Should she creep back downstairs and summon help? It seemed the most sensible course of action and quickly too before the mummy realised he'd been spotted. The Crusader hurtled on through space, dodging meteorites and shooting stars as it zoomed towards twenty-first century New York. Just as Greta descended the stairs the bus hit a cloud of gas and wobbled causing her to fall and bash herself against the handrail. She howled, waking the mummy. He was instantly up on his feet and hopping, as best he could with his legs so tightly bandaged, towards her staring menacing, his flail in one hand and his crook in the other.

The captain made use of her self-defence techniques and swinging back up the stairs, gritting her teeth determinedly she threw a punch, winding the mummy and then hurling him to the ground with a kata guruma shoulder throw. Equally determined he rose up and struck her on the face with his crook. Greta retaliated with a taekwondo kick to his head, sending him swirling to the ground and causing him to black out. The commotion woke up everyone downstairs and taking two steps at a time they leapt up the stairs, jumping on the stowaway and using strips of cloth from his own mummy body tied him to a seat.

The captain was congratulated for her timely action.

"First time for everything! I've never floored an Egyptian mummy before!" She laughed.

"Your 10th dan Liatram Rainbow Belt came in useful after all!" Jack chuckled. Juan was otherwise engaged, taking a good look at their unwelcome guest.

"I know this guy. This is Osiris, God of the Underworld and the Dead."

"Is that the same as the Afterlife?" Jack asked.

"Exactly that. Osiris oversees resurrection and regeneration for the recently deceased."

"I thought Osiris was something to do with the Nile's annual flood, making the land greener," Edward proffered.

"Yes, indeed. The flood is known as the inundation and it occurs between June and September each year bringing fertile silt to the region. Osiris, as you suggest, is linked to harvests and anything cyclical like the river flooding and of course, death too!"

Osiris was regaining consciousness so before he opened his eyes they all took a step back.

"Hello friend," Juan greeted him like an old mate. "What in space are you doing on my bus?" The iguana and Osiris chatted for a short time while Captain Greta, standing nearby, nursed a painful gash on her face where Osiris had struck her with his crook.

"Oh yeah! Sorry about that. I didn't mean to hurt the lady. It's just my instinctive reactions!" The mummy spoke English and actually had feelings!

"Listen up everyone!" Juan called out. "Osiris is the son of my old pal, Sun God, Ra. I also knew his mother back in the 4th Dynasty, Goddess Nut. Osiris has been sent to deliver a message. Apparently, we're guilty of a serious misdemeanour. Entering the sacred Sphinx was tantamount to declaring war on the ancient Egyptian world. The Gods aren't happy with us! We're to present ourselves at the, Palace of the Heavenly Cloud, in the sky somewhere above the ancient City of Thebes ... to be punished for our crime!" Juan was having difficulty keeping a straight face, his mirth doing nothing to quell their worries.

"It just gets better," Emmie sighed. "We'll probably lose our heads!"

"I'll never get to my dental appointment," Floss mumbled.

"I just knew there'd be trouble if we entered that Sphinx!" Edward muttered, wanting to stress how right he'd been all along.

"Where's this Thebes? I've never heard of it before," Lily asked.

"Thebes no longer exists," Juan began, "It was once an ancient Egyptian nerve centre that was later incorporated within Luxor. From Thebes the gods used to look down from above on mankind and see what it was up to, sometimes intervening if they didn't like the way things were going."

"Are we going to be the gods' prisoners?" Floss asked glumly.

"Indeed not!" Juan rebuked her for presuming he'd allow anything like that to happen. "Hawkins, get me King Ra on the ancient world blower. Let's see what the old man has to say about this nonsense, shall we?" Lieutenant Hawkins dashed away to the cockpit returning with an earpiece. Juan engaged God Ra in repartee, lightening the mood. Osiris was feeling dejected at not being taken seriously and he sat in silence with his crumpled ostrich feathers in his lap, damaged during his tussle with the captain.

Juan's contacts extended to the illustrious leaders of the spirit world and once again he was able to speak to the right person at the right time!

"Good. All settled. Full speed ahead!" Juan exclaimed. Fabio checked his space map making sure they were still on the correct course. "All a big misunderstanding. My good friend God Ra was totally unaware that Mr Magnus was hiding in the Sphinx!"

"How come they didn't know he'd been dossing there from time immemorial and yet when we enter, within half an hour they're onto us?" Floss was bemused. The iguana contemplated this and then made a phone call to the Dead Spirits Government Office to get an adequate answer for her.

"I'm told Gregor Magnus persuaded the Spirits of the Dead to make him imperceptible to the supreme gods, that's the ones in charge of all the lower rated gods such as our Osiris here. We, on the other hand were easy to detect because people-lets like yourselves have a pungent body odour that the gods find obnoxious, and which alerted them quickly to our presence. They reasoned that by learning the secrets of the Sphinx's inner sanctum we would be sure to reveal them to the outside world. They could not allow that to happen. We had to have our memories wiped clean!"

"You're telling us that these ancient Egyptian deities didn't realise it was you, Sir Juan of Malachite, renowned warrior and acclaimed statesman?" Jack teased.

"It would seem that way." Nothing ever seemed to make sense in Juan's world.

"What shall we do with the mummy?" Floss asked, regarding the sack of dishevelled rags sitting on one of the bus's seats.

"Ah yes. Come Osiris, let's enjoy a mug of fizz and chew the cud before we drop you off," Juan beckoned his friend to sit with him.

Juan and Osiris chatted animatedly until Fabio abruptly interrupted them.

"Sir, we're nearly clear of the Egyptian dynasties. We've just three minutes left of the late 31st Dynasty and we're currently passing through 342 to 332 BC. This would be a good time for Osiris to leave us. The next epoch will be the Romans when we veer off through the 120s BC and fly over Hadrian's Wall, which is currently under construction." Edward was beside himself with excitement. Hadrian's Wall! He wanted to see it and the Roman soldiers guarding it too! History was his bag.

"Ed, I'm sorry to disappoint. It's imperative that we stay on course," Juan told him sternly and then turning to Osiris he invited the god to prepare to exit the Crusader. The period they were travelling through right now was a time when ancient people still worshipped the gods. If Osiris arrived later, in a more modern age he'd be mocked and laughed at. He picked up his crook and flail and saying a few hurried goodbyes and muttering some enchanted words, disappeared in a puff of smoke back to the Afterlife.

Jack, the computer gamer and the one with the most vivid imagination shared his thoughts.

"I'm wondering if we've just allowed a golden opportunity to slip through our fingers." Jack was speaking to anyone who wanted to listen. "Osiris would have made the most impressive exhibit ever in the British Museum's Egyptology room!"

"Jack, really! I don't believe you just said that. Not that long ago I remember you being worried about the future of the zebafe should the academics get hold of him," Lily carped.

"And what about Rosie and Rodrigo? I seem to remember you were concerned about the general public finding out they were getting married..." Edward added.

"Alright! I get it. I'll remember to keep my big mouth shut in future!" Jack stomped off taking a seat at the back.

Juan still had some explaining to do where Osiris was concerned.

"When Gregor Magnus kept asking for his mummy, that mummy was Osiris. Legend has it that Osiris was cut to pieces by Seth, his jealous brother. Osiris' wife searched high and low for her husband's body parts and when she found them she wrapped them up like a mummy, entombing them in a secret compartment of the Sphinx. Gregor has been trying to get pally with Osiris for years because being the God of the Afterlife and Regeneration, the despot hoped that he'd take pity and resurrect him after his own death allowing him to go forth and create havoc all over again."

"Was that likely after all the damage he's done to the space community?" Floss asked.

"Absolutely out of the question. Osiris is a sensible fellow at heart and wouldn't be so stupid as to give a terrorist the privilege of another shot at universal domination."

"Fancy being the King of Dead People," Jack remarked. "It can't be much fun, can it?"

"Not true Jack! Living in the Afterlife is like living in paradise. Osiris leads the life of Riley! There's absolutely no reason for you to feel sorry for him," Juan explained.

"Whose Riley?" Lily asked.

"It's just a euphemism..." Emmie, their friendly linguist told them.

The Crusader was still hurtling through space.

"Operation Lizard was successful and you are invited to attend an important event in Manhattan. Please enjoy your new-found fame," Juan told them tantalisingly. New-found fame? What was that all about? Even their families were unaware of their mission, in fact, their parents were more likely to buckle up with laughter if someone had told them their offspring had been prime movers in an intergalactic war. "Once in New York your heightened senses will return to normal. Secret places such as the Retipu's codebreaking centre at the top of the Washington Arch and the field hospital under Washington Square Park will no longer exist. UNDER NO CIRCUMSTANCES are you to go looking for them. Do you understand? Only trouble will come of it if you do." Juan was deadly serious.

"Orders is orders," Jack barked back.

"Exactement!" Juan agreed.

Chapter 21

Yankee Doodle

The Crusader tore through space hitting the Roman period at full pelt. The Dark Ages followed with King Arthur and his Knights of the Round Table and then King Alfred burning the cakes. The Norman Conquest then the Tudors and Stewarts flashed past as the bus approached more modern times. They hovered momentarily over some famous historical events giving the young astronauts a glimpse of the French Revolution and the bloody scenes at the guillotine, making them gasp in horror. The Crusader slowed again as it flew over tall ships carrying English convicts to Australia. They saw men, women and children being transported, destined never to set eyes on their families again and mostly for trivial offences like stealing a loaf of bread because they were hungry.

"I've just seen a pig fly by," Jack stuttered, jettisoning his drink over Edward sitting beside him. The girls laughed. Jack must be seeing things!

"Don't be daft!" Edward reprimanded him, shaking juice from his khakis shorts.

The two boys were squaring up to each other for an argument when Hawkins intervened.

"Jack did, indeed, see a pink flying animal but it was an elephant not a pig," he assured them. "Baby pink space elephants travel this way to the elephants' sky nursery."

"Get out of it!" Jack was questioning his own sanity now, feeling sceptical about what he thought he'd seen.

"Trust me! It was a baby space elephant. Around this time in the galactic calendar we travel through the aurora of the modern centuries. Baby space elephants are a common sighting during this period, a bit like shooting stars. However, very few humans have been privileged to witness the nursery migration so you're very lucky, my friends. Keep looking. I think you'll see their nanny bringing up the rear. She's a large white elephant.... ah, yes, just coming into view now," Hawkins shrieked, pointing at a large white tusker just entering their sightline.

Crusader's passengers couldn't take their eyes off the elephantine, hard skinned pachyderms flying through space as though they were as light as a feather.

"Lieutenant, why are these elephants flying to an elephant nursery?" Emmie asked.

"Haven't you heard the saying, the *elephant in the room*?"

"We've all heard that stupid saying," Lily spoke first.

"It's not stupid," Hawkins replied deadpan. "Those little pink elephants will grow into large whites and become those very elephants in the room that people refer to."

"You'll be telling us next that when people want to solve an *elephant in the room* situation they just have to make a trunk call!" Jack giggled unstoppably until the elephants had vanished from view.

The USA beckoned and the teenagers' excitement was growing.

"How long will we be staying in New York?" Floss called out to Juan in the cockpit.

"And Juan, will it be possible for me to say, *goodbye*, to my Retipu team?" Emmie asked.

"And I need to find someone special at the hospital," Lily added, remembering Jack's mum, Staff Nurse Barbara Stanley. "How can I do that if the hospital's gone?"

"There'll be time to tie up loose ends," Juan sounded confident. "Whilst we're in the city I also have an important job to do. I need to disband our termite armies and permit them to return to their humdrum nest building existence the world over until the next intergalactic cataclysmic situation arises," Juan explained.

"Why don't they go back to their original planet, Pruna?" Floss asked.

"The generals may do that but the rest will want to be with their families who are now scattered across Earth's continents. Naturally, PUPA keeps accurate records of where they set up home so it can call them back into action at a moment's notice," Juan explained.

Lily was still glued to her window hoping the elephants might reappear but instead another equally mystifying sight took shape outside. Four children popped into view, flying through space as if it were the most natural thing in the world. Three of them wore nightwear and the fourth was dressed in green from top to toe. They waved to the Crusader's passengers. The children were Wendy, John and Michael Darling and they were accompanied by Peter Pan on their way to Neverland. Peter Pan, the boy who would never grow up was Lily's favourite pantomime story. The main character was athletic like herself and he cared about the lost boys, protecting them from Captain Hook and the ills of his world. Lily loved that kind of fairy tale and it was unfolding in front of her eyes in the middle of space.

Hawkins was likewise excited at spotting the characters from Peter Pan, which he loved too.

"We're just passing through the 11th October 1911, the original publication date for Peter Pan. A mother somewhere in England is reading the story to her children. We often see Peter taking the Darling children to Neverland. And quick, look over there," the lieutenant was pointing at what looked like a twinkling star flying behind Peter Pan. "See that sparkling light?" They looked. "That's Tinkerbell!" The lieutenant purred. Lily had goosepimples. This was their second sighting of a genuine fairy within twenty-four hours. "Do you believe in fairies, ladies?" Hawkins prattled on. "I love the bit where Peter tells Wendy that every time a child says, *I don't believe in fairies,* a fairy dies...." Hawkins laughed out loud as though it was meant to be funny. Having met the friendly Starlight the girls were not impressed. They looked daggers back at him.

They were soon passing through 1912 with RMS Titanic on her maiden voyage from Southampton to New York below them. The ship had hit an iceberg and was sinking fast into the freezing waters of the North Atlantic four hundred miles off the coast of Newfoundland. It was the night of the 14th of April and Juan seemed totally unconcerned at witnessing such an awful tragedy.

"We're putting down in the New York Yankee Stadium," he told them, without a whisper of anxiety for those drowning.

"Cool!" Edward and Jack voiced in unison.

"Babe Ruth played for the Yankees," Jack informed them all. "He wore the no.3 shirt."

"No football, please," begged Emmie.

"Football!" Stammered Jack. "The Yankees are a famous baseball team if you don't mind!"

"Oh, how I'd love to play baseball with the Yankees," Lily, the sportswoman hankered.

"There'll be no time to play ball games," Juan warned.

Floss felt wretched. No one was paying attention to the Titanic crisis unfolding below them.

"Juan, We HAVE TO GO BACK and save those people!"

"Floss, you know what I think about changing the course of history!" Juan reminded her of his important well-meaning principle. Floss had gained Edward's attention and he felt morally obliged to support her.

"Nevermind all that old tripe, Juan. Floss's absolutely right. This time we simply don't have a choice. WE MUST HELP THEM!" The iguana knew that unless he acted on their request he wouldn't have a moments peace and being nagged to death was not an exciting prospect so, resigned to breaking the habit of a lifetime he ordered the brigadier general to stop and hover mid-air.

Juan gave the order to rescue the survivors swimming aimlessly about in the ocean. If truth be told he was glad to do it.

"Fabio, drop to two hundred and fifty metres and hover under a cloak of invisibility just above the heads of those poor souls in the water," The Crusader spun round and nosedived like a peregrine falcon after its prey, zooming down towards the Atlantic Ocean. The moonlight was dancing romantically on the water belying the horrific drama engulfing the stricken ship's passengers. Lopez turned on the bus's spotlights picking out survivors splashing ineffectually, frantically trying to stay afloat. The shafts of light surprised the swimmers. Aircraft were still on the drawing board in 1912 so the shimmering lights, they thought, must be moonbeams.

Fully immersed in such mind numbingly freezing temperatures the swimmers could only survive for minutes at most. Many had already expired, their bodies bumping up against others barely alive who were managing to doggy paddle and in doing so were using up their precious energy reserves. Those still alive struggled to keep their heads above the waves. Juan knew from historical records that the rescue ships wouldn't arrive until the next day by which time most would have perished.

"Do we have any magic bubble wrap on board?" Juan asked Captain Greta.

"We do sir."

"Great!" Juan turned to Major Gubby, "Gulliver, we need your assistance!" Gulliver? Gulliver Gubby! No one commented. The rescue operation must not be delayed. Gulliver Gubby stepped forward, his ears growing larger and resembling wings as they had done on several previous occasions. Stepping into a spacesuit with a parachute attached and being careful not to tread on his ears he secured the bubble wrap to his belt by a gold thread and signalled for Hawkins to open the door. Major Gubby took a leap of faith and in the darkness floated down to those whose lives were in jeopardy.

"Good Chap!" Juan shouted after him. "You know what you must do!"

Major Gubby was invisible to those floundering about in the water. First he gathered up those close to death using great care not to cause them further distress. He wrapped them in the insulating bubble wrap and placed them into empty lifeboats bouncing about on the inhospitable ocean. Once these were full up he made use of flotsam, jetsam and ship's debris such as planks of wood floating aimlessly on the waves. Engulfed in the bubble wrap the weak souls might just stand a chance of staying alive until the following morning. Those saved were numbed by the cold and their minds addled making them confused, lethargic, stupefied. They had no idea that they had just been lifted from death's door. The bubble wrap was programmed to dissolve just as help arrived in the morning. No one would ever know that an intergalactic rescue mission had taken place, or Juan hoped, that he'd made an executive decision to change the course of history. The major returned to the Crusader to a round of applause.

The Crusader flew on veering right to the Bronx and New York's Yankee Stadium.

"How many Titanic survivors were there?" Floss asked, casually.

"I believe about a third of the passengers and crew survived. In truth, I would have to admit more lives were saved because the Crusader was in the right place at the right time, passing overhead at that fatal hour. If that hadn't been the case…who knows how many souls would have been lost!"

"So, am I correct in thinking that you foresaw that we'd insist on rescuing the Titanic's passengers?" Floss asked in playful fashion.

"I may have presumed you'd adopt a Florence Nightingale approach to saving mankind!" The iguana said, looking smug.

The sun was rising by the time the Crusader touched down in the middle of the Yankee's hallowed field. The Carshalton team ran out and pretended to hit invisible baseballs with make believe bats. Juan found them some proper equipment and as the sun rose higher in the sky the sound of cork filled balls on metal bats echoed around the playing field. Emmie's attention span for any ball game was short lived and feeling bored with what she saw as pointless running around, she left the others and went to the top rows of seats where she could survey the ballpark from its highest point. She imagined she could hear the fans clapping and, even though ball games were not her thing she felt elated at just being in the place the Yankees' called home.

Floss followed Emmie's lead and went for a wander finding an unlocked door into the players' changing rooms. Coat hooks held towels and shirts from a recent game, left behind, she wanted to believe, by famous players. She bet the fans would go crazy to be standing right where she was now! Even though the place was empty the air seemed charged with electricity. Walking along the corridor she admired several mannequins dressed in Yankees stripes and thought of Lily. What a pity the stadium souvenir shop was shut. Outside she could hear the joyous screams of Lily, Jack, Edward and the rest of Juan's team playing on the field. Floss explored further arriving at the Terrace Cocktail Bar. She gingerly went inside and sitting down at a small table pretended to be a rich businesswoman able to afford anything on the menu.

Emmie joined Floss at the Terrace Cocktail Bar.

"I'll have a Manhattan with plenty of maraschino cherries please," Floss addressed an imaginary waiter in her poshest voice.

"I'll have the Bloody Mary and don't go sparing on the tomato juice," Emmie ordered, giggling uncontrollably until a chilling, clanging noise like glasses banging together came from behind the bar making them almost jump out of their skins.

"There's something very much alive over there," Floss whispered, her heart knocking against her chest. They stood up slowly with the intention of creeping out unnoticed when Emmie clumsily kicked the leg of her chair and sent it crashing to the floor. Mortified, they hoped it was just an early morning bar worker making preparations for the day ahead. The worst that could happen was they'd be asked to leave the premises, wasn't it? It was a nurse holding two full glasses of fizzy lemonade who made herself known to them.

"My dears, please take some refreshment," the nurse fussed over them, oblivious of the fright she'd just given them. "Now, where's my Jack? I expected you all to arrive yesterday!"

Floss and Emmie were startled but then recalled Lily telling them about Staff Nurse Barbara Stanley, Jack's mum. Jack still believed the remark the girls had made about his mum joining them on Operation Lizard had been a wicked joke.

"Mrs Stanley, it's our fault we're late. We stopped over the North Atlantic to save some of the Titanic's passengers." Jack's mum was one of the team so there couldn't be any harm in sharing their heroics with her.

"Wow! How wonderful. Please call me Barbara. I bet you're both wondering how I came to be here?" The girls were doing just that. "Well, short story, Sir Juan sent me to New York to assist Lily. He's such a thoughtful chappie isn't he? Didn't want me to worry about my Jack so didn't let on that my lovely son was here with you until much later. I thought he was staying with his friend!" The nurse laughed. "I'm so proud of you all!" She exclaimed, kissing them both noisily on their cheeks. The exuberant nurse urged them to finish their drinks quickly. "We must return to the Crusader, sharpish. Sir Juan wants a roll call." The girls were shocked. It seemed Barbara had a direct line to the boss. "Juan talks to me using telepathy!" She said, noticing their questioning expressions.

"Mind reading!" Floss deduced.

"Yes, I know. What fun!" The nurse was loving her intergalactic experience.

Juan was waiting for Floss and Emmie in the Pitcher's Box along with Lily, Edward, Jack, Captain Greta, Clive Hawkins, and the man they now knew as, 'Gulliver' Gubby. They arrived just as the Crusader lifted off on its way to Geospace to find a secure garage for the bus. Brigadier General Lopez waved goodbye to them all from the cockpit as the Routemaster went under a cloak of invisibility and disappeared. The five were filled with a sense of loss wondering if they would ever fly through time again. Nurse Stanley made a beeline for Jack.

"What the hell are you doing here, mumsy?" Jack shrieked. He was shocked but at the same time pleased to see she was safe and not under a pile of bricks in May Tree Close.

"Jack dear, please don't forget I'm a skilled nurse practitioner and Sir Juan needed my help to fix the broken termites and Triangular Midget Men," she explained stoically.

"And I couldn't have done it without her!" Lily welcomed the nurse into their circle.

"I'm so glad that's sorted out. Can we get on now?" Juan exclaimed as Jack threw his arms around his mum forgetting the others were present and gave her the biggest hug.

The teenagers were still wearing their thin desert clothing and shivered in the chilly New York early morning temperature. Desert khakis in springtime Manhattan also looked odd and was not serious clobber for the big city. Greta, being practical appealed to the iguana to use his wizardry and transform their hot weather gear into fashionably warmer togs. He did. In moments they were looking like any other New York adolescents, sporting jeans and denim jackets. At the same time Juan and his aides took the opportunity to dispose of their own heavy military uniforms making it possible for them to roam the city incognito too. Juan led them steadfastly through the stands to a gate marked, Exit To Street.

Chapter 22

Towards Home

Juan and his party left the Yankee Stadium and boarded a metro train to 151 West 34th Street, the stop for Macy's department store. Emmie's eyes lit up. Finally, they were going shopping! Manhattan was crowded. Office workers on their brunch break were almost tripping over each other to get into their favourite coffee bars for a burger and a flat white. Juan was wearing a floppy sombrero to conceal his iguana features and with Barbara and the kids in tow they took their first real look at New York's hustle and bustle. Greta, Hawkins and Gubby mysteriously left Juan's protégées enjoying the city's hurly burly to organise, they claimed, a function at City Hall.

Macey's was awash with beautiful floral displays heralding summer. The girls checked the store plan. Women's Wear was located on the first floor. They took the escalator leaving the boys still figuring out where they wanted to go.

"How exciting is this then?" Emmie asked.

"Not as good as spending time on the Yankees' turf," Lily argued.

"No Lily, you're absolutely right. It's better!" Emmie laughed. The girls and Barbara split up, each wending their way to their preferred fashion labels. Floss wasn't really into designer wear. She didn't know one label from another and not wanting her friends to think she was a complete country bumkin tried to look interested in a range of silk blouses. Lily wanted a smart tracksuit and Emmie, who'd waited ages for this chance to shop till she dropped, headed for the prom dresses. School proms were popular at home and Emmie's dance was scheduled for July. She wanted to look gorgeous.

Juan had told them to let their hair down as on this occasion money was not an issue. The iguana had given them each a special credit card and said they were free to choose whatever they wanted because PUPA was footing the bill. Emmie chose a lemon taffeta gown with a lacey neckline and hem. It was magnificent. She would be the belle of the ball! Lily purchased a purple and black tracksuit, several running vests, a striped baseball jersey much like the sort the Yankees wore and a baseball cap. Floss bought two of the beautifully embroidered silk blouses, one for herself and the other for her mother and then worried about how she would explain where the money had come from. Barbara was doing her own thing. Nobody had clapped eyes on her since they had parted at the top of the escalator.

The shopping spree was too exciting for words as far as Emmie was concerned but she did manage to direct her friends making sure they forgot nothing.

"Shoes next!" Emmie told them taking them down to footwear on the ground floor where they found a glittering array of silver and gold high-heeled shoes and sparkling trainers. Even the flip-flops were diamante studded. They agonised over what to select. Emmie chose a pair of two-and-a-half-inch heeled lemon shoes with a diamante brooch on the front of each one to match her lemon dress. She was ecstatically happy with her purchases. Floss would definitely not be attending the prom so stuck to what some might call a boring pair of black patent low heeled shoes. Lily, surprise, surprise, went for an expensive pair of gym shoes studded with blue and purple sequins leaving her friends wondering whether she would ever actually wear them, tending as she did to stick to her tired, smelly old trainers.

Shopping done, they rode the escalator up two floors and found the boys waiting for them at the instore McDonalds. The lads had declined the opportunity to buy new clothes choosing electronic games and fashion accessories instead. Jack had insisted that Edward lighten up and experience the world of make believe! Edward had burst into laughter at Jack's suggestion. To anyone outside their group their recent adventure with the iguana would seem to be totally make believe! For once though, Edward agreed with Jack that perhaps at times he appeared a tad too serious. With Jack's coaxing he purchased a video game for himself called, *Egyptian Chronicles 1: First Dynasty Mummies Strike Back,* an appropriate keepsake he thought. Jack chose a game for Harrison to say thanks for all the hours he'd spent at his house playing on his games console. He did make one other purchase for himself, a pair of cool dude designer sunglasses with blue lenses.

McDonalds was buzzing. Everyone in New York City seemed to be there. The boys had managed to get a table and called the girls over. Edward did the gentlemanly thing and carefully placed their parcels underneath the table to prevent them being accidently kicked by passing customers. Jack went up to the counter and ordered fries and soft drinks for everyone. For the first time since leaving May Tree Close the pals felt totally at ease. They ate their food and chatted, loving every minute until Juan summoned them back to the ground floor. With so many packages, for their descent they opted for the elevator finding the iguana waiting for them at the bottom, his head still hidden beneath his large hat making him look out of place in a department store. A yellow cab idled outside Macy's ready to whisk them away to an important appointment.

"We need to put all this stuff in the boot," Lily said.

"You mean, trunk!" Jack remarked, feeling upbeat. He couldn't remember a time before when he'd been allowed to buy whatever he wanted without worrying about the cost.

The cab set off for City Hall without Barbara Stanley.

"Anyone seen my mum?" Jack asked, worried.

"Staff Nurse Stanley is on a secret assignment," Juan told him. "I could tell you where but then I'd have to kill you," he said laughing.

"You can't send my mum out alone on one of your dangerous missions in this jungle of a place!" Jack cried out, concerned for her welfare.

"Jack, I've the utmost respect for your mother. She answered an emergency call with such dignity and eagerness. I would NEVER put her life in danger. Oh ye of little faith. Trust and faith, Jack, trust and faith!" Jack's friends were also wondering what might have befallen Barbara. "My dear people-lets, Jack's mum is having lunch with her heartthrob, Brett Jacobs, her choice not mine. Apparently, Brett's been her pin-up since his days playing James Bond!" The iguana revealed. Jack nodded, recalling her fondness for the 007 secret agent.

The girls empathised with Barbara's choice of pin-up but they had their own heroes.

"Greg Sandiford, the long jumper is mine," Lily informed everyone.

"Mine's the gorgeous film star, Louis Vander! He's so handsome...," Emmie sighed. Floss didn't have a pin-up.

She preferred the term, muse. Could an airline pilot like Captain Jackie Ambrose be considered a muse?

"What about you, Ed?" Lily asked

"Haven't got time for such silly nonsense," he said impetuously.

"Can we get back to the whereabouts of my mum, please?" Jack was impatient.

"Your mother's dining at a top-class restaurant in Manhattan," Juan said, flipping his elaborate Malachitian space phone to video mode and showing Jack moving images of Barbara and Brett chatting easily together and dining on lobster.

The girls studied the screen.

"Do you see what Barbara's wearing?" Emmie screeched.

"I think you're right," gasped Lily. "Jack's mum is wearing a beautiful *House of Zachary* creation." Floss now felt more ignorant about fashion than ever but she had to agree Barbara's gown was quite splendid.

"I love that shade of blue and those multi-coloured sequins appliqued onto the fabric are magnificent. Absolutely stunning. That dress must have cost a million bucks," Emmie shrieked.

"Close!" Exclaimed Juan. He'd just settled the credit card bill. Barbara looked like a Hollywood film star. Jack's eyes moistened.

"Hey look, they're drinking champagne and its only 2 pm," Lily squealed.

"And, why not indeed. Joie de vivre! Barbara is living the dream!" Juan exclaimed.

The taxi chugged along at a snail's pace. Every time they turned a corner they hit another traffic jam and the team watched as the fare meter went on ticking, clocking more dollars.

"My dad would've made us get out and walk in traffic like this," Edward admitted.

"My dad wouldn't have taken a taxi in the first place," Floss added.

"The Mayor of New York City is footing the bill! No need to fret," Juan told them. The cab drew up in Chambers Street outside City Hall and the gates opened automatically as they approached. The security guards saluted as they drove into the compound. It was as though they were famous. They looked up in awe as they studied the magnificent building. Seconds later they were welcomed by Abigail Morley, City Hall's chief of staff. Abigail wore a smart navy suit with tiny iguanas printed all over a white blouse - the girls did a double take. Abigail told them something about the building's history, which gave Edward the chance to admire the architecture. Jack, too, considered the entrance hall but not for its architectural aspects but as a skate park!

Abigail acted as their tour guide telling them about the building's history.

"This City Hall is the only one left in the USA that's still being used for its original purpose. It's actually the third such building on this site. And, did you know several of our leaders have lain in state here following their deaths?" The boys grimaced. They had seen quite enough dead bodies albeit insects, plants, and glass heads for now. "Please follow me to the gowning room." Abigail led the way. They dutifully followed but gown up for what? They thought they were there for a sightseeing tour. Juan pushed them forward. Abigail took them up City Hall's famous floating marble staircase passing George Washington's desk along the way. Edward was lost for words. A steward in the oak panelled gowning room who was wearing old fashioned ceremonial breeches tied at the knees, graciously offered them each a pair of smart leather shoes and a full length red velvet cloak with what looked like a mink collar.

"I hope this isn't real fur," Lily whispered to Emmie.

"It's not. I'm sure of it." Emmie was allegedly an expert.

"It looks like real fur to me," Lily grumbled. The steward approached.

"It's fake my dears. Even the Mayor of New York can't afford real fur!" He told them.

Chapter 23

A Glorious Tribute

Five happy teenagers paraded about the room in their ceremonial robes, giggling and wondering what such shenanigans might be leading to. The steward lined them up in a specific order and suddenly it all seemed a bit too organised, predetermined even. Florence Roberts, Director of Operations was placed at the head of the procession followed by Knight Commanders Edward and Jack with Supreme Code-Breaker, Emmeline Taylor and Surgeon General, Lily Gibson bringing up the rear. They processed towards a pair of ornate rococo doors, Juan watching with pride until he caught sight of Lily's footwear. She had rejected the official smart leather shoes in favour of her tatty old pumps. The iguana halted the parade.

"Awful footwear. Most inappropriate. We can't have that!" He said, shaking his snout and chanting a spell transforming Lily's disgustingly, lived-in trainers into respectable polished leather shoes much more suited for such a grand occasion. The procession restarted.

Footmen attired in silk damson suits trimmed with gold braid opened the doors bowing deferentially as the guests of honour processed serenely into the Blue Room. The beautiful assembly room was full of TV cameras, journalists and dignitaries from all over the Universe who burst into spontaneous applause accompanied by much stamping and tapping of feet as the stars of the show made their entrance. They were guided to their seats on a flower bedecked stage. New York's Mayor, Bobby Winton stepped up to the microphone.

"Mr President, may I say that we're delighted that you and your wife were able to make time in your busy schedules to attend today's important award ceremony." The guests of honour gasped. The President of the United States of America, Mr Frank Collins and Sylvia, his First Lady, were there sitting right in front of them in the first row.

Next to Frank Collins and his wife sat the British prime minister, The Right Honorable Mrs Lucy Murray and her husband, George. Sitting next to them was a nervous Barbara Stanley, now wearing a cream two-piece with a pink blouse. Brett Jacobs was beside her, holding her hand. Juan, not wishing to hog the limelight took his seat at the end of the first row.

"All the great and the good are here," whispered Floss to Emmie.

"I know! And I'm so pleased that Jack's mum is flying the flag for British fashion."

"I've no idea what you're talking about!" Floss mouthed back, trying to be inconspicuous whilst sitting on a stage in front of hundreds of guests.

There were several other dignitaries seated close to the American president. The high commissioners of several of the collaborative worlds felt it important to be represented at the awards ceremony. The British teenagers' efforts had secured their futures as free planets and stars. The Star Kibas foreign secretary, known as the kratonga, sat at the end of the row having travelled seventy five thousand light years to be with them at short notice. The event was simply too important to miss. PUPA's members might need help in the future if or when another unscrupulous slimeball turned up to wreak havoc in any of their celestial communities. Showing their gratitude now seemed a good idea.

The Star Kibas contingent included Percina and Buttercup, two of Lily's hard-working senior nurses, were seated in the fourth row beside multi-tasker, Brigadier General Fabio Lopez. They were no longer lookalikes for Barbara Stanley but resembled instead a well-known female athlete, one of Lily's sporting heroines she'd talked about incessantly whilst attending to her patients at the field hospital. The nurses had ditched their uniforms in favour of their national costume, a glittery blue and silver wrap-around ankle length dress decorated with moons and stars. They looked charming.

Next to the kratonga sat the Malachitian Supreme Governor, Lord Rollo de Landseer wearing the Stewart tartan. The *de Landseer* part of his name demonstrated his appreciation of Sir Edwin Landseer, the Victorian painter and his Monarch of the Glen creation, a famous painting of a red deer with mighty antlers that reminded him of his own similar protrusions spouting from the top of his head. Lord de Landseer's antlers were taking up a lot of room preventing those in the second row from getting a good view of the stage. Fellow guests were complaining so he removed them. Apart from the antlers, Lord de Landseer looked like any other middle-aged gentleman, discounting his unruly orange hair. If Juan ever stopped being an iguana the teenagers wondered if he would look like the supreme governor.

Generals Felipe, Joaquin, Gonzalez, and Admiral Mathias were seated in the second row behind the presidential line-up looking splendid in their ceremonial uniforms, their chests littered with medals. Colonel Eva, being of short stature sat beside them on a well-padded crimson cushion enabling her to watch the proceedings comfortably.

Starlight of the Nile, to use her official title was there too, perched on one of Major Gubby's ears and next to him were Lieutenant Hawkins and Captain Greta. It seemed at first glance that no one had been forgotten. The traitor, Alvaro, was no longer mentioned in polite society.

"Where are the Retipu?" Emmie sent an intercranial message to her friends sitting beside her on the stage. "Surely they're here somewhere? We couldn't have broken the enemy's codes without them." Just then a commotion broke out at the back of the room. The doors were thrown open and in walked Treah, Azure and the other bears from Emmie's trusted team. Abigail showed them to their seats beside the Star Kibas nurses.

Mayor Winton kicked-off the proceedings.

"Mr President, we're assembled here this afternoon to honour five humble souls for their courage, bravery and unerring support in ridding the intergalactic community of our common enemy, Gregor Magnus. They've allowed us to feel safe in our beds and for our democracies to remain free." Mayor Winton paused and smiled at the stars of the show before continuing his opening address. "Mr President, I will shortly call on you to say a few words and then with the help of Prime Minister, Lucy Murray, present our conquering champions with the highest honour the Parallel Universe Peace Association can bestow, the Libra Congressional Medal. PUPA, as we all know, exists to uphold the universal right to freedom, justice, and peace for all. These youngsters have made sure we can continue doing this." The Blue Room resounded with thunderous applause as the mayor beckoned President Collins to step up onto the stage.

President Collins waited for the applause to fade away before speaking.

"Thank you everyone for attending here at such short notice. I'm sure our young heroes get the message that our universal community is eternally grateful for their determination to see Operation Lizard through to the end. I'd like to echo Mayor Winton's sentiment and thank them personally for delivering victory over evil. Moreover, I think children everywhere will read about their exploits for years to come." President Collins glanced back at the teenagers before continuing. "My dearest wish is that the youth of tomorrow will look up to you as shining examples of good citizens. This can only be good for society in my view." President Collins looked down at his notes before continuing. "During my presidency I intend to nurture a caring attitude amongst the American youth, forging a community that is kind-hearted and responsible towards those that need help. I want the young to *lead the charge* in showing true friendship to all in need, whatever their age, shape, colour or creed." More rapturous applause followed with Juan clapping the loudest!

The British prime minister, the Right Honourable Mrs Lucy Murray was invited to come to the podium for the next part of the ceremony. A small table with five small white silk lined boxes containing gold medals depicting the Great Sphinx was lifted onto the stage. Lucy Murray smiled fondly at the medal recipients telling everyone that the British people owed them a great debt of gratitude. After their roller coaster adventure she wondered if they would ever be able to settle down to serious study at school again. The audience chuckled politely. First up to receive her award was Floss. President Collins shook her hand then Mrs Murray pinned a medal to her red cloak but as she made to return to her seat Mrs Murray gently stopped her.

"I pride myself on being a very good judge of character, young lady," she spoke quietly, "I'll be tracking your progress at home because I intend to ensure that you reach your full potential..." Floss returned to her seat, mesmerised by the prime minister's words. Lily, Emmie, Edward and Jack received their own medals to heartfelt clapping but without the personal epithet from their prime minister.

Time seemed to fly by so quickly and soon the official part of the event was over. They looked around the room at the auspicious guests and had to admit they had made some interesting friends since meeting Juan. When the time came it would be hard to say goodbye. They disrobed and rejoined their guests for a sumptuous buffet getting stuck into canapes, sandwiches and the like whilst chatting until it was time for their guests to leave for their distant planets and stars. As the evening drew to a close the teenagers were dizzy with excitement. They waited at the bottom of City Hall's steps for their ride to a posh hotel costing over a thousand dollars a night, paid of course by PUPA.

"I loved those tiger prawns," Edward gushed contentedly. Their friend's preoccupation with food made them all laugh. They had hobnobbed with the American president, the British prime minister and some of their galaxy's greatest citizens and all Edward could comment on was the food!

"Do you think all this fame will change us?" Jack asked the others.

"Not at all," Floss reassured him. "Once we get home we'll sink back into oblivion and just get on with our lives as we did before."

A horse drawn carriage arrived to take them to their super-duper overnight stay. They climbed in and waited for Barbara who was saying her own farewell to Brett at the top of the steps. It was a windless evening and Brett's words could just be overheard.

"Now don't forget, Babe. Call me whenever you need to. Understood? Here, take my card. It has my personal contact details. You can get me on my cell at a moment's notice." The film star kissed her tenderly before disappearing to a waiting limousine.

"Did you hear that?" Jack whispered. "Brett called my mum, Babe!"

"You misheard. He said Babs!" Edward joked.

"Jack heard correctly. Brett called her, Babe, right enough!" Emmie said firmly.

"Your mother's a woman in a million," Juan intervened, as if Jack needed reminding. Barbara re-joined them placing Brett's card safely in her handbag. No one noticed the tears slipping slowly down her cheeks as they set off for their hotel.

"I can't wait to soak in a tub full of perfumed bubbles," Emmie announced.

"Oh yes please!" Agreed Lily, "I want to be surrounded by candles and I want one of those fluffy white bathrobes..."

Chapter 24

Once More Unto The Breach...

The next morning Lily, energetic as always, was up with the lark and fancying a dip in the hotel's swimming pool. She called Floss on the internal phone.

"Come on Floss! A splash before breakfast will do us both good," she urged.

"I don't have a swimsuit!" Floss didn't feel like swimming.

"The hotel shop has plenty to choose from and it opened at 8 am. I'm coming to get you now..." With Lily's nagging Floss caved in. Barbara had risen early and gone for a walk on Broadway, mingling with New Yorkers rushing to work. She wanted to make every second of her short stay in the city count. Emmeline, fashionista, had opted for a bit of pampering and had booked the beauty salon for an early slot. A massage and pedicure before facing up to the rigours of their return to London sounded just divine. Edward and Jack slept in, agreeing to meet for coffee and bagels after the normal breakfast rush had died down.

The boys met as planned. Jack was still feeling bleary eyed from the excitement of the night before but when Edward divulged his game plan for the morning he was soon wide awake and hanging on every word.

"I'm going back to Grand Central Station. I want to see it as a regular punter," Edward told Jack. "I can still smell those delicious aromas in the food court. They're making me feel hungry just thinking about them."

"Don't be ridiculous! Surely, you've seen quite enough of that place? Anyway, Juan deliberately told us we weren't to go back to any of the command centres and orders is orders!" Jack reminded his friend. Edward thought differently. What harm could there be in innocently strolling around a train station? Where was the danger?

Edward was not dissuaded by Jack's argument.

"I'm interested in the station's architecture. I'm considering studying it as a career," Edward explained. Jack still wasn't convinced.

"Our quarry may be behind bars but Gregor Magnus and Effria have nasty friends out there. Best not provoke another war. I, personally just want to get home to my rabbits," Jack told him. Edward wasn't listening.

"Cornelius Vanderbilt built the Grand Central Terminus. He was the eighth richest man in the world, once upon a time," Edward rambled, shutting his mind to Jack's misgivings.

"How do you know all this stuff?" Jack's brain wasn't attuned for a lesson on railway station history so early in the morning. He just wanted to spend their last few hours bathing in the memories of the night before.

"Oh well, you know… I googled it," Edward told him, his urge to step back inside the train station undiminished. Jack felt uneasy. Without back-up it appeared foolhardy. "I just want to take some pictures, that's all. They'll come in handy when applying to colleges," he added, his pleading falling on stony ground. "Look, I'll pop along on my own. I'll be back in time for the airport, I promise," Edward said, rising and walking briskly towards the hotel's main exit without giving Jack a second glance.

Jack rejoined the girls around midmorning just as Colonel Eva was bidding them farewell.

"Well, here we all are again," the bird squeaked. "Well almost," she corrected, realising that Edward was missing. "I just wanted to say what a pleasure it's been to meet you folks but like they say, all good things must come to an end!" The lobby was full of people and not one of them seemed to think it odd that the teenagers were conversing with a wading bird!

"You're leaving us, colonel?" Floss was truly sorry to hear Eva's news.

"You can drop the colonel bit now… just call me Eva. The war's over! I have to go. When I left home Noah, my mate, was sitting on our eggs. They'll be hatching about now. Three little beauts!" The avocet was so excited.

The teenagers hadn't received news on how Rudy the cat was faring. Jack took the opportunity to ask the avocet if she knew anything.

"Is Rudy happy in his new life at Buck Pal, do you know?"

"I'm so glad you asked me that, Jacko," she replied. "Rudy's not what you might call a happy bunny. Oops! Sorry about my choice of words," she apologised, remembering Jack's anguish over Rosie and Rodrigo. "Rudy's pining."

"Pining?" Floss exclaimed, surprised. "He lives with the Queen of England as one of her most cosseted pets, eats at her table and sleeps on her bed!" She couldn't understand why any pet might be so unhappy when living in the lap of such luxury.

"Her Majesty's renamed him, White Heather. The cat thinks it's a bit sissy. Know what I mean? And then there are the rats! Thousands of them. Eighteen inch long rats from head to tail! The cat claims they're as big as horses!"

Floss had fought to get Rudy a comfortable new home and was disappointed to hear he was so unhappy. They would shortly be going home to Carshalton and the opportunity to help him would be lost, leaving the cat imprisoned in Victorian London forever.

"Eva, could I take Rudy home with me? Could we get him back from the 1880s, kidnap him if necessary?" She begged Eva to think hard and fast.

"There might just be a way," Eva said, loving a challenge. "First though, I'd need to get permission from PUPA. Once peace is declared us lower ranking military personnel aren't allowed to use time travel willy-nilly. There has to be a particularly good reason for doing so. We've a couple of hours before you leave for the airport. Let me think about it." A janitor held the hotel's door open for more arriving guests and Eva took the opportunity to fly out onto the busy street. No one in the foyer even bothered to look up.

The teenagers were in the hotel's games room when Juan caught up with them. Still wearing his floppy hat he looked flustered. Floss sensed something was up.

"Hi, Juan," she said kindly. Juan nodded.

"We may have a grave situation developing," he whispered. Jack and Lily were playing pool and Emmie was perusing a fashion magazine. They didn't notice Juan arrive.

"Oh no! We're flying home on garden chairs again?" Floss joked.

"No! I have something far more serious to occupy my thoughts. I'm concerned about Edward. Do you know where he is?" Floss didn't.

"Jack spoke to him last… said he went out after breakfast." Floss rose to fetch Jack.

"He rushed off to Grand Central saying he wanted to become an architect and needed photographs for his CV. Why, what's up? He should be back any time now," Jack said, checking the hotel's clock.

Juan shook his lizard-like head making his hat wobble.

"I sense something bad is in the offing. I've been trying to message Edward and all I get are loud engine noises like trains racing over rickety tracks. I'm concerned for his safety."

"Grand Central's got plenty of trains! Maybe you're picking up an echo?" Jack was doing his best to be helpful.

"I told you all to keep away from all war zones and command centres and that included Grand Central Terminus. Danger is ever present!" A glum looking iguana reproached them. Jack and Floss immediately volunteered to accompany him to the terminus to search for Edward. Lily was fully occupied with getting The Harlem Globe Trotters autographs having seen them arrive at the Reception desk and Emmie was totally immersed in her fashion magazine. There seemed little point in trying to get their attention so Juan, Floss and Jack decided to go it alone.

The rescue party rose to leave when Eva scuttled across the carpet to them.

"I have the *purrfect* answer to the Rudy problem," she chuckled. "I've consulted with PUPA's constitutional lawyers and they'll allow a trip back to Victorian England provided we can prove it's for a, *Special Being That Transcends the Galactic Boundaries* and that the necessity for the time travel goes beyond *the Conceptual Sphere.* There! I knew we could find a way of getting Rudy back." The bird was so very obviously proud of herself. Juan was desperate to get to the railway terminal.

"Dearest Eva," he began. "I believe you're interpreting the laws too loosely here," pouring cold water on her literal translation of the rules.

"With respect, sir, I think we can work the clauses to our own advantage," she remonstrated. The avocet wouldn't be beaten. Jack took Juan to one side.

"Juan, it's a no brainer! I know Rudy's just a scruffy old moggy but if this simple act of kindness will make both Floss and the cat happy why not just do it?" Jack had found Juan's soft spot.

"Yes, yes, alright, let's do it," Juan spluttered, knowing he wouldn't win in any case.

The iguana told Eva to go ahead with her plan and took the opportunity to inform the bird of their latest predicament. Eva immediately put out a call to Fabio Lopez, currently engaged on a mopping up operation with his termite team somewhere in New York. As always the brigadier was up for another challenge, delighted at the chance of one final adventurous fling into the face of danger. Juan, Floss, Jack and Eva rendezvoused with Fabio at 42nd Street from where they continued on together to the Grand Central Terminus.

"Three quarters of a million people pass through this majestic edifice every single day. It's the biggest railway station in the world with its forty-four platforms and more in the making!" Juan told them as they surveyed the glorious architecture.

"Yes, that's what Ed was telling me," Jack explained, as the search party followed Juan to a small secret room being used as Operation Lizard's Disbanding Centre. Juan requested they stay there and await news of Fabio's termites who were investigating every nook and cranny of the eight hundred and forty miles of track and swarming through the four hundred stations and tunnels across the network leaving no stone unturned. Edward would be found!

Jack was very concerned for his friend's safety.

"No news is good news. Isn't that what they say?" Jack was sounding more anxious.

"It'll be OK!" Floss tried to comfort him but screams heard on one of the remaining monitors in the decommissioning room suggested something seriously wrong on Track 61. Fabio's crack team moved fast in Track 61's direction.

"Track 61 can't be far from where we are now," Jack reasoned. "I'm going out there and don't try to stop me." Juan was vexed. He didn't want to lose another of his team.

"Jack, There's something I must tell you. Track 61's no longer used by real trains," he paused. Jack was listening.

"It was built for President Franklin Delano Roosevelt during the Second World War. Crippled by polio he didn't want the public to think of him as disabled. Having his own special track meant he could board trains without them seeing him in his wheelchair. That was a long time ago and although there are still trains using that track, they are ghost trains! It's a closely guarded secret known only to those at the top of the transit corporation's hierarchy. Can you imagine how the public would react if they thought their trains were full of supernatural goings-on?" Juan's speech made no difference. Jack was going it alone. "OK! Just remember that the ghost trains run to a schedule and they don't have drivers or emergency stop handles!" Jack had to understand what he was truly up against. Juan's warning just made Jack more determined to rescue his buddy.

"What kind of phantom trains are they, electric, diesel, steam?" Jack was presenting a brave front.

"They're electric."

"Oh good. No chance of mistaking them for the Hogwarts Express then!" Jack laughed, sounding as cool as a cucumber whilst his insides felt like jelly.

Jack checked the station map Juan had given him and then made off in the direction of Track 61. Big wooden gates barred his access but Juan had told him the magic words to open them. He'd memorised the ghost train timetable and walking swiftly along in the darkness soon found himself at the far end of a longer than usual platform. He could hear cries for help in the distance so he increased his pace, jumping down onto the track and cautiously keeping to the middle to avoid electrocution. A train was due in the next eight minutes. Juan had given Jack his chronometer so he could accurately pinpoint the train's arrival giving him a better chance of survival.

Hundreds of termites were scurrying along Track 62 but so far none of the Fabio's patrols had broken through to Track 61. Jack was on his own. Besides the intermittent crying Jack's ears were picking up every new sound. A beetle scuttled past giving him a fright. He stopped for a second, leaning up against the tunnel wall to get his breath back until an even louder screech filled the void. It was Edward. It just had to be. Quickening his pace Jack remembered Juan's warning that the ghost train could do just as much damage as a real one. He checked the chronometer. He'd been walking for five minutes so the train was due in three. Something or someone was threshing about on the track ahead of him. A few more steps and he could see it was definitely Edward, bound, blindfolded, and gagged and his six legged assailant was still there, tying him to the rails.

Jack steeled himself knowing he must remain strong, his friend's life depended on his next move. Leaping into action and caring little for his own safety he hurled himself at Edward's captor sending him flying. There was a thud as the latter's head hit a metal rail followed by silence as he was knocked unconscious. Jack worked fast, untying the ropes binding Edward to the rail and dragging his pal to safety. He pulled off Edward's blindfold, removed the gag and untied his hands and legs then helped his dazed friend to his feet. Once completely clear of the rails he allowed Edward a moment to recover his balance. The hellish roar of an approaching train filled the empty train shaft and just then an army of small feet approached with Juan and Floss bringing up the rear. The termites had finally arrived. They lifted Edward effortlessly up onto their shoulders and carried him horizontally to safety just as the ghost train hurtled by. Danger over, Jack cast his eyes back to see Edward's assailant lying motionless, his head severed and his thorax and legs having been completely and utterly squashed beneath the ghost train's wheels, a train that had disappeared into thin air.

The hotel seemed tranquil after Edward's railway hell. Lily, Emmie, Barbara, the latter just back from her stroll around the city, and Eva welcomed him back.

"So, the wanderer returns," Lily joked.

"Where were you?" Emmie asked. Both girls were unaware of the near-death situation Edward had so recently been prised from.

"It's a long story," Edward sounded weary and just glad to be alive.

"Try us," Emmie pushed. Edward massaged his ankles, sore from being tied to the track.

"It was all down to my purely selfish desire to indulge myself. I just wanted to wallow in the station's architecture but as soon as I stepped foot inside the terminus Alvaro turned up, pushed a laser gun into my back and frogmarched me to a pigeonhole of a place where he interrogated me. He wanted to know the whereabouts of Gregor Magnus and Effria. I didn't tell him a thing!" He proudly told them.

"General Alvaro!" Emmie and Lily shrieked. To hear that the despicable traitor was still up to no good was a complete shock.

"He's no general. We stripped him of his rank," Jack reminded them.

"I should've sensed that turncoat would cause us more trouble," Juan groaned.

"Too right, mate," Eva screeched, forgetting she was addressing her field marshal.

"I'm pleased to tell you all we don't need to worry about Alvaro anymore," Jack sounded confident. "That bug is a mere fraction of his former glory. The tunnel's bats will enjoy scraping him off the rails and eating him up!"

"And, thanks to Jack," Juan chirped, making sure Jack received his rightful praise, "Edward has the chance of living to a ripe old age. It was Jack who pulled Edward from the railway line in the face of the on-coming train." Barbara listened until she could no longer contain herself and flinging her arms around Jack, suffocated him with kisses.

Chapter 25

Flying High

A mini-bus arrived to take Juan, his victorious conquistadors and Barbara to the airport. The iguana sat up front with the driver. Out again in public he felt it necessary to cover his head with his hat concealing his true identity. He chatted incognito with the cabby, the latter insisting on telling him about some of the weird people he'd ferried around New York over the years. The teenagers wondered what he'd think if he took a long hard look at his present front seat passenger! Their departure from New York was tinged with sadness. Eva, Lieutenant Hawkins, Major Gubby and Captain Greta had said their goodbyes at the hotel, which had already made them feel miserable and dreading their return to normal Carshalton life.

"It'll be nice to see mum and dad again," Floss voiced without a hint of excitement.

"I'll be glad to get back to my studies, I suppose. I'm really missing my Latin classes," Emmie lied, feeling woeful. The boys gloomily hung their heads. Returning to the drudgery of school life was not exactly an exhilarating prospect.

Emmie tapped Juan on the shoulder pleading for a stay of execution.

"Could we take a last look at Washington Square Park?" Juan was in an agreeable mood and told the taxi driver to make a detour. Emmie et al except for Barbara who remained in the cab with Juan, alighted to the sounds of musicians playing trumpets and other instruments in the park and who were themselves surrounded by families listening to their music or simply enjoying watching the many street performers juggling, blowing giant bubbles, or doing conjuring tricks. In the centre of the park was a grand piano and a pianist playing Debussy's Clair de Lune. The tune floated around them. Emmie looked up at the arch. The small window from where she had watched New Yorkers going about their everyday lives was gone. Back then she'd had butterflies in her stomach and she did now as she walked around the arch admiring the statues of George Washington, remembering that he too had been a commander of armies, albeit human beings rather than creatures from outer space. The cab tooted and they hurried back to complete their drive to the airport. As they left the square Floss felt sure one of the jugglers winked at her. It was as if he knew their secret.

At John F Kennedy airport the newly famous medal holders were met by the airport's celebratory Meeter and Greeter and escorted to the VIP lounge. The lads were overjoyed at seeing platters of free food laid out for them to nibble.

"This fame thing isn't half bad!" Edward said, munching a sausage roll and holding a choc au pan in his other hand. Barbara was finding it difficult to relax. She felt the need to get up and hand the food around.

"Mum, stay put! It's your turn to be waited on hand and foot. Let the stewards serve you for a change!" Jack told her. The girls were nodding in agreement as the steward asked if they would like blankets for their knees. Contemplating a life of such luxury was something Floss's mum would never have allowed. There were always jobs around the house or errands to run!

The teenagers' sojourn in the VIP lounge was short lived and with mixed feelings about leaving New York they followed the steward out to their awaiting aircraft.

"Welcome aboard! I'm Captain Jackie Ambrose," The cheerful captain shook hands with each teenager as they entered. She was wearing a Royal Air Force uniform with four stripes on her sleeve denoting her seniority. The last time Floss had met Jackie Ambrose she'd been flying a commercial passenger airliner. "We feel privileged to be taking you home today. The prime minister has made her private jet available for your flight," the captain told them. Relief spread across their faces. A luxury aircraft was taking them home and not one of Juan's inventions.

"Flight Lieutenant Melissa Cranfield will show you to your seats. Please let Melissa know if you need anything. We'll certainly do all we can to make your flight home smoother than the one that brought you to New York!" The captain sniggered. "Those garden chairs were a hoot and I'm betting, uncomfortable!" She winked knowingly.

Settling into their seats the teenagers were pleased when Melissa brought them complimentary drinks, pillows, blankets, and earphones - all the normal stuff given out on a transatlantic flight.

"It's a little chilly in here just now," Melissa apologised. "Our flight over from the UK was hit by a swarm of insects and the little blighters blocked up the heating ducts! The engineers are working to restore it as I speak. We should be off in a jiffy! We're so sorry for the delay."

"What kind of insects?" Floss asked, recalling the accident that had destroyed so many of General Felipe's SSS enroute from Dover to New York.

"Large ant-like creepy crawlies, I believe," Melissa advised.

Once airborne Floss pushed her service button. Melissa responded.

"Miss Floss, how can I help?"

"I'd like to speak to Captain Ambrose." Floss held her breath hoping her request wasn't a step too far.

"Indeed miss, you may! The captain's very keen to spend time with you too." No time like the present thought

Floss and unbuckling her belt she galloped down the aisle towards the cockpit with Melissa in hot pursuit. The flight deck appeared at first glance to be an unending mass of controls.

"Wow!" Floss gasped, fully amazed.

"Captain Ambrose at your service!" The captain saluted her as she stood stock still in the doorway. "Come on in and take a seat." There were so many switches, dials, knobs, levers, and screens that Floss moved cautiously, careful not to touch something inadvertently and be responsible for crashing their plane! Floss noticed the co-pilot was watching her like a hawk. The captain sensed her anxiety. "It's OK. We won't let you do any damage."

Floss sat in the pilot's seat and glanced around noting the bird's eye view.

"I'll explain the controls to you," Jackie said. Floss's dreams had all come true at once. "For starters, this is what we call an instrument panel," Jackie pointed to the switches and dials in front of her. "We've two engines on this jet and an auxiliary power unit we refer to as an APU. We start that up first and that gets the big engines beneath the wings firing. We have three fuel tanks. One in each wing and a main tank in the fuselage, a fuselage is..."

"I know what a fuselage is, captain," Floss interrupted, wanting her to know that she'd not been completely idle since the Paris trip.

"Well now, let me see... ah yes, this aircraft has advanced navigational aids and our radar is in the plane's nose cone. We've antennas, thrust reversing capabilities and a gyroscope to read acceleration changes..." There was so much to take in.

Floss now wanted to be a pilot more than ever and was interested to know more about the captain's career progression.

"Captain, why did you leave Rise Airlines to become a military pilot?" She enquired.

"I was head hunted by the RAF because I'm an expert on PUPA's latest jet design. It's still under wraps so I can't say too much about it right now. What I can tell you is that a few years ago I worked for PUPA on their orbiting space stations. These monitor situations on member planets. They track illegal spaceships and listen in for unusual activity that could disrupt fragile peace agreements."

"The RAF knows about PUPA then?" Floss asked, amazed.

"Indeed. The RAF works hand in hand with PUPA. In fact, Prime Minister Murray..." The captain wasn't allowed to finish.

"Mrs Murray makes secret trips to PUPA meetings, yes I know."

"Why yes, she does. I bet Juan told you that didn't he?" Jackie asked, bursting into laughter. Floss nodded, not at all surprised to learn that Jackie was another of Juan's acquaintances.

Floss's time in the cockpit whizzed by and in no time at all she was back in her seat for supper where she found her friends daydreaming about their futures. Emmie's ambition was to work with PUPA as an intergalactic spy following in the footsteps of Colonel Eva. Lily foresaw endless opportunities for equalities work on far-flung planets such as Ice Leonard. She didn't know if they employed social scientists on Malachite or anywhere else in space but it was something worth aspiring to. Edward's goal as an architect was to improve the Malachitian pod design, making life more interesting for their developing wormsicals whilst Jack's horizons had been much broadened. The Machiavellian warfare they had witnessed had dimmed his interest in virtual games. He wanted to know everything there was to know about sustaining life rather than destroying it. The notion of doing something for the environment attracted him. Saving the oceans by designing underwater robots to monitor the seabed, saving species from extinction, or even learning how to make plastic more biodegradable? There was so much he could do and he was eager to get started.

Saving the Universe had been an exhausting business. Floss picked up a paper napkin and borrowing a pen from Emmie scribbled a simple ditty.

May Tree Close

I long to be in May Tree Close,
The place I really love the most.
I've seen New York and met a moggy,
- a prison cat, and very stroppy.

My mum and dad will be waiting at home,
Impatient as always by the phone.
I just wish they'd met the Persian cat
They'd have loved him, I'm so sure of that.

I'll become an aviatrix and fly the skies,
Sometimes I'll fly Emmie, Lily, and the guys.
Outer space is where it's at,
Pity I had to leave the cat.

I'm travelling home but what will I find?
Piles of rubble or homes that are fine?
New York was exciting, no doubt about that,
I'm sad I'll never again see Rudy the Cat!

Emmie watched Floss composing.

"Floss come on, read it out to us," she begged.

"It's not good enough."

"Oh yes! Come on, let's hear it," Jack called out.

Embarrassed Floss reluctantly recited her little poem. Everyone loved it and started composing their own short rhymes, Edward being the exception. He was busy scratching his sunburnt legs. His sensitive skin had suffered badly in Egypt. Wearing shorts and standing in the strong sunshine he'd suffered sunburn. He was peeling.

"Gross!" Emmie screeched.

"Stop doing that!" Lily yelled. Melissa arrived with a tube of soothing ointment.

Chapter 26

So Good to be Home

The teenagers were welcomed back at Heathrow Airport by the British foreign secretary, The Honorable Mr George Dobbs. Mr Dobbs accompanied them in their chauffeur driven limousine towards central London, debriefing them along the way. Barbara and Juan, his hat still firmly planted on his head travelled in a separate vehicle. Mr Dobbs wanted to be sure that national security hadn't been compromised. Reassured by their answers and delighted to know that Gregor Magnus had been satisfactorily dealt with, he thanked them for their service to the nation and the wider intergalactic community and left them at Parliament Square. They continued on to Carshalton in their luxury limo.

The May Tree Close neighbours, local town councillors, businesses owners and schoolteachers were out in force to welcome them home. They were celebrities in the UK too! Looking around, they saw the ruined houses had been fully restored to their former glory and even improved upon. Fresh coats of paint, new roof tiles and gleaming front doors were on show. The front gardens had been grassed over and planted with roses, delphiniums, lupins, and all sorts of flowers strangely in full bloom considering they were officially still in springtime - obviously, all down to Juan and his people. The little green island's trees were standing tall again with Floss's favourite cherry tree festooned in pink blossom. Life had returned to normal, relatively speaking!

The Welcome Home Party gave the heroes a standing ovation, clapping like it was going out of fashion. Floss ran to her parents hugging them tightly, not wanting to let them go.

"Hi mum, dad. I can't tell you how good it feels to be home and to see you've both woken up without any side effects," Floss spoke without first engaging her brain. Her parents cast her a strange look and then glanced at each other. What was she talking about? Woken up? Floss glanced across at Juan who was looking more human than ever before. He winked and she knew instinctively that he had taken care of everything, even expunging her parents' memories.

Lin Roberts was the first in the queue to congratulate her daughter.

"We saw you on the telly at City Hall. We're so proud of you and your friends," she whimpered, reaching for a tissue to dry her eyes. Floss's much loved granny was next in line for a hug and gathering her up in her arms she embraced her. Remembering that Juan wanted to be introduced to her gran she brought them together. The two old timers got on like a house on fire sitting beneath the cherry tree, having a good old chinwag. Floss's brother, Toby, was still on his way home from uni so a family reunion was planned for the next day.

After chatting to Granny Molly Juan sauntered around, smiling at everyone. He was still an iguana underneath his disguise but on the face of it he looked like anyone's granddad, around sixty-five years old with silvery, rumpled hair and a few whiskers where it looked like he hadn't shaved. His trousers were baggy and held up with braces presenting an overall lived-in look. Even though his hat was still hiding his iguana shaped head and he'd taken care to replace his thin reptilian fingers he still looked like an iguana to Floss. Ever inquisitive, Mr and Mrs Roberts wondered who the strange chap in the hat might be.

"Floss dear, who is that? He seems to know you all," Lin Roberts was pointing at Juan.

"Oh! You mean John! He's connected to the White House. He's one of President Collins' undercover agents. He escorted us here just to make sure we arrived safely. He'll be going home soon. Best not speak to him, mum. You know, spies and their secrets and all that. Might make it difficult for him…" Floss chuckled deep down inside at her little white lie.

"Yes of course, dear. I understand!" Her mother replied, tapping the side of her nose twice just like Juan did sometimes and indicating that she would keep his secret.

Lily received an equally charged emotional welcome home from her own parents. Now dressed in the black and white striped jeggings and the long white blouse that she had worn at the start of their adventure, having changed in the car following Mr Dobbs' departure, she raced over to them. They were waving both the Union Jack and the Japanese flag at the same time so they were easy to pick out from the crowd.

"Hello Mum and dad," Lily said. "How are you?"

"We're fine, sweetheart," her mum replied.

"We've been so worried about you," her dad admitted.

"There was no need for that. We've been well looked after," Lily said cautiously.

"Someone called, John did his best to keep us in the loop. We trusted him to bring you all back safely, and here you all are!" Bill Gibson exclaimed. "We're so honoured that out of all the teenagers in the UK you five were chosen for such an important mission," he sounded so proud. "We must thank John for keeping his word. Is he with you?"

"Eh, no. Sorry dad. He has an important assignment in the US…he hasn't got time…" Lily hoped her savvy reply would throw her dad off the scent.

Floss, Emmie, and Edward overheard the Gibsons and wondered how Juan had kept in touch with their parents. Chatting to their neighbours the impression gained was that everyone believed they'd been acting as international youth ambassadors not warriors, battling fierce intergalactic enemies. Juan was so clever! On the little grassy island stood a table with a tea urn powered by electricity from 71 May Tree Close, the home of Mr Wainwright, a widower and retired electrician by trade. The tea was being served by the normally grumpy Miss Makepeace. Today, unusually, she was grinning from ear to ear. Planning the homecoming party had brought these two lonely hearts together. Mr Wainwright and Miss Makepeace had fallen in love. Even Miss Makepeace's poodle, Harriet had found a friend in Mr Wainwright's pooch, a brown mutt called Lawson.

Floss collected up their medals and laid them out on the table for the neighbours and local dignitaries to admire. The heroes chatted with well-wishers and tucked into gigantic wedges of Victoria sponge oozing with strawberry jam. The relevance of the cake's name was not missed on Floss who was now considered the, *Honorary Special Adviser to Her Majesty, Queen Victoria on the Rehoming of Pet Cats.* The memory made her smile. Barbara was enjoying the party looking smart in her elegant two-piece suit as she mingled confidently, happily knowing Brett Jacob's card was safe in her handbag. Life was looking up for the Stanleys. Juan had warned the exuberant Barbara not to spill the beans on the finer details of Operation Lizard and absolutely forbade her to mention that her patients had been termites, glass headed midgets or aggressive Ailhad plants. He also reminded her that she had signed PUPA's secrecy agreement and not abiding by its terms could see her wind up in prison. The very suggestion she might be locked up in a cell next to Gregor Magnus was an effective deterrent for the usually chatty nurse.

The Welcome Home Party had taken them all by surprise and caused Jack to forget about Rosie and Rodrigo. Edward reminded him.

"By the way Jack, have you checked on Rosie?" He whispered, not wanting to draw the attention of the neighbours since Juan had specifically advised against discussing the rabbits' wedding in public.

"Hell no!" Jack replied, panicking and rushing off in the direction of his back garden with Edward in close pursuit. Floss, Lily and Emmie watched in horror at the boys' sudden departure and thinking something must be wrong put down their plates of cake and followed, entering Jack's back garden via a side gate. There they found a large wooden hutch big enough for a whole family of rabbits standing in the middle of the lawn. Jack lifted up the hutch's hinged roof and peered inside. There was nothing to see except a load of old bedding straw. A queasy feeling gripped Jack's stomach. Where could they have gone? Had Rodrigo kidnapped Rosie and whisked her away to another planet? He would never see her again! Jack's friends felt his pain and Edward put a comforting arm around him. Normally at such times they'd lighten the mood by telling jokes but Edward couldn't think of any. They had commanded armies putting a spoke in the wheel of the most feared megalomaniac of all time but he didn't know what to do to comfort his old friend on his sad loss. There just were no words.

It was bad enough that Jack was feeling depressed and his friends were struggling to think of a way to cheer him up but then Barbara started screaming. Charging up the garden they burst into the kitchen through the back door. Shock horror, the Stanley's kitchen had been completely re-furbished during their absence. New wall tiles, the latest range of kitchen cupboards, spanking new built-in cooker and so on all in Barbara's favourite colours, beige and autumnal red. It looked chic. Barbara was still screaming and is wasn't because she loved her new kitchen so much. The teenagers walked through to the hallway, redecorated and with a brand new radiator adorning the wall. Juan had kept his promise. The Stanley's house now had central heating and winters would never feel so cold again.

Barbara's scream turned to sobbing as she stood in the doorway to her dining room, her hands cupped over her face as though she couldn't bear to look. Jack gently pulled his mum to one side to see what was causing her so much unhappiness. The room was a foot high in mucky hay and with piles of rabbit dung steaming in the corners producing an odour normally found in cow sheds. The room had become an enormous rabbit warren and happily skipping around were eight black and white angora kittens, the official term for baby bunnies. Jack's mouth hung open. His friends were similarly aghast. Floss thought her own mother would have reacted in much the same way at finding her home trashed by furry animals. It didn't bear thinking about. The girls ushered Barbara into the next room whilst Jack decided what to do.

Rosie and Rodrigo sat resplendent in the middle of a pile of smelly hay, a quizzical look affixed to their faces wondering what all the fuss was about.

"Hi Jack," Rosie called out. "We're so glad you're home safe and sound." The new mother looked tired after chasing around after her babies all day and all night long. "It's OK, we'll get it all cleaned up," she added, sensing displeasure at the mess. "The house was empty and what with all the rain…"

"Rosie, you must take your family outside right now! My mum will have a heart attack if you stay here a moment longer," Jack remonstrated.

"It's all my fault," Rodrigo butted in, apologetically. "I made the decision to come inside. We didn't think you'd mind. I can sort everything out. I would've done it sooner but we didn't expect you home for a few more days and we've our beautiful babies to consider. They're still young." Rodrigo purred, sounding every bit the devoted father. Eight baby bunnies continued to scamper about in the hay.

Jack did some quick sums on his phone's calculator. A pair of rabbits could produce up to fourteen babies each time they bred and could mate again as soon as a litter was born, which could be every thirty-one days. In Rosie's case, she currently had just eight young but if next time she produced more and his calculations were correct, over a period of say four years Rosie, Rodrigo and their offspring who can reproduce at around five months old could produce millions of rabbits!

"Hell's bells!" Jack shrieked. It wouldn't be just his dining room he would have to worry about. His whole house and the entirety of Carshalton would be knee deep in rabbits! He shut his eyes and meditated for a second or two, calming his nerves.

Jack had an important question to ask the rabbits.

"Have you tied the knot yet?" He asked, recalling their promise to await his return.

"We said we'd wait and we have. Our word is our bond," Rodrigo said snottily. "In any case, Rosie wants you to give her away." They hadn't forgotten Jack after all. "We've everything arranged for next week but we can bring it forward if you like?"

"What about today?" Rosie shouted excitedly. Rounding off the day with a wedding sounded fun. All his friends were present except Harrison, but he'd never understand and was now outside Jack's close circle.

"Bring it on!" Jack cried out joyously, "but, not before you've vacated my home! I want this place looking spick and span and that includes a new carpet. I don't want to see a single stalk of hay or poo left behind." Jack was serious.

Rodrigo used his magic to return the dining room to its former clean and tidy state. A whirlwind of hay and other unmentionable stuff was swirling around the room causing Jack to run like the wind to throw open a door that opened onto the garden allowing the pongy twister to escape into the fresh air and so avoid causing damage to the newly redecorated house. Rosie dutifully led her offspring out into the garden and on hearing the good news, Barbara's palpitations subsided. Tranquillity had been restored.

The wedding ceremony was scheduled for 8 pm that night when it would still be light but when the neighbours would be indoors watching TV, suspecting nothing. Juan agreed to act as the celebrant conducting the marriage. The rabbits' hutch was bedecked with flowers and ribbons and Rosie's four bridesmaid daughters made daisy chain tiaras and posies of dandelions. Rosie's wedding dress and lacy veil were fashioned by Emmie from a piece of white net curtaining Barbara found in a drawer. Rodrigo worked superfast to distribute invitations inviting their friends and some of Juan's acquaintances to their impromptu joining of paws. A certain amount of magical methodology was put into play to get the guests to May Tree Close in time. All of Juan's incredible time limos were brought into service. Queen Victoria, because of her age, was allocated the comfortable and roomy Crusader Routemaster. The Queen never travelled lightly and even on this occasion she was accompanied by a host of ladies-in-waiting, private secretaries and copious Red Boxes containing government papers needing her attention.

At 8 pm the wedding guests gathered around Rosie and Rodrigo. Juan said a few formal words after which the rabbit couple made their promises to each other.

"I call upon these persons here present to witness that I, Rosie Stanley do take thee, Rodrigo Rabbit to be my lawful wedded husband…" Rodrigo was asked to make a similar declaration. Following this, Juan invited Rodrigo to speak in earnest of his love for Rosie.

"There was once a fluffy toy rabbit that wanted to be real. A rocking horse told him that he would have to be loved for a long time before that could happen. The toy rabbit didn't care. He just wanted to be loved unconditionally..." Rodrigo went on to tell everyone that he too, wanted to know what it felt like to be a real rabbit rather than a cricket, to love and be loved unconditionally and he believed that united with Rosie, he could be certain of it. "I will make Rosie happy and will always love her. In return, I hope she'll always love me even if my fur falls out and my eyes become dim." Rosie's nose twitched and she blushed at Rodrigo's romantic words. Their guests were pulling out their hankies to stem the flow of happy tears, it was so emotional. The ceremony ended when Juan pronounced Rosie and Rodrigo, buckhus and doeif, the rabbit language for husband and wife and presented the newly-weds to the gathered throng to rapturous applause, as Mr and Mrs Rodrigo and Rosie Stanley.

A musical quintet made up of Rodrigo's old cricket friends launched the wedding reception party using their buzzing wings to play a waltz for the bride and groom's first dance as husband and wife. Queen Victoria shed a tear as she remembered her own dear, departed, Prince Albert who had died many years before in December 1861. The nuptials were everything they should've been - merry and joyful with excited guests coming from far flung places and different time zones. Captain Greta, Lieutenant Hawkins and Major Gubby were there, lost in the music and dancing like they'd never danced before. Some of Rodrigo and Juan's old friends from Costa Rica had dropped everything to make the journey. Speedy the Sloth, screeching capuchin monkeys, opossums, agoutis, the latter a rabbit like rodent and genetically one of Rosie's ancestors, and Andreas the Kinkajou. Eva was absent. She was stuck in Australia with her feathers moulting, unable to fly and with eggs to incubate. The elderly termite generals were also missing from the list of attendees. At their mature age they just couldn't face the razzmatazz of a wedding shindig. They sent their congratulations and apologies via the monkeys.

The five friends had walked through fire to preserve universal peace but the affair of Juan's heart was still unresolved. The iguana was still alone, believing that this was how he would be for eternity. It should have been his wedding! He was, naturally, very happy for Rosie and Rodrigo and knew that the latter had made a great sacrifice to have Rosie by his side. The cricket-turned-rabbit was prepared to live in a hutch in Jack's back garden in order to have the love of his life beside him. Before Rosie had entered Rodrigo's life he had traversed the Universe as a free agent. All that was gone. He'd left his itchy feet behind and gained a family that he could cherish. Juan just had his memories of Ani.

The baby bunnies grew tired of dancing early on in the celebrations and returned to their hutch, passing a stack of wedding presents piled high in their run. There were no tea towels, toasters, sheets or pillowcases that might have been suitable gifts for a human wedding. Their gifts were rather more practical rabbit accoutrements such as water dispensers, food bowls and bunches of carrots for the large family. Nestling down in the soft, sweet, smelling hay the bunnies were soon fast asleep. The cricket quintet played on and as the guests swung to the music there came a kafuffle at the back gate. A muscly five foot bouncer termite especially bred for such security work was dealing with a gate-crasher. Edward went to investigate.

A beautiful femme fatale with golden tresses and wearing an elegant red floaty dress and silver shoes stood weeping at the gate. The toned, six-pack security guard was adamant that this siren was not coming in. No invitation meant no entry to the best party May Tree Close had ever witnessed. By the time Edward arrived tears were streaming down the lady's cheeks causing her mascara to smudge. Edward gallantly led the lady to the wooden bench beneath the cherry tree and wiping away her tears with a paper hanky, chatted, trying to establish her identity.

The lady refreshed her make-up and began her story.

"I've come a long way to be here," she began. "Andreas the Kinkajou told me about Rodrigo's wedding. We set out together but I lost him over the Caribbean Sea and I rather fear for his safety. Kinkajous are not the most seasoned travellers," she said sadly.

"'You can stop worrying about Andreas. He's here ahead of you. He apparently bumped into a couple of black backed gulls and they let him hang on to their tail feathers whilst they debated the pros and cons of forest living against that of swimming in the sea!" Edward chuckled. The lady relaxed, a smile brightening her face.

"What's your connection to Rodrigo?" Edward asked.

"I've known him since he was a lava. I watched him wriggle his way to adulthood."

"He's an angora rabbit now!" Edward laughed heartily.

"Yes I'd heard," she answered quietly.

The beautiful lady sat beside Edward in silence for a few seconds before continuing.

"To tell you the truth I was really more a friend of Juan's. We were engaged to be married until a wicked creature named Gregor Magnus, you won't have heard of him, cruelly trapped me inside the feathered body of a bird, and a bird that couldn't fly far. This meant I couldn't be with my fiancé. That barbarian brute did it to hurt Juan but I'm pleased to tell you my captor's been caught and the spell's broken, so here I am!" There wasn't any doubt in Edward's mind as to the lady's identity.

"My name is A....," she began.

"Ani, as in groove billed ani bird!" Edward blurted out, unable to hide his joy. "Juan talks about you fondly all the time. He'd given up hope of ever seeing you again. Come, you have a party to go to."

Edward took Ani to the party where they found Juan sitting under an apple tree looking sad and seemingly unaware of the merriment going on around him.

"Shove up Juan. I want to sit next to you," Edward ordered. Without even looking up Juan moved along the bench, making a space. Edward beckoned Ani to sit beside him, which she did taking the iguana's hand in hers. Juan silently raised his face to see Ani smiling back at him. They linked their minds and told each other their stories until the band played their favourite Malachitian love song. Juan kissed Ani tenderly, afraid that she might once again slip through his fingers and disappear. The couple danced together for the rest of the night whilst Juan's alter egos who had shown meteorite rises from naïve school kids to mature, interstellar commanders of the Universe, looked on, satisfied that their much respected new friend had been reunited with his sweetheart at long last.

Midnight approached and it was time for the wedding guests to bade Rosie and Rodrigo farewell and return to their homes on distant planets or across Earth's seas to foreign lands. Juan made to leave with Ani.

"Iggy!" Jack cheekily called Juan stopping him in his tracks. "Thank you for keeping your promise and giving me and my mum central heating!" Juan shook his head as if to say it was nothing. He was in love! Juan, still man-sized curled his arm around Ani as they slipped out through the back gate and disappeared into the night.

"Don't worry, Jack. Look on the bright side. Juan and Ani have a wedding to plan and I'm sure we'll all be invited," Edward consoled his friend.

Lieutenant Hawkins and Major Gubby were ready to leave for Malachite aboard the Crusader, parked in a copse of sweet chestnut trees in Carshalton Park.

"Sorry gang! We need to make a move. Dear old Queen Vic is looking tired and we've been asked to take her back to the palace," Hawkins said, shaking hands with the teenagers and adding, "we're really looking forward to working with you five again soon!" Floss was sceptical. How often did intergalactic emergencies occur? Major Gubby, much the worse for wear after all the dancing, continued jigging all the way to the back gate singing at the top of his voice. He stopped to pump up his ears in readiness to fly Hawkins and Queen Victoria, one on each side, over the house tops to Carshalton Park and the Crusader. The Queen's servants would have to walk!

Captain Greta hung back hoping for a few minutes alone with Jack. They chatted, promising to keep in touch via space email. Greta would speak to Juan about setting up an account for him. Jack kissed Greta on the cheek and they parted company, Jack smiling contentedly. The garden was suddenly, eerily quiet. Jack thanked his fellow team members for their support in what had been both a difficult and satisfying few days rolled into one and then the friends left. Jack locked the back gate behind them.

Floss, Edward, Lily and Emmie strolled across to the green and chatted for a while longer until Edward offered to walk Emmie home. Lily and Floss wearily made their way to the Roberts' house where Lin and Pete Roberts were coming to the end of a pleasant evening soiree with their friends, the Gibsons, a get-together to celebrate the safe return of their daughters. They were just finishing a Chinese takeaway when the girls walked in.

Floss heard a familiar conversation as she and Lily walked along the hallway .

"I hope there wasn't any monosodium glutamate in that sauce. I hear it can cause side effects such as headaches and nausea," Lin said.

"That was banned years ago," Yumi reassured her. Floss smiled. Juan had wiped their memories clean starting from the time of the original Chinese takeaway right up till their Libra Congressional Medal investiture at New York's City Hall. She anticipated no inquisition would follow into the finer details of their time spent with Juan. They joined their parents for coffee, munching the remaining prawn crackers. It was late and the girls had school the next day, which neither was looking forward to.

"Alas, see you tomorrow, Floss..." Lily sighed, giving her friend a hug as the Gibsons left for their short walk home.

Floss couldn't settle. She slipped outside to the silent green and sitting on the bench pondered the last few days. Floss's eyes searched the sky knowing that enumerable new worlds, planets, stars, and moons teeming with life of one kind or another were up there just waiting to be discovered. The stars looked like sparkling pinpricks hundreds of light years away. She was privileged to know that these new worlds were within easy reach of those vested with magical powers such as Juan and his circle of special friends.

"Hello little stars. I wonder how many there are of you up there?" Floss whispered. Star Kibas, Optima,

Malachite… Juan had promised to take her to Malachite one day and she dearly hoped that day would come soon. "Always believe that something wonderful will happen," Floss repeated the words Juan had once said to her, hoping they would ring true.

The colder night air started to bite and as Floss walked back home her mobile phone rang. It was Edward.

"Hi Floss. Hope I didn't wake you! Sorry about ringing so late. Would you like to come with me to see a film on Saturday night?" Adrenalin whizzed around Floss's body. She still liked Edward!

"Yes please!" She replied without hesitation, and then… "Ed, how's your sunburn?"

"Completely gone! Melissa's ointment did the trick. I read the list of ingredients on the tube and guess what, it contained marberry extract. Can you believe that?" They both burst into laughter.

Floss changed into her pyjamas, brushed her teeth, and pulled back her duvet ready to enjoy a deep sleep when she heard a mewing coming from outside. She opened her window to find a white Persian cat sitting on the windowsill. Rudy had been whisked forward through time from the nineteenth century to the present day by PUPA's specialist time travel force. Queen Victoria had so enjoyed the wedding and seen for herself what a happy place May Tree Close would be for an old cat that she had readily agreed to the moggy being airlifted into the twenty-first century. Floss lifted Rudy inside, placing him on her bed. He had just one request to ask of his new owner.

"Please don't call me a silly name like, White Heather," he begged.

"Now, let me think about that," she teased him. "OK! I've thought about it. I'll call you Rudy," Floss hugged him, feeling delighted at having gained both a cat and a new friend. She would square it with her mother in the morning.

Floss Roberts, ex PUPA director of operations laid her head on her pillow with her arm curled around Rudy and felt her brain mysteriously start to crackle. Was Juan speaking to her? Unlikely since he was preoccupied with Ani. The crackling stopped and was replaced by the sound of waves splashing and crashing on a beach. In her mind's eye she saw an image of Queen Elizabeth Tudor and the number, 1589? Another adventure? Of course not. She must be dreaming!